• • • • • •

"Anything you tell me to do, I'll probably do the opposite," Korah said as she watched him.

"Well, in that case *don't* go out with me again," Brick said. "*Don't* invite me into your home, and certainly *don't ever* come to my home – or my ranch."

He offered his fork with a juicy bite of lobster speared. Rather than lean over the table and allow him to feed her, Korah took the fork from him and fed herself. She returned his utensil as she chewed the delicious morsel.

"Is that really your ranch?" she asked, "on your website?"

He nodded. "It's been in the family for years. It's all mine now."

"And I guess you have horses and cows and stuff?"

"No cows," he said, hypnotizing her with his intense gaze again. "But I do have horses. Would you like to go one day? You wanna ride my horse?"

Korah did not miss the innuendo, nor did she back down. "Where is it located?"

"Lewisville. I have a ranch hand who lives there full-time. He takes care of things while I'm away."

"What else you got on your ranch?" Korah asked.

"Actually, I could show you better than I could tell you," Brick said. "Are you saying you *do* wanna ride my horse?"

His boldness made Korah's clit quiver.

"I haven't ridden a horse in years," she replied. "I'm worried I might fall off."

"You gotta hold the reigns tight," Brick advised. "You gotta wrap your legs around him and squeeze a little, with your thighs. And if you do fall off, you gotta get right back on, and we'll take it a little slower."

Korah grinned. "I don't know what you're thinking about, but I'm only talking about riding a horse."

"Oh, well here, have some more wine," Brick said and commenced to fill her glass.

Korah couldn't help but laugh at that.

• • • • • •

BRICK HOUSE

BRICK HOUSE

KEITH THOMAS WALKER

KEITHWALKERBOOKS, INC
This is a UMS production

BRICK HOUSE

KEITHWALKERBOOKS

Publishing Company
KeithWalkerBooks, Inc.
P.O. Box 331585
Fort Worth, TX 76163

For information write
KeithWalkerBooks, Inc.
P.O. Box 331585
Fort Worth, TX 76163

ISBN-13 DIGIT: 978-0-9882180-5-5
ISBN-10 DIGIT: 0988218054
Library of Congress Control Number: 2014912007
Manufactured in the United States of America

First Edition

Visit us at www.keithwalkerbooks.com

KEITH THOMAS WALKER

This book is for Michele Halsey Hallahan

MORE BOOKS BY
KEITH THOMAS WALKER

Fixin' Tyrone
How to Kill Your Husband
A Good Dude
Riding the Corporate Ladder
The Finley Sisters' Oath of Romance
Blow by Blow
Jewell and the Dapper Dan
Harlot
Plan C (And More KWB Shorts)
Dripping Chocolate
The Realest Ever
Jackson Memorial
Sleeping With the Strangler
Life After
Blood for Isaiah

NOVELLAS

Might be Bi (Part One)
Harder

POETRY COLLECTION

Poor Righteous Poet

Visit keithwalkerbooks.com for information about these and upcoming titles from KeithWalkerBooks

ACKNOWLEGMENTS

Of course I would like to thank God, first and foremost, for giving me the creativity and drive to pursue my dreams and the understanding that I am nothing without Him. I would like to thank my wife for being my first and most important critic, and I would like to thank my mother for always pushing me to be the best I can be. I would like to thank Janae Hampton for being the best advisor, supporter and little sister a brother could ever have. I would also like to thank (in no particular order) Denise Bolds, Sabrina Scott, Beulah Neveu, Jason Owens, Sharon Blount, BRAB Book Club, and Uncle Steven Thomas, one love. I'd like to thank everyone who purchased and enjoyed one of my books. Everything I do has always been to please you. I know there are folks who mean the world to me that I'm failing to mention. I apologize ahead of time. Rest assured I'm grateful for everything you've done for me!

BRICK HOUSE

CHAPTER ONE
THE MORNING AFTER

The morning after.

Ugh.

Korah's nostrils flared as the delectable aroma of biscuits and sausage and possibly hash browns made it all the way from the kitchen to her large, sundrenched bedroom on the second floor. She frowned rather than smile at the thought of a man cooking for her. She did not look forward to the conversation she and Quincy would have when she went downstairs to greet him.

She rolled over and squinted at the alarm clock on her nightstand. It was 7:22 am. She should've been up and amongst the working world by now, or at least in the midst of the morning commuters. She rolled back over to her other side, thankful that she didn't have a headache. All things considered, she felt pretty good – which was not usually the case when she drank as much as she did last night.

She wondered how Quincy managed to weasel his way into her home and her bedroom in the wee hours of the morning, but of course she knew. It all started with her tight red dress that ran out of material midway down her thighs and the look of utter foolishness Quincy wore when she answered the door for him and he ran his wolf eyes up and down her curvy frame.

Yesterday was his birthday. Korah and Quincy had been broken up for months, but they remained cordial. So she wasn't opposed to accompanying him to the Red Flamingo for a big party he and his friends planned. Last night Quincy looked surprisingly dapper in a new Armani suit, and Korah complemented him as the perfect arm candy. Her hair was down and flowing. Her legs were long, her dark cleavage plentiful. She garnished just as much attention as the birthday boy, much to her and Quincy's delight.

They were having so much fun, she didn't protest when Quincy began holding her hand when he introduced her around the room. As the night progressed, he kept an arm possessively around her waist as they strolled the lively locale, and Korah didn't put a stop to that either.

She should have, but she didn't.

The alcohol no doubt played a big part in it. The Red Flamingo Club had a signature drink called *"Paradise."* It was pink in color and sweet to the taste and loaded with vodka, gin and rum. Korah was sufficiently buzzed after her second one. But Quincy kept ordering them, and she kept drinking. It was a party, after all.

As the clock struck midnight, and the party kicked into second gear, Korah and her ex-boyfriend tripped the light fantastic. She wasn't the best dancer, but she was better than Quincy and most of the other women who hit the dance floor that night. Quincy was absolutely gushing with appreciation for her accompanying him. And Korah had to admit she was having a lot of fun as well.

They grinded under the strobe lights like lovers, and at some point Korah stopped shooing his hands away when they slipped from her waist to her hips down to her swollen derriere. She kept her arms around Quincy's neck and stared into his eager, hungry eyes. Korah's brown orbs were low and intoxicated. Her lips were full and moist. Quincy's skin was dark and smooth like polished mahogany. He pulled her hips very close to his, and he hummed in her ear when Korah didn't protest that either.

She felt how hard and how badly he wanted her. She knew she shouldn't dip her toes in those forbidden waters, but sometimes (if there's enough time passed and alcohol involved) familiarity wins out over good judgment.

When Quincy drove her home in his sleek Mercedes E-Class, it was nearly two am, and his hormones had been raging for hours. He didn't attempt a pickup line when he killed the engine. He simply leaned over the center console for the kiss he'd been yearning for, and Korah met him halfway. His tongue slipped into her mouth immediately. Spurred on by the unexpected green light, his hand boldly moved from his lap to hers, in search of the blazing heat between her legs. He rubbed the outside of her panties with long, skillful fingers, and then he slipped her panties to the side.

He grunted when he encountered her incredible moistness, and he commenced to finger her while they made out like teenagers.

Korah thought his tongue tasted like Paradise. She sucked his lips and bucked her hips against his hand. She rode his stiff fingers until her chest was moist with sweat and the volume of her moans drowned out Ralph Tresvant, who was crooning on an oldies R&B station.

Though I love the girl, I know that the best thing is for us to be apart...

Korah's breathing became heavier and heavier, until her orgasm thundered like cannon fire, leaving her squealing and numb and tingly all over.

She still didn't agree with her choice of partners for the night, but as she shielded her face from the sunlight the next morning, she couldn't help but smile at the memory.

By the time she and Quincy made it inside her home, his dick pitched a mighty tent in his slacks. Korah was sufficiently plastered, but did have sense enough to make him return to his car to get a condom. Aside from that, she let Quincy have her any way he wanted to. He came too quickly, as was his tradition, but he made up for it when Korah rolled him onto his back and straddled his face.

Oooh.

That memory made Korah moan aloud and squeeze her legs together as a sweet aftershock rolled up her thighs and made her clit swell pleasantly. She grinned as she pulled her sheets up over her shoulders, content to traipse down memory lane a while longer.

By the time Quincy got hard again, his mouth and cheeks were slick and glistening with Korah's essence. She looked down at him with both hands gripping the top of the headboard, thinking he was such a sloppy eater. Quincy grinned up at her and then moved to a more dominant position behind her.

Korah appreciated his enthusiasm, but by then she was exhausted, nearly to the point of passing out. Quincy grabbed hold of her thighs and hiked her hips up as she lowered her face onto her pillows. Quincy wasn't necessarily *packing*, but he knew how to work with what he had. He never filled her completely, but he maximized his movements, ensuring his dick provided constant stimulus to her clitoris with each stroke.

It was around this time that Korah began to contemplate the folly of her actions. She and Quincy were not in a relationship anymore. He had courted her for four months, and it took approximately that long for Korah to decide they were already in a rut. It wasn't Quincy's fault. He was hardworking and successful and cultured. But Korah longed for something *different*.

Something exciting.

She didn't need him to be a mafia hit man, but Quincy's boring life as an accountant didn't fit the bill, either.

Unfortunately, like a few other men Korah dumped in her lifetime, Quincy was forever hopeful that they could reignite the fires that once kept their love blazing. He would no doubt think he was working his way back into her life as he worked his dick between her hot, wet walls – and that was a problem.

Any hopes that he would understand (as Korah did) that this was a one-time thing were dashed when she awakened to an empty bed and the smell of biscuits and sausage and possibly hash browns wafting from her kitchen. She knew Quincy was preparing the meal with a fool-hearty smile pasted on his face, and she knew he'd paint her out to be a bitch when she went down there to burst his bubble.

Ugh.

Korah sighed, her smile completely gone now. She threw back the sheets and sat up in bed. She was completely nude. Her slight movement brought with it the first throbs of a mild headache.

Her bedroom was big and beautiful – not nearly as disheveled as she thought it would be. Her dress was on the floor in the doorway. Her bra was a few feet away from it. She only saw one of her heels, and she had no idea where her panties were. Knowing Quincy, they were probably balled-up in his pocket, which was another good reason to put him and his birthday bash behind her.

She checked the clock again. It was 7:30 now. Korah rose to her feet and stopped by the bathroom to grab a robe before she went downstairs. She found Quincy in the kitchen putting the finishing touches on her breakfast plate. In addition to the biscuits and sausage, he made her eggs and split a grapefruit in half. Korah didn't see the other half of the grapefruit anywhere. She hoped that meant he had already eaten, because she didn't want him to leave upset *and* hungry.

Quincy was barefoot, but he wore his slacks and tee shirt from last night. He was of average height and build. He sported a short afro that Korah wasn't particularly fond of, but she did like his smooth, dark skin and the way he kept his moustache and beard trimmed perfectly. He turned and smiled when he heard her bare feet on the tiles behind him. He turned the stove off and placed his spatula on the counter before he approached her.

He wrapped his arms around her waist and held her tightly, like they were newlyweds. Korah grimaced as he nuzzled his face against her neck. She didn't mind his affection, just as she didn't mind the pleasure he provided last night. But it was never easy with this man. A simple smile could take his heart on a journey.

He backed away and frowned when he noticed her expression.

"Good morning. What's wrong?"

"Nothing," Korah said. "You been up for a while?"

"Yeah." Quincy turned and hefted her plate. "I made you breakfast." He presented to her as if she was a sex goddess, and it was an offering.

Korah didn't care for greasy foods first thing in the morning, but she didn't want to be rude. She plucked one of the small sausage links from the plate and ate it. She even managed to smile.

"Thank you very much. Don't you have to be at work this morning?"

"I called them," Quincy said. "It's okay if I'm a little late."

"Hmmm. Not me," Korah said. She tied her robe straps together and stretched lazily. "I gotta get a move on."

"Oh, that's okay," Quincy said. He smiled. "Thanks again for coming to my party. You looked so good last night. You look good now, too."

"Thank you," Korah said. "But I know I look like crap."

"Hell no you don't," Quincy said. "Even in your robe, you look better than most of the women I see on a daily basis."

At five foot, eight inches, Korah was roughly the same height as Quincy. And like him, she had rich skin, like coffee with just a hint of cream. Even the fluffy robe wasn't enough to hide her curves, which Korah had to admit were pleasing to the eye.

At 46 years of age, her breasts weren't as perky as they once were, but they were nice and round, and even a cheap bra gave her mountains of cleavage. Her hips were spread enticingly, and her ass was soft and round. Korah's natural hair was shoulder-length. Her cheeks had sexy dimples that she didn't fully appreciate until she became an adult.

She told her ex-boyfriend, "I'm about to jump in the shower. Are you gonna leave before I get out, because I wanna lock the door."

"I don't have to," Quincy said with a dopey grin that reinforced Korah's thinking that he was about to get his feelings hurt. "I can jump in the shower with you, if you don't mind..."

"You can use the shower down here," Korah offered. "I'm already running late. I don't need any of your *distractions*." She smiled, hoping to soften the blow.

Quincy smiled too. "Alright. I get it. Last night is over, and you're ready to get back to your regularly scheduled life."

Korah raised an eyebrow, thinking he wasn't as lovesick as she thought. "Yeah. That's what I want."

"Okay," Quincy said. He removed his cellphone from his pocket and accessed the calendar app. "I was wondering if you wanted to catch a dinner at the new steakhouse that opened downtown. I'm busy for the rest of the week, but–"

"No, I don't think that's a good idea," Korah said, stopping his thumb in mid-swipe.

He looked up at her. "Oh. Um, why not?"

Korah rolled her eyes inwardly. "Because we're not together anymore, Quincy. We broke up two months ago. We shouldn't go on dates."

His smile fell. "Yeah, but, last night..."

"I know," Korah said with a sigh. "I knew it was probably gonna be trouble, but I–"

"There's no trouble," Quincy interjected, shaking his head. "I had a good time. I thought you did, too."

"I did," Korah said. She smiled. "I had a great time with you last night."

"But you're saying it's over?"

"Well, yeah," she said. "Today's a new day. I gotta get to work."

"I'm talking about us."

Korah brought a hand to her face and rubbed her eye sockets. "Quincy, you know we're not together anymore. You asked me to be your date for your party, and I said I would. I drank a lot more than I should have, and—"

"So that was all about you drinking? Now you wanna blame it on the alcohol?"

"Quincy, I don't have to blame it on anything. We're both grown. I didn't say I was drunk. I'm just saying I drank more than I should've, and I didn't think things through."

"So you are saying you wouldn't have slept with me, if you were sober..."

Korah shook her head in exasperation. "Quincy, sleeping with you is not the problem. What's happening right now is the problem. We had a good time last night, and you're about to ruin it by—"

"I'm ruining it?"

"Yes, you're making this very awkward," Korah confirmed.

Quincy returned his phone to his pocket and folded his arms over his chest. "Well excuse me for thinking that when two people kiss and hold hands and make love it probably means they're in a relationship."

"It was your birthday," she said. "We had a good time. No need to end it on a sour note."

"So it meant nothing to you. That's what you're saying, right?"

Anger was getting the best of him, but Korah was undeterred. His temper was another reason she broke up with him in the first place. And she couldn't stand his clinginess. Quincy didn't realize that putting both of these characteristics on display this morning only bolstered her negative feelings about him and made her feel less like a heartless bitch for hurting his feelings.

"It certainly didn't mean we were getting back together," she said plainly. "Now, if you want to shower before you go—"

"You're acting like a real *bitch*," Quincy decided.

Korah grinned. She knew that would be the end result, no matter how she tried to schmooze this little talk.

"And you think it's funny," he spat.

"No, Quincy. I think you're acting really immature right now. And I'm thinking this will be the last time I agree to go *anywhere* with your crazy ass. We shouldn't have slept together. I get it. Now could you please leave, so I can get ready for work?"

All of his resolve dissipated right before her eyes. "I'm sorry, Korah. I didn't mean to get upset. You're right. I read too much into it. I don't wanna leave here on bad terms."

Too late for that.

"Okay," she said. "It's fine. So did you wanna take a shower before you go, or..."

"Um, no," he said "I know you're in a rush. I'll just grab my things and stop by my place on the way to work. I gotta get some clean clothes anyway."

"Okay," Korah said.

She waited in the living room while he gathered his shoes, shirt and jacket from the bedroom. He approached her a few minutes later, fully dressed and hoping to make amends, but Korah was sick of his stupid face by then. She clenched her teeth when he gave her a kiss on the cheek on his way out.

When did booty calls get so complicated? she wondered as she locked the door behind him. *I'm getting too old for this.* But that didn't seem right, either. Korah still felt young enough to take the world by storm.

She decided Quincy was the one at fault when she stepped into the shower. By the time she got out, she was able to put the whole silly incident behind her – except for her orgasms. She didn't know when she'd reach that level of contentment again, so she held on to the memories of their lovemaking for a little while longer.

• • • • • •

When she finally got dressed for work, it was after eight, and Korah had to return three business calls she'd missed. Her son Devin seemed to have the most significant issues, so when she rolled out of her driveway, Korah pointed her Pathfinder in his direction.

Devin Jr. served as foreman for the construction company Korah added to the family business four years ago. Prior to that, Texas Builders functioned only as a general contractor. They had to hire a construction team to work the sites Korah won bids on.

Establishing their own construction company increased profits dramatically. Not only was her squad guaranteed to work their properties, but Korah also sent them to work for other contractors who still had to outsource their manual labor.

The date was Monday, September 8th. The weather in Overbrook Meadows was warm and cloudy, but not too humid that morning. The cloud cover was expected to blow over by noon, leaving ideal conditions for Devin's 30-man crew. Today they were erecting a 7-11 at the corner of Hemphill and Sycamore School Road.

The worksite was bustling with activity when Korah arrived at the property, but she had no problem spotting her son. At six-foot-four inches tall, Devin stood head and shoulders above most of his employees. He was fair-skinned, like his father, and he had long arms and broad shoulders that made him a force to be reckoned with when he played ball in high school and college.

Devin Jr. could've taken his hoop dreams further if he gave it his all, but working for the family business had been his only dream, ever since he was constructing mini-malls out of Lego building blocks when he was in grade school. His father's death reinforced this legacy thirteen years ago, despite Korah's assurances that Devin Jr. was free to be whatever he wanted to be.

Seeing him now, Korah knew that she never really had a say in the matter. Her son was born to build things, just like his dad. At only 26 years of age, Devin Jr. was already fully in charge of multi-million dollar projects and was completely comfortable with the role. He was well-respected by his crew. And even though some of the business owners who hired them seemed unsure of the youngster when they first met him, by the end of the job they were always impressed and appreciative of Devin's work. In many cases, they were genuinely awed.

Korah parked her Navigator next to a large sign that read:

TEXAS BUILDERS
General Contractors
Construction

Renovations
555-225-6623

There were identical signs currently planted at six different construction sites throughout the city. Korah's chest swelled with pride, no matter how often she saw them.

She stepped out of her SUV wearing jeans with a tee-shirt that had their company logo printed prominently on the front and back. Korah snatched her hardhat from the backseat and pushed it down on her head before she stepped into the construction zone. She wore steel-toed boots, rather than pumps, but she still looked very feminine on the male-dominated property, despite the fact that she wore no makeup at all.

All of the construction workers knew that Korah was their boss' boss (and mother), and they were very respectful and quick to acknowledge her presence as she approached.

"Morning, Ms. Stewart!"

"Great to see you today!"

Korah smiled and nodded at their pleasantries. "Morning, boys. Gonna be a great day today."

"Yes Ma'am! Everything's coming along just fine."

Korah's smile faded when she reached her son, because Devin was not in a good mood at all. He briefly made eye-contact with her before he turned away slightly and continued yelling at whoever was on the other end of his cellphone.

"Who the hell told him to go down 35? What the hell do y'all do, just plug it in your GPS and take the shortest route? Everybody knows 35 is jacked up this time of morning. He could've hit 820 and been here by now!"

After a pause, Devin said, "That's not my fuc–" He caught himself and turned away from his mother even more. "That's not my fucking problem," he grumbled. "I got my concrete crew out here *right now*. Every minute your guy is late is costing me money! And if that batch is no good by the time it gets here, we're gonna have some serious problems..."

As she waited, Korah marveled at how much her son looked like his father. Devin kept his hair cut short, and he wore no moustache or goatee. The major difference between him and Devin Sr. was his irritability, but Korah didn't fault her son for that. His way of getting things done had proven successful time and time again.

Some bosses earned their employees' respect with perks and bonuses. Others preferred intimidation tactics. Devin Sr. built the company from the ground up without every raising his voice. Devin Jr. chose a different path.

When he got off the phone, he turned and gave his mother a brief hug.

"Hey, Mama. Sorry about that."

"What's wrong?"

"Concrete truck is stuck in traffic," Devin reported. "He added water to the mix twice already. The consistency will probably be all messed up by the time he gets here. And I got a crew of guys just *waiting*. It'll take another hour, if they have to get a new batch."

Korah turned and saw a group of strangers milling around the front of the store. They were all Hispanic, with brown, sun-beaten skin and work clothes that already looked soiled.

"I thought you had some concrete guys on your crew," Korah said, not happy that they had to look elsewhere for a portion of the labor.

"Everybody's tied up today," Devin said. "I wanna knock this parking lot out as soon as possible. This crew can get it done, if we ever get the damn concrete."

Korah saw that the foundation and rebar had already been laid perfectly. All they needed was the wet stuff.

"How many trucks are coming?"

Devin gave her a look. Korah caught herself and grinned. She knew he hated it when she got too deeply involved in his construction work. As a contractor, her role was to hire a construction company and let them do the job. She wouldn't normally poke her nose into their business unless there was a major problem. But it was hard to back off, since the construction crew was run by her baby, and it was part of her overall brand.

"So what you're telling me is we don't have a problem..."

Devin nodded and smiled brightly. "That's right, Mama. We do *not* have a problem."

Korah narrowed her eyes. Back when she used to outsource for construction, some of the foremen she hired would tell her the same thing when there was indeed *plenty* to worry about. As a rule, construction companies never want contractors to know how bad things really are.

"Alright," Korah said. "You hungry? You eat breakfast today?"

Devin patted his flat belly, still smiling. "Yes Ma'am. I ate a big breakfast. I'm full of energy."

His smile made Korah want to pinch his cheeks, but of course she would never do that. Not in public, anyway.

"When are you getting the windows installed?" she asked instead.

The store was nearly complete, with all four walls and the roof erected.

"As soon as we get the concrete work finished," Devin said. "The glass man should be here any minute. The electricians are coming today, too."

"You're doing a great job," she told him. "Have I told you how proud I am of you?"

"Yes, but you can say it again, if you wanna."

The boy would never know how much he meant to his mother. Korah loved him so much, it made her heart sigh.

"I'm very proud of you," she said. "But if that concrete doesn't get here in the next thirty minutes—"

"Mama, you—"

She held a finger up to silence him when her cellphone rang. Korah fully expected to see Quincy's number on the Caller ID, but the call came from her main office.

"Hey, what's up?"

"Good morning, Korah."

It was Priscilla, vice president of Texas Builders. The sound of her sweet voice put a genuine smile on Korah's face. Priscilla was 65 years old. She had been with the company since Korah's husband founded it in 1989. That was twenty-five years ago. Priscilla had been mentioning retirement for the past couple of years. Korah did not look forward to the inevitable day they would lose her expertise.

"Ms. Priscilla. Good morning! How are things?"

"Great!" Priscilla said. "Got good news about the bid."

Texas Builders had a dozen or more bids being considered at any given time, but Korah had no doubt as to which one Priscilla was referring to. This was The Big One: A new high school for Overbrook Meadows school district. The winner of the bid would be contracted to complete what would be the biggest project in the history of Korah's company. The school district had already set aside fifteen million dollars for the development. That kind of money made Korah's heart flutter.

Texas Builders had done well for themselves over the years, constructing churches, convenience stores and even a shopping center and a few small Walmarts. But the school district contract would take them to another level – especially since the contractor with the winning bid would also get first crack at other work in the district, which already included a new middle school and countless renovations.

This was the kind of job Devin Senior dreamed about many years ago, when all he had was a pocket full of ambition and a head full of dreams.

"What's the good news?" Korah asked, her heart light in her chest.

"We're in the top two," Priscilla announced. "We actually have a good chance of winning this thing."

Korah's face flushed with heat. She couldn't hide her elation. Even Devin Jr. loosened up when he saw the smile on her face.

"Are you coming to the office?" Priscilla asked.

"Yeah, I'm on my way."

"See you soon," Priscilla said and disconnected.

Korah regained her professional demeanor when she put her phone away. "I'll be back later," she told Devin. "I gotta check on a few things."

"What's going on?" her son asked, following her to her truck.

They both wore the same jeans and Texas Builders tees, but Devin was nearly a foot taller than his mom, and his shirt stretched nicely over his broad shoulders and prominent pectorals. His tool belt hung on his hips like a gunslinger. It was well-worn, sunburned leather, but it was still beautiful. It once belonged to his father.

"What are you so happy about?" he asked.

Korah looked back at him, her eyes glistening under the bib of her hardhat. "I think we might get the school," she told him.

"Oh yeah?" Devin's chest swelled with hope as well.

"You think you could build a school?" Korah teased as she opened her car door.

Devin offered his hand and helped her up into the cab of the truck, although it wasn't necessary. Korah placed her hardhat on the passenger seat and brushed her hair down with long, slender fingers.

"I reckon we can build one just as good as any of the others," Devin said, his big hands resting on the open window frame. "When will they make an announcement?"

"In about three weeks," Korah said.

He frowned. "I ain't got time to be anxious for that long," Devin said, backing away from her truck. "Got too much to do." But the delight in his eyes said otherwise.

"Well, get to it then," Korah said. She started her car and winked at him as she threw it in gear.

CHAPTER TWO
TEXAS BUILDERS

Korah met Devin Stewart Sr. during her junior year at Finley High, nearly three decades ago. Devin was a recent transfer from west Texas, and he was the talk of the school within a week of his arrival. All of the girls were attracted to his rugged, country boy looks, and many of the jocks hoped Devin's height and brown skin would translate to a new weapon on the basketball court or football field.

Much to their disappointment, Devin wasn't into organized sports. He participated enough to pass gym, but it was shop class that made his heart go pitty-pat. He and Korah were paired together for the menial task of building a birdhouse, but no construction assignment was menial for Devin.

Two weeks later they turned in a triple-decker monstrosity that was big enough to house a murder of crows. Korah had done little more than paint their birdhouse (she went with pink, against Devin's protests), but that was enough to garnish her a 100 for the assignment and an A for the course overall.

Korah and Devin didn't spend much side-by-side time working on the birdhouse, but they did see each other often enough to create a sense of intrigue on both sides. Korah wanted to know more about the first boy she ever met who took shop class so seriously, and Devin was smitten with Korah from the moment the teacher assigned her as his partner. Korah was tall and pretty with a bright smile and pink lip gloss that smelled like bubblegum. But she wasn't an airhead, like most of the other gorgeous girls at the school.

Devin was so nervous around her, it took him nearly a month to ask if she wanted to have lunch with him one day. The cafeteria served casserole and cornbread that afternoon. Devin couldn't eat one bite while sitting with Korah, which she thought was the cutest thing ever.

They were officially a couple throughout their senior year of high school, and many of Korah's fondest memories could be traced back to those magical times. Devin bought her the biggest, most beautiful mum for Finley's homecoming game that year, and he looked very debonair in the tuxedo he rented for their senior prom. Korah lost her virginity to Devin that night, and after graduation she began dreaming of the life they would one day share together.

Korah and Devin began college together at Texas Lutheran University in 1986, but an unexpected pregnancy caused Korah to put her collegiate career on hold the following year. This was the only aspect of their relationship Devin was not pleased with. But rather than desert her, he made a vow to always be there for Korah and their son. By then she trusted him fully. Even as a young man, Devin had the integrity and work ethics of a man twice his age.

He and Korah married in 1990, which was a big year for a number of reasons. That was the year Devin graduated with a degree in Construction Management, and it was also the year he founded the family business, Texas Builders. Success was not immediate, but it was also never in doubt – as far as Korah was concerned. The young couple welcomed their second child into the world in 1995. This time it was a girl. Devin named her Stephanie.

The next few years were filled with so many blessings, Korah forgot how precious each moment was until tragedy visited the Stewart household in 2001. A routine physical revealed an abnormality on Devin Sr.'s prostate gland. Further tests concluded the prostate gland was enlarged, cancer was the cause, and it had already spread to his colon and lymph nodes.

There wasn't much light for Korah in those gloomy days. The only thing she was thankful for was that the disease didn't prolong Devin's suffering. They fought the cancer with an aggressive regimen of surgery and chemotherapy. Devin was upbeat and courageous, but he lost the battle within five months of the original diagnosis. Korah became a widow at the tender age of 33.

Depression and despair never had a chance to take a foothold in her life, however, because Korah still had children to raise, and allowing her late husband's legacy to die with him was never an option. Prior to his death, Devin Sr. spent most of his time in the hospital training Korah to be the best unlicensed contractor the state had ever known. At times she became upset with him, urging him to put his business ledgers away and focus his energy on his recovery. But Devin would have none of that.

"Baby, please listen to me," he told her, on more than one occasion, while stretched out on a hospital bed at Jackson Memorial. "Texas Builders is my life, and it must not end with me. You can keep this thing rolling. You have to try your best."

It became increasingly hard to maintain focus, but Korah wiped the tears from her eyes and absorbed everything he taught her. After Devin's death, Korah returned to school to complete her higher education. Initially she wanted to be an English teacher, but she changed her major and graduated two years later with a degree in Construction Management, just like Devin.

Korah got her license and fulfilled her promise to not only keep the family business operational, but she also expanded Texas Builders much sooner than her late husband's projected goals. She would forever give Devin Sr. all of the credit for everything Texas Builders had become, but their vice president, Mrs. Priscilla Levin, was solely responsible for keeping the business afloat in the two years following his death. She taught Korah more about the construction game than any of her college professors, and Priscilla made sure the main office remained open throughout Devin's illness and Korah's time in school.

Each day that Korah showed up for work and saw Priscilla sitting behind her desk was a great day. She offered her the CEO position many times over the years, but Priscilla was content with running the show from behind the scenes.

Korah was currently training her nineteen year old daughter, Stephanie, to take Priscilla's place, but everyone knew that Priscilla was irreplaceable. Her expected retirement was something no one in the office wanted to accept or even consider.

● ● ● ● ● ●

Korah arrived at her office after nine a.m., which was late by her standards. But she was the boss, and technically she could get there any time she very well pleased. Unlike many of the other contracting companies in the state, Korah's front office was run entirely by women. That was totally coincidental, but it was also something she couldn't help but take a little pride in.

Korah had taken over her late husband's role as owner and CEO. Priscilla was the best vice president the construction game had ever known. Yolanda was Korah's personal assistant, and Stephanie was the company's administrative assistant. As with Devin, Korah assured her daughter that she did not have to get involved with the family business, but Stephanie never had a goal that didn't involve Texas Builders. She was currently studying construction at Texas Christian University.

Korah was greeted with appreciation and warmth that felt very familial as she headed for her corner office.

"Morning, Ms. Stewart!" Yolanda called.

"Hey, Mama!" Stephanie said.

"Korah, I am so excited!" Priscilla said.

Within seconds all three employees had entered her office. Korah took a seat behind her desk and looked up at them with a broad smile.

"Good morning, ladies! Nice to see everyone in such a good mood on a Monday."

Priscilla took a seat in the chair directly across from Korah, and Stephanie sat down in the only other chair in the room. She rolled it close to her mother's desk and continued to grin at her.

Korah reached and brushed a few stray hairs away from her daughter's eyes. Stephanie was beautiful. She had rich, smooth skin like Korah, and she had her mother's smarts and drive as well. Stephanie was short and pleasingly plump. She wore bold-rimmed glasses, and she always dressed smartly.

Priscilla was Jewish with long, dark hair and stylish reading glasses that were typically parked on the tip of her nose. She was always dressed modestly, with long dresses and pumps, and she preferred pearls over diamonds.

Korah's personal assistant, Yolanda, stood in the doorway cradling her iPad. She was the most beautiful of the crew, with long, sensual legs she chose to show off with skirts on most days.

Yolanda was brown-skinned. Her long hair was braided this morning and wrapped up in a professional bun. She never needed more than a scant coat of lipstick to accentuate her perfect lips and teeth. Nearly every man who had cause to stop by the office found themselves growing enamored with Yolanda, including Korah's own son Devin Jr.

"I can't believe we're this close," Priscilla said. She rubbed her hands in her lap anxiously.

"I can't either," Korah said. "How do we know? I know they're pretty tight-lipped about the whole process."

"I found out," Stephanie said with a hint of pride. "I talked to Anthony last night, and he told me."

Although Korah lived less than 30 miles away from the university, her daughter opted to live on campus, so she would be immersed in the true college experience. Korah hated to see her go, but she was all for the decision.

Stephanie was currently a freshman, and she already had her first college crush. Interestingly, Anthony's mother just happened to be the secretary for the school district's superintendent. Stephanie's relationship with Anthony wasn't enough for the superintendent's decision to be biased, but it was enough for Korah and her crew to get an inside scoop about which bids were at the top of the list.

"When did he tell you that?" Korah asked.

"Last night," Stephanie beamed. "His parents invited me to dinner yesterday."

Korah raised an eyebrow, still smiling. "Really? How was it?"

"Awesome," Stephanie said. "Mrs. Rangel is a great cook. She made meatloaf and cabbage and cornbread."

"Wow, that sounds nice," Korah said. She knew that Stephanie had only been dating the superintendent's secretary's son for a couple of months. "Was that your first time meeting his folks?"

"Actually it was the second time they invited me over," Stephanie said.

"Anthony must talk about you a lot," Korah ventured.

Stephanie blushed.

"Um, what about the bid?" Yolanda asked from the doorway.

"I'm getting to that," Korah said. "But it's not every day that my little girl gets invited to meet her boyfriend's parents. This is a big deal."

"The bid is a big deal too, Mama," Stephanie said. "We're about to be in the big league."

Korah tried her best to slow her beating heart. She still didn't want to get her hopes up – no matter how promising things looked. "Okay, how did our company come up?" she finally asked.

"Anthony told his parents about you already," Stephanie reported. "While we were eating dinner, Mrs. Rangel said, 'So, Stephanie, I understand your mother owns Texas Builders...' I was nervous at first, because I didn't know what she was going to say. But then she smiled and said, 'We've heard great things about them. Your mother offered a bid for the new school we're building.'"

"Oh, Jesus." Korah clasped her hands together over her mouth. Her elbows rested on her desk.

"What's wrong, Mama?"

"I don't know if I want to hear this," Korah said. "You're giving me the shakes."

Stephanie laughed. "I told you it's good news."

Priscilla's smile confirmed this.

"I know, but it's a lot to handle," Korah admitted. "I can't believe she talked to you about it so candidly."

"She didn't," Stephanie said. "But I asked Anthony about it after we got back to school. He said his mom told him we're in the top two. He said it was probably going to be us or Brick House Construction."

Korah closed her eyes and exhaled slowly. She wished Devin Sr. could be there at that moment. She wished he could feel what she was feeling right now. But then she had to catch herself. She got over-excited before, and sometimes it didn't end well.

"Who's Brick House Construction?" she asked.

Yolanda approached with her iPad. "Here they are." She handed the device to the boss.

Korah stared down at the screen and then frowned in confusion. "What is this?"

"That's Brick House Construction," Yolanda said with a snicker. "That's their website."

Korah's smile became curious. "What is this?" she asked again. "This looks like an Abercrombie and Fitch ad."

Yolanda shook her head, grinning knowingly. "Nope. That's them."

Korah stared at the tablet in more detail. The website Yolanda had pulled up was clearly for Brick House Construction. But rather than their logo or one of their constructions or simply links to the appropriate pages, there was a huge photo of a man covering the top half of the screen. He was wearing jeans and a white button-down and a *cowboy hat* – a Stetson. He was leaning against a wrought iron gate that was part of a beautiful entryway to the majestic Avery Ranch. Korah knew the name of the ranch because it was mounted above the gate in dark, iron lettering.

The cowboy was black and strikingly handsome, rough and rugged. His skin was caramel colored, his face clean-shaven, his jawline hard and rigid. He had a serious expression. The way he stared at the camera gave Korah an unexpected chill. Behind him, she could see the ranch, which was stunning, but it seemed to pale in comparison to its apparent owner.

On the bottom right portion of the photo, Korah saw the words

Brock "Brick" Avery
CEO Brick House Construction
Pure Texan

Korah's mouth was hanging open by the time she looked up from the iPad. She stared at Yolanda, unable to articulate the thoughts in her head.

Stephanie leaned over to get a better look, and her eyes widened as well.

"He's a looker, ain't he?" Yolanda offered.

"I'm not worried about what he looks like," Korah managed. "I just can't believe this is their actual website. Seems a little..."

"Caught your eye, though. Didn't it?" Yolanda said.

Korah rolled her eyes at that.

"They're the real deal," Yolanda told her. "They've built a lot of nice properties – and even a school."

Korah's hopes were instantly dashed. Her company had never built a school. That was one of the reasons this job was so important.

"I can't believe this Brock guy has his picture this big on the front page of their website," Korah said, looking at the iPad again. "That's what he wants to lead with – his..." Her eyebrows bunched as she was forced to acknowledge the obvious. "...his, *good looks*? He should call himself *Prick* instead of Brick." She chuckled at her own joke.

But it wasn't funny, and she knew it. Prick Avery might take her dream job! Korah already hated his stupid, handsome face.

"Looks aren't everything," Priscilla said, hoping to regain some of the enthusiasm Yolanda's iPad took away. "The superintendent's people are looking at numbers, not his picture."

"I know," Korah grumbled. "But if he's built a school, he's already got an advantage over us." She finally clicked the link that showed off some of his properties and renovations. Every set of photos turned the day into just another dumb Monday.

"We're still in the top two," Stephanie said. "Maybe if his bid is too high, they'll go with the company with the lower bid, even if we're not as established."

"We're just as good as Brick House," Yolanda argued. "They're impressive, but they can't do anything we can't do."

"That's right," Priscilla said, and Korah's heart dared to beat quickly again.

"If all else fails, maybe Stephanie can nag Anthony so much, he'll make his mom suggest you," Yolanda said with a grin.

"I can do that," Stephanie readily agreed.

"No, please don't," Korah said, shaking her head.

"I was just kidding," Yolanda said.

"I'm not," Stephanie said. She was brimming with excitement over her new task. "I can work on Anthony. Like, for *real*. I'm ready to take one for the team!"

Her smile faded when she saw the look of revulsion her mom fixed on her.

"I wasn't talking about *sex*, Mama," Stephanie said, reading her mind. "Dang. Get your mind out the gutter." She smiled coyly.

CHAPTER THREE
THE COWBOY

Forty miles away in his office on the east side of Dallas, Brock "Brick" Avery sat behind a huge cherry wood desk with an inquisitive look on his face. Brick was a tall man, topping off at nearly six foot four inches. He wore a tan button-down with faded jeans and camel-colored work boots that had steel-toe reinforcements.

He hadn't shaved in a couple of days. His strong cheeks and squared chin were sparsely covered with a burgeoning beard. Brick's eyes were dark, his complexion fair. His hair was short and faded on the back and sides.

His office was huge, decorated with earthy tones and a western theme. The chandelier hanging above him was constructed from iron, shaped by hand. A small end table next to his desk had a cowhide cover with three crooked antlers acting as legs. A coiled lasso hung decoratively on one wall.

Above Brick, there was an original Charles Russell mounted professionally. The painting depicted an intense scene; a group of cowboys huddled in the middle, weapons drawn, eyes wide as they struggled to defend themselves from a swarm of bloodthirsty Indians, who were circling the "good guys" with much a hoot and holler, like in the old western movies.

The painting was given to Brick as a gift. He often shook his head at the irony of the scene when he took the time to admire it. The invaders and land-takers had somehow become the victims, and the Native Americans were depicted as ruthless savages.

Only in America.

But politics aside, the painting was a masterpiece, and like everything else in the office, it instilled Brick's visitors with a sense of Texas pride that generally translated into more construction projects coming his way.

Across from Brick's desk sat his second in command; an old friend and longtime employee named Isaac Kennedy. Isaac was dark-skinned, short and stout. He wore a short beard with wire-rimmed glasses that had thick lenses. He kept his hair shaved completely bald.

Brick had known Isaac since their college days at Texas A & M. Isaac studied accounting while Brick earned his degree in contracting and construction management. When Brick started his own company a year after graduation, Isaac was reluctant to join him, but he eventually quit his job and moved his family to Dallas. Brick could be very persuasive. Twenty years later, Isaac would tell anyone that it was the best move he ever made.

The hot topic this morning was a bid for a new school in Overbrook Meadows. Brick wasn't that hopeful when Isaac first informed him of the opportunity, but they crunched the numbers and gave the best offer they could. Surprisingly, it appeared they had a good shot at pulling off an upset. Isaac had sources in the school district who told him Brick House was currently at the top of the list. There was only one other company offering serious competition.

"Well I'll be damned," Brick said, leaning back in his executive chair. His smile was moderate, but on the inside, his brain was racing.

Brick House built a school before, but it was for a much smaller district, valued at close to five million. This new project would be worth three times as much. Plus if his company won the bid, they would be a shoe-in for additional projects in the school district.

Brick and Isaac had been trying for years to elevate their company above the rank and file. Isaac felt like their time had finally arrived. Brick was reluctant to agree, but there was no denying this was the big one. This project was every contractor's dream.

"Who are your contacts?" Brick asked his vice president. "Are they reliable?"

"Members of the school board," Isaac said. "And yes, they are."

"How did we get ahead of Industrial Works?" Brick asked, referring to their top competitor.

"Their bid is too high," Isaac reported. "Plus they had some problems with Arlington ISD."

"Really? I didn't hear about that."

"Yes you did," Isaac said. "Remember that stadium that went a year past their projections? All of the Arlington high schools had to play a whole season at Layne Field. Everybody was pissed about that."

"But the stadium turned out very nice," Brick recalled. "Overbrook Meadows is holding that against them?"

"When it gets this tight, everything comes up in the meetings," Isaac told him.

"Hmmm." Brick chewed on a toothpick that was poking out of the corner of his mouth. "And McIntosh? I know they put a bid in for this one, too."

"Actually they withdrew it," Isaac told him. "They just picked up a dozen warehouses in Azle that are gonna keep them tied up for the next few years. They don't have the manpower for anything else right now."

Brick narrowed his eyes, looking for more reasons to remain cynical.

"What's the matter?" Isaac asked with a grin. "You're looking like this isn't the biggest thing that's ever happened to us."

"It is," Brick said with a sigh. "That's why I don't wanna get my hopes up. I don't have that kind of luck, Isaac. Never have. It's never this easy."

"Luck doesn't have anything to do with this," his friend said. "We put up the best bid, and we're definitely qualified to do the job. We deserve this. You know that."

"Yeah, but we're not the *most* qualified," Brick countered.

"Every company that's building schools nowadays started off somewhere," Isaac said. "And my people tell me Overbrook Meadows is looking for some new blood. They wanna keep the money in Texas. And they are in a budget crunch, so the lower bids are getting a lot of attention, even if they're from less established contractors."

Brick inhaled and blew it out slowly.

Isaac chuckled. "Do I gotta light a fire under your ass to get some excitement in here? I tell you we got an excellent shot at winning this thing, and all you got to talk about is why we shouldn't get it..."

Brick smiled and let go of some of the tension eating away at him. "So it's your intention to get me fired up about this?"

Isaac nodded. "Yes, sir. I'd say that's entirely appropriate."

Brick laughed and let go of his lingering doubt. "Alright. I'm in. We're gonna bring this baby home."

"That's right," Isaac said. "I've got no doubt about it."

Brick's chest swelled. Isaac never gave him that much of an endorsement unless he was positive, or very close to it. In his mind's eye, Brick saw their company logo prominently displayed at major construction sites, like concert stadiums and high-rise office buildings. It was much too soon to fantasize about such things, but he couldn't help it. He wanted it all.

This was part of the reason Brick didn't want to get his hopes up. Now that he claimed the victory in his heart and mind, he would remain obsessed with the bid until the superintendent made the official announcement.

"How much longer before they call it?" he asked his vice president.

"Three weeks," Isaac said.

Brick frowned at that. "Are they still taking more bids in the meantime?"

"Yes, the cut-off isn't until next Friday. But all of the powerhouses have already weighed-in. No one's gonna come and snatch it out of our hands at this point. A few out-of-staters might try, but it's like I told you; they wanna keep the money in Texas."

"Are we at the very top of the list?" Brick asked. "No one else even close?"

"No, I didn't say that," Isaac replied. "We're at the top with one other company – but they're not gonna beat us."

"Why not?"

"They're too small," Isaac explained. "They have a cheaper bid, but they've never built a school before. They're untested."

"Then why are they being considered?"

"Because they do have a lower bid."

"You went over our proposal again? We can't lower ours at all?"

Isaac shook his head. "Not if you wanna make money off this thing."

Brick actually didn't need to get rich off this one job. Once they built the school, the notoriety would make them much more money down the road. But he couldn't say the same for his staff. Isaac deserved to be compensated for his hard work, and so did their construction team.

"Well, who's our competition?" he asked. "Is it someone we've gone against before?"

Isaac shook his head as he reached for his laptop that was perched on the corner of Brick's desk. Isaac disabled the screensaver and offered the computer to Brick. He already had a website pulled up.

"*Texas Builders...*" Brick mumbled as he read the screen. "How long they been in business?"

"Twenty-five years," Isaac informed him.

"Any notables?" Brick asked as he perused their website.

"Probably nothing you've heard of," Isaac stated. "A lot of nice houses, churches. I think they have a line with 7-11. They built 12 of them in the past couple of years, from Houston to Oklahoma. They got a few restaurants. They built the new YMCA in Beaumont."

Brick raised an eyebrow. "Impressive." He was referring to both Isaac's comments and the pictures he was now shuffling through on their website. "Who's the big man at Texas Builders?"

"Not a man," Isaac said. "It's a woman."

Brick looked up at him with a grin. "No shit?"

"It's 2014," Isaac replied. "You shouldn't be surprised by that."

"Construction is still a man's game," Brick grunted. He began searching the website for biographical information about the owner.

"Construction used to be a *white* man's game," Isaac replied. "Especially in Texas. Mrs. Stewart is no more an anomaly than you are now."

"*Mrs. Stewart?*" Brick said. His smile deepened when he pulled up the page he was looking for. "Oh, she's nice," he drawled.

Isaac rolled his eyes.

"She been running this company for 25 years?" Brick asked.

"Her husband founded it," Isaac told him. "He died some time ago. Mrs. Stewart has been running things ever since."

"*Korah*," Brick said. He moistened his bottom lip subconsciously. "That's a pretty name – for a pretty lady. I think I need to meet her."

Isaac scratched his forehead. "And what would be the reason for such a meeting?"

"I don't know," Brick said. "I'll think of something."

He continued to stare at the small photo of Korah on her website. She wore a pants suit that wasn't all that flattering, and the picture was black and white. But Brick didn't need a lot of help when it came to uncovering a woman's beauty. The suit couldn't hide the seductive spread of Korah's hips or her bountiful bosoms, which beckoned to be free of the confining outfit. Korah had dark brown skin, full lips, serious brown eyes.

According to her biography, she was educated and fully qualified for her role as contractor, but Brick still found it interesting that she stood at the head of such a successful company. That was no doubt due to his upbringing. He was a country boy from a small neighborhood in Lewisville. The way he was raised, men did the hard work; the heavy lifting, car fixing and home building. Brick knew that women were making great strides in the workplace nowadays, but there were still occupations that seemed better suited for men.

Or maybe he was wrong about that.

The longer he stared at Korah's photograph, the more convinced he was that he had to see her in person. He looked up from the laptop and smiled at his vice president.

"Isaac, ready the Batmobile. I'm going to Overbrook Meadows."

Isaac laughed at him.

Brick pushed a button on his desk phone. After a short beep, a sweet voice responded: "Yes, Mr. Avery?"

"Persia, I'm going to Overbrook Meadows." He gave her the address for Korah's main office. "Program that into my GPS," he instructed.

"No problem, Mr. Avery," the voice on the other end of the line responded.

"Also, look up this website," Brick continued. He gave her Texas Builders' URL. "I want to check out some of their properties on the way there. Plug a few of them into my GPS as well, if you don't mind."

"Of course I don't, Mr. Avery."

Brick pushed the button on his phone to end the call.

Isaac was giving him one of those looks when they locked eyes again.

"What?"

"What is your plan?" Isaac wanted to know.

"I think I'll tell her I *really* need this job, for my daughter's cancer treatment. Maybe she'll drop out of the running."

Isaac blinked at him. "That's got to be the most ridiculous thing I've ever heard."

Brick laughed. "Why are you being so negative?"

"You don't have any children," Isaac pointed out. "And that smile of yours will only get you in trouble, if you try your wheeling and dealing with this woman."

"Wheeling and dealing is what I do for a living," Brick replied smugly. He leaned back in his throne and grinned mischievously. "I do believe you underestimate me, sir."

CHAPTER FOUR
FAULT FINDING

Brick drove a Ford F-150 King Ranch. The interior was immaculate. The V8 engine was strong enough to yank a barn from its foundation and drag it to another county. Brick took the scenic route down I-30, past the Texas Rangers Stadium and Six Flags amusement park in Arlington.

His GPS directed him to a few convenience stores along the way that had been constructed by Texas Builders. Brick parked in front of the buildings and took his time inspecting the exterior. He had several projects under construction at the moment, but like Korah, his company had its own construction team. Brick didn't have to check up on his foreman, and he knew he'd get a call from Isaac if something unexpected occurred.

The 7-11's built by Korah's company were perfect, but Brick wasn't impressed. Major chains always had specific architectural designs and schematics, leaving little guesswork or creative liberties for the contractor. Brick did concede that the designs had been followed perfectly, and there were no blemishes he could see from the outside.

When he reached Overbrook Meadows, Brick stopped briefly in the Forest Hill neighborhood and found a community center Korah's company completed earlier that year. The structure was once again flawless, from the main building to the basketball courts and soccer field in the back.

But that didn't mean Korah's company was in any way exceptional. As a contractor, she bid on jobs and delegated the responsibilities to others. She would be responsible for any mistakes that occurred, but if there were no mishaps, then a contractor's job could be fairly easy.

Brick realized he was on a fault finding mission, and his next stop proved equally fruitless. Sunrise Baptist Church was located on the south side of Overbrook Meadows in a neighborhood that appeared to be on the decline. There were no prominent businesses along the main thoroughfare, only pawn shops, liquor stores and fried food joints.

The church was tucked deeply in the neighborhood, on the corner of Illinois and Hattie Street. Brick's eyes widened when he rounded the corner and saw the steeple poking above the tree line encircling the property.

Brick saw the church on Texas Builders' website already, but the photos didn't do the building justice. The horn-shaped roof was an architectural masterpiece. It flowed majestically from the tip and began to curve outward towards the middle. The glasswork followed this pattern seamlessly. The building was designed with brick and redwood, with stained glass windows on either side of the vestibule and a collection of smaller classroom buildings out back. The landscape was immaculate. Every tree and shrub grew in perfect alignment.

Brick parked near the main entrance and exited his vehicle for a closer look. He was strolling down the south side of the building when he noticed a landscaper watching and then heading his way on a riding mower. Brick continued his inspection until the stranger came to a stop within ten feet and put the mower in park. He killed the engine and hopped off the vehicle gingerly.

Brick turned and gave him his full attention. The man looked to be in his early sixties. He pulled a handkerchief from his pocket and wiped the sweat from his dark brow. He smiled and offered a hand to shake when he was within touching distance.

"Morning. What can I do for you?"

Brick was surprised that a groundskeeper was asking him to state his business, but he understood that crime was surely a problem in the neighborhood.

"Morning," he said, shaking the man's rough hand. "My name is Isaac Avery," he lied, borrowing his partner's first name for the alias. "Just stopping by to take a look at your church."

The man smiled genuinely. He rubbed a sore spot on the small of his back as he turned and admired the structure himself.

"She's a beaut, ain't she? Brand new. Had her for about five years. Sometimes I come out here just to stare at her. I never dreamed something this beautiful would be standing on this piece of land. You should've seen the church we had before. I loved that place. Sho' did. But *this* church... Can't nothing compare to this."

Brick grinned at the gleam in the man's eyes. These days it was rare to find someone who truly appreciated quality architecture.

"I'm Pastor Davis," the man said. "Assistant Pastor."

"Oh, well it's nice to meet you," Brick said. He regarded the man oddly. The confusion must have shone on his face.

"Eh heh. I know I don't look like much," the older fellow said. "Don't worry. I clean up pretty nice, come Sunday morning."

Brick chuckled. "I'm sorry. I thought you were the groundskeeper."

"I'm that, too," Pastor Davis said. "We got some youngins here that help out on Saturday afternoon, but for the most part it's just me. I do it by choice. I been mowing these grounds for over twenty years. It's a hobby, at this point. Keeps me out of the wife's hair," he said and laughed again.

Brick nodded, his smile growing wider. He liked this man. Pastor Davis had a good sense of humor, and Brick respected anyone who wasn't afraid of a little manual labor.

"You're doing a great job out here," he told him. "I haven't seen anything on this side of town that looks as good as this place."

"Thank you kindly," the pastor said. "This church is my life. It means a whole lot to the community."

"I'm sure it does," Brick said, then, "If you don't mind me asking, how'd y'all get the funding for this project? This looks like it could go for three million – easy."

The pastor nodded, still smiling. "That ain't nothing but God," he said. "We got a nice-size congregation. We was saving up for years. Our old church had a lot wrong with it; bad foundation, leaky roofs. Towards the end, the water wasn't even safe to drink. The pipes was so bad, rust was coming out the water fountains.

"We got a small grant," the pastor said. "It was part of the city's overall renovation project. They restored the north end of Evans Street and threw a lot of money at Cobb Park, too. But even with the grant, we still didn't have enough to build something like this. But Korah, God bless her, she took the job because her mother used to be a member here. We buried Mrs. Clemmons a year before the new church was built; God rest her soul."

Brick's throat caught at the mention of Korah's name. He wasn't sure why. It wasn't like he didn't know this already. "Korah?"

"Look at me talking like I know her personally," the pastor said and laughed. "Ms. Stewart owns the construction company that built this church. I was in close contact with her during construction. Awesome woman. I don't think she made much – if anything – from this job. I never asked her directly, but I know how much money we had, and I know what we ended up with. I think she did it out of the goodness of her heart; out of respect for her mama."

Pastor Davis was a virtual treasure trove of information. The more he listened, the more Brick came to respect the woman who might beat him out of his dream job.

"Excuse me for bumping my gums," the pastor said. "My wife always says if you wanna get me to talking, ask me something about this church." He chuckled. "Now, what was it again that you needed, young man?"

At forty-five years of age, Brick was rarely in a position to be referred to as a "young man." That made him like the talkative pastor even more.

"Just bought me some land in Venus," he said, with absolutely no qualms about lying to a pastor on church property. "I'm thinking about hiring Texas Builders to build a house and a barn for me. I looked them up on the computer and wanted to check out some of their properties first."

The older man's eyes lit up. "Oh! Well you already know about Miss Korah then."

Brick shook his head. "Actually I don't know any more than you just told me. She sounds like an awesome woman, though. Not too many contractors out there willing to put community service ahead of the almighty dollar."

"Ain't that the truth?" the pastor said. "Miss Korah is one of a kind, for sure. She's beautiful, *and* she's single. Are you married Mr....?"

Brick chuckled. "Avery," he said. "And no, I'm not."

"Either way, you'd enjoy working with Miss Korah," the pastor said. "Very nice on the eyes, that woman is. Do you need her business card? I'm pretty sure I got one in the church somewhere."

"Oh, well I, uh–"

"Hey, you know what?" The man produced his cellphone. "I bet I still got their number saved. I haven't talked to them since they finished up work here, but I don't think the number has changed..."

Before Brick could respond, the pastor not only found the number for Texas Builders, but he dialed it as well.

"Hello? Hi. This is Assistant Pastor Keith Davis, from Sunrise Baptist Church on Illinois. Mmm hmm. Yes Ma'am. Thank you. Everything's just fine, thank you. Oh, no. No, there's no problem. The reason why I'm calling is there's a man here who came to check out our church, and he says he wants to hire y'all to do some work for him. Mmm hmm. Yes, Ma'am. He's right here. Do you want – uh, okay. Well, hey, let me let you talk to him directly..."

The pastor offered the phone to Brick. "Here you go. I got 'em on the line."

Brick took the phone and cleared his throat. "Hello?"

"Good morning," Stephanie said.

"Morning."

"I understand you're interested in getting some work done..."

"Yes," Brick said. "I just bought twenty acres down in Venus. Nothing at all on it. I'd like to build a home for my family and a nice barn, too. Maybe a stable. Thinking about getting me some horses. I went to your website and thought I'd check out some of your work myself, before I gave you guys a call."

"Oh, that's great," Stephanie said. "I hope everything you saw was up to par."

"I'm very impressed," Brick said honestly. "Especially with this church. You guys do great work. Is Mrs. Stewart available? I'd like to meet with her today."

"Um, I can make an appointment," Stephanie said. "Could you hold for a moment?"

"Sure can," Brick said. In the interim, he watched the pastor, who was grinning at him like a damned fool.

"What is your name?" Stephanie asked when she came back to the line.

"Avery," Brick said. "Isaac Avery."

"Thank you, Mr. Avery. I can make an appointment for tomorrow morning, if you like."

"Actually," Brick said, "I'll be out of town tomorrow. Is there any chance of meeting with her today?"

"You're welcome to stop by our office today," Stephanie offered. "You can meet with Ms. Stewart's assistant or our vice president. Either one of them will be happy to–"

"Actually," Brick said, "I'd like to meet with the head honcho herself. Sorry, I'm a little old-fashioned," he said with a chuckle.

If Stephanie was offended by the comment, she didn't let on. "I'm sorry," she said, "but it's not possible to meet with Ms. Stewart today. She's out of the office. I can schedule an appointment for ten a.m. tomorrow morning..."

"I'll be in Oklahoma tomorrow morning," Brick lied. "Is there no way I can meet with her today? If she's working, I don't mind meeting her at one of your worksites."

This time Stephanie was clearly irritated when she told him, "Hold on for a moment."

While he waited, Brick continued to smile at the pastor, who looked disappointed that he might not be able to steer a paying customer Korah's way.

"Mr. Avery," Stephanie said when she came back to the phone.

"Yes. I'm here."

"Ms. Stewart said you can meet her at a project we're building on Sycamore School Road. She said she'll be there for another hour. Will you able to make it there in time?"

"Yes Ma'am," Brick said. "Do you have the exact address?"

Stephanie gave it to him and added, "That may not show up in a GPS yet."

"It's okay," Brick told her. "I'm familiar with the area. Thank you very much."

"I appreciate that," he told the pastor when he returned the phone. "You've been quite helpful."

"No problem," the older man said. "Miss Korah is a special lady. She deserves all the blessings God has planned for her."

"I'm sure she does," Brick said. *As long as those blessings don't have anything to do with my bid on the school!* "You take care."

He turned and headed back to his truck. Brick still didn't know what he would say to Korah when they were face to face, but incidentals like that were never a deterrent. His brain worked very well on the fly.

● ● ● ● ● ●

When Brick got to the site, he was not happy to see a contractor's sign posted out front that was not his own, but he was excited to see construction work going on. He parked on the street and stepped out into the warm morning sun. The smell of wet concrete and the exhaust fumes from heavy machinery made his pulse quicken.

Brick felt at home on any construction site. Growing up in Lewisville, he'd done all sorts of work with his hands. His father was an auto mechanic, and his uncle was a carpenter. Brick recognized the wonder and power of tools before he could speak.

He was grateful that his mother encouraged him to put education first, but Brick never looked down on men who broke a sweat and bruised their hands for a living. Even as head of his own small empire, Brick still rolled up his sleeves and worked alongside his men on a regular basis.

Before he could make it too far onto the property, Brick was approached by an impressive young man who wore a hardhat and jeans and a tee-shirt with the Texas Builders' logo stitched on the breast.

"How's it going?" the man asked. "What can I do for you?"

"Morning," Brick said. "I'm looking for Korah Stewart. I was told I could find her here. My name's Avery."

"Oh, hey, how's it going?" the man said. "I'm Devin. You called about a job in Venus, right?"

"Yes, I did."

"I'm head of construction at Texas Builders," Devin said. "What kind of work do you need done?"

Brick raised an eyebrow. This company was full of surprises; a woman CEO and a twenty-year old running construction. But as Brick studied Devin's face, he saw similarities between him and the photo of Korah on their website. It only took a few moments to deduce that this was Korah's son. The father's death no doubt shook up the company, but they had adjusted and were thriving without him. Brick was impressed.

"I think Stephanie mentioned a house and a barn..." Devin prompted.

Brick didn't want to spin his web of lies any further, and luckily he didn't have to. Behind Devin he saw a woman and a man round the corner of the building, heading their way. The woman was dressed for work in jeans and a tee shirt and – did she have on steel-toed boots? Brick's eyes widened in astonishment.

Even with a hardhat planted firmly on her head, Brick could tell this was Korah. But she looked remarkably different than she did in the suit she wore for her website photo. Her shirt was tucked in, and her jeans were a little baggie. Her mission was not to impress, but she certainly had Brick's attention. The tee shirt couldn't downplay the sensual swells of her breasts or her hourglass figure. Her smooth skin was without a blemish.

Her lips curved into a smile as she spoke to the man she was walking with. He wore khakis with a golf shirt. His loafers were not suitable for construction, and, despite his hardhat, Brick could tell the man wasn't there to work. Brick thought he might be the property owner. He and Korah shook hands and then headed in separate directions.

Devin looked back to see what had stolen their new customer's attention. When his eyes returned to Brick, they were narrowed and suspicious. Stephanie already told him this guy seemed cagey over the phone.

"Mr. Avery?"

Brick continued to ignore him as Korah approached. When their eyes met, hers registered confusion, and then she looked suspicious as well. Brick didn't like to see that look directed at him – not from her at least. He would prefer that she smiled at him, like she did with the property owner a few moments ago.

"Hi, Ms. Stewart?" Brick said when she came and stood next to her son.

"Brock Avery," Korah said, a little disdainfully, Brick thought.

"Please, call me Brick."

Devin looked from the stranger to his mother. "You two know each other?" he asked Korah.

"No, but Brock is the CEO of Brick House Construction," Korah informed her son. "Can't imagine why he'd want us to build something for him."

Now Devin looked angry and protective. Brick thought he might take a swing at him. That made him smile, for some reason. He couldn't help it.

"Please, call me Brick," he insisted.

"What can we do for you, Mr. Avery?" Devin asked. He folded his arms under his chest, making it clear that the question was rhetorical. They weren't going to do a goddamned thing for the likes of him.

"Do you have time to meet with me?" Brick asked Korah. "For a late breakfast? I can see that you're busy. Won't take but a minute of your time..."

Devin's frown intensified, but Korah's curiosity was piqued. Just this morning her team was contemplating how Brick House might steal their dream job away from them. Now the CEO of Brick House was here in the flesh, and he wanted something from her. What could it be?

Korah checked her watch before saying, "I got ten minutes."

Devin turned and stared at her. He opened his mouth but was respectful enough not to question her in public.

"There's a Mimi's not too far from here," Brick suggested.

"There's a Jack in the Box right there," Korah said and pointed to the restaurant across the street.

"That'll work, too," Brick said, still smiling. "Got my truck parked right over there." He threw a thumb over his shoulder. "I'll bring you back safe and sound."

Devin blew hot fumes from his nostrils.

Brick gave him another antagonizing grin.

Korah checked out his bad ass truck before saying, "I'm sure I can make it over there just fine. Go ahead. I'll meet you there."

CHAPTER FIVE
INDECENT PROPOSAL

Brick was already seated at a table when Korah entered the fast food restaurant. She didn't have her son with her – which was a surprise. After the terrible first impression, Brick didn't think Devin would let her come alone.

Korah left her hardhat in the car, revealing her shoulder-length hair that was wavy and vibrant. Brick found her very attractive, despite her lack of makeup. He waved in her direction when Korah looked his way. She headed to his table with a blank expression. The moment she sat down, Brick heard the cashier call his number.

"Excuse me," he said and rose from his seat.

Korah frowned and cocked her head slightly. Brick smiled at her.

"I ordered us some breakfast," he said. "I'll be right back."

"Thank you, but I don't want anything," Korah told him.

"I already paid for it," Brick said. "If you're not hungry now, you can take it with you."

Korah started to respond, but Brick had already walked away and was spared from seeing her reaction.

The nerve, she thought. She was already convinced Brick was an arrogant asshole, and every move he made seemed to reinforce this assumption.

He came back a couple of seconds later with a tray full of food. He placed a wrapped sandwich in front of Korah and then served her a medium coffee and finally a hash brown. This was the second time today a man offered her breakfast that she did not want. However the coffee did smell heavenly, and the aromas from the hash brown made her stomach growl. She cursed her body for the natural response. God, she really was hungry. But she wouldn't give Brick the satisfaction of watching her chow down on the meal he provided.

He took his time placing his own breakfast on the table before settling into his seat. His slight movements caused his cologne (or maybe it was only deodorant) to waft from his body and find Korah's nostrils. She found the scent pleasing, but she didn't feel the same way about Brick. She sighed impatiently when he finally returned his attention to her.

"Sorry," he said, unwrapping a croissant sandwich. "I'm really hungry." He took a huge bite and hummed graciously.

Korah cleared her throat and said, "Um, so what exactly can I do for you?" she asked.

Brick smiled. "All business, huh?" he asked around a mouthful of food.

"I'm busy," Korah said flatly.

"Okay," Brick said and put his sandwich down. He finished chewing the food in his mouth and reached for his coffee. He took a few sips and swallowed everything down and smiled cordially. He plucked a napkin from the dispenser on the table and took his time wiping whatever crumbs might have been lingering on his lips.

"That's a good sandwich," he said. "I think you should eat it."

Before Korah could respond, he added, "And I think we got off on the wrong foot."

"That's bound to happen, when you lie during your introduction," she told him.

"I apologize," Brick said. "I know that wasn't right. I just wanted to meet you, is all. I didn't know if you'd be willing to talk, if you knew who I was."

"Well, I'm here," Korah said. "So could you please tell me what you want?"

"How'd you know who I was?" Brick asked instead. "Have we met before? I'm sorry, if I don't recall..."

Korah frowned and shook her head. "No, we've never met. I saw your picture on your website."

Bricks smile grew wider. "Really? You checked out my website?"

Korah nodded. "I did."

"Why?" Brick asked. "Do you need some work done?"

He laughed when Korah didn't respond. "I'm just kidding," he said. "You probably looked me up for the same reason I looked you up."

"And what reason might that be?"

"Your bid on the new school for Overbrook Meadows ISD," Brick said. "I talked to some people who said you're close to the top of the list. Congratulations."

"Thank you," Korah said. "And congrats to yourself."

"Do you think you'll win the bid?" Brick asked. "What do you think your chances are?"

Korah was surprised by the question, but she didn't miss a beat. "About as good as your chances," she told him.

Brick grinned. "Yeah, you might be right."

Korah didn't like his confidence or the twinkle in his eyes, but at the same time she found both of these characteristics compelling. This man was bad news, plain and simple. And he was also smart and conniving. If he was planning something that affected her business, then Korah wanted to know about it. Otherwise she wanted to walk out and leave him sitting there with that smug expression on his face.

"What'd you think of my website?"

Another curveball. The more impatient Korah became, the less she could hold her tongue.

"I think you're arrogant," she replied.

Brick didn't flinch. "Really? How come?"

"Because of the picture on the home page. The first thing you want people to see is *you*."

"I'm the owner of the company," he explained.

"What difference does that make?" Korah asked. "Your work is most important. It doesn't matter what you look like."

"I disagree," he said. "And Paula Deen has her picture on the front page of her website. So does Beyonce. Why shouldn't I?"

"I am not your media consultant," Korah snapped. "Why do you care what I think?"

"You have a picture of yourself on your website," Brick stated.

"Not on the front page."

"I think it looks nice," he said. "You should put your picture on the front page. You're a very pretty lady."

Korah's forearms sprouted goose bumps despite her growing contempt for this man. She checked her watch. "Well, it's been fun..."

Brick laughed. It was a hearty, manly laugh. He had nice teeth, perfect lips. His humor was disarming, though Korah was doing her best to keep her defenses up.

"I checked out some of your properties on the way here," he said.

Korah was about to rise from her seat, but that comment stopped her. Brick was more successful than her, so she was interested in his opinion. But she didn't want him to know she was interested, so she didn't offer a response.

"You do great work," he said. "You already know you got those 7-11's down pat. I was also impressed with the community center in Forest Hill. But the best thing I've seen today is that church on Hattie. That is a spectacular construction, Ms. Stewart. If I had a hat on, I'd certainly tip it for you."

Korah was momentarily taken aback. She had merely scrolled through his website, but Brick took the time to visit some of her properties personally. She was clearly at a tactical disadvantage, and she didn't like that at all. But she was also flattered that a contractor of his caliber had good things to say about her work.

"Wh, why are you visiting my constructions?" she asked.

Brick leaned forward and placed his strong forearms on the table. His closeness gave Korah another unexpected crop of goose bumps. She subconsciously leaned away from him.

"Can I be honest with you?" he asked.

That gave Korah a genuine chuckle. "You know how to be honest, Mr. Avery?"

He smiled. "I deserve that. The truth is when I learned how close you are to snagging the school job, I was a little worried, and I thought I'd check out the competition. I won't lie: Initially I was looking for flaws in your work. But I'm happy to say I didn't find any. You built that church with your own construction team?"

In truth, her mother's church was the most ambitious architectural design Korah had ever attempted. Devin's crew managed to complete most of the work, but they had to bring in another company to construct the unusual design of the roof. Korah had always been proud of the finished product, but now she felt embarrassed to admit that she couldn't do it without help.

And why should she admit it? She didn't owe this man a thing.

"What does that have to do with why you're here?" she asked. "Listen, Mr. Avery, if you don't tell me what you want–"

"Why can't you call me Brick?" he asked, almost pleadingly.

"I'm gonna call you a lot more than that, if you don't–"

"Okay, okay," he said. "I'm not trying to drag this out. I just wanted to get a read on you. You're not at all what I expected."

Korah desperately wanted to know if that was a good or bad thing, and she cursed herself for caring.

"What I wanted to ask is if you think we could work together," Brick said.

Fat chance, Korah thought.

"On what?" she asked.

"The new school," he said. "I think it would be mutually beneficial if we came to some sort of agreement before the school board makes a decision."

Korah wanted to tell him to go to hell, but on a business level she felt that she had to at least hear him out.

"How is that supposed to work?" she asked.

"Well, it's like this," Brick said. "From what I hear, one of us will most likely get the contract. I don't know about you, but this is a big deal for my company. This is an opportunity we don't want to lose out on. If you feel the same way, then I suggest we come up with an agreement that would guarantee *both of us* involvement in the project. Does that sound like something you'd be interested in?"

"I still don't see how that would work," Korah said honestly.

"Well, let's say one of us drops out of the running," Brick said, "with the understanding that the other company will hire them for some of the construction work when they win the bid."

That was so ridiculous, Korah couldn't believe he said it with a straight face.

"So what you're saying is," she surmised, "you're willing to drop out and let me win the bid, and in return I'm obligated to hire your company for construction?"

"Or *you* could drop out," Brick countered. "And, yes, I would hire your company to complete *some* of the construction."

"Why would I drop out, when I have as good a chance of winning as you do?" Korah wanted to know.

"Because if we do it my way, we'd both be guaranteed inclusion in the project," Brick said. "Whereas, as it stands, there will be only one winner, and the loser gets nothing."

"But why in the world would I hire you for construction work after I win the bid?" Korah asked. "I have my own construction company, and you do, too."

"There will be enough work for two or even *three* crews," Brick explained. "No sense in being greedy. And if *you* drop out, I give you my word you'll be included in the project."

Korah thought his proposal was preposterous. Surely Brick knew that his *word* meant absolutely nothing to her. She didn't know him at all, and he'd already proven himself to be a liar. Even if they wrote up a legally binding agreement, she still wouldn't trust him.

But on the other hand, Brick's offer did make sense. Why should one of them lose completely when they could share the victory? But then again, why would Brick want to share the victory? Stephanie said his company was the front-runner. Did he know something they didn't know?

At the very least, Korah thought she should run the idea by her team. She already knew Devin wouldn't like the idea. If they won the bid, he'd want all of the spoils for himself. He didn't like Brick, and he wouldn't want any Brick House employees on his site. But Devin was a hothead, and bad tempers should never be involved in a business decision.

"I'll think about it," she decided. "I'll get in touch with you."

Brick reached into his pocket and produced a business card. "My cellphone's on here."

Korah took it and tucked it inside her purse without looking at it.

Before she rose to her feet, Brick said, "So, are you originally from Overbrook Meadows?"

Korah shook her head. "No, I'm from Chicago."

"Beautiful city," Brick mused. "Do you ever think about returning, or are you pretty much settled in here?"

Korah was not comfortable with the new direction of the conversation. She checked her watch again. "Mr. Avery, I'm sorry, but I have to go."

He reached across the table and touched her hand. The unexpected contact made Korah's throat catch. The serious look in Brick's eyes made her breaths stop altogether.

"Korah, please, call me Brick," he insisted.

Their closeness brought a lot of observations to the forefront of Korah's mind, like how pretty his eyes were, how big and strong his hands were, how nice he smelled and the way confidence oozed out of every one of his pores.

Brick filled her head with so many contradictions. She hated his arrogance, but at the same time, it was starting to turn her on – and she hated that, too. She politely withdrew her hand.

"Okay, *Brick*. I have to go."

His nostrils flared as he took a deep inhalation. "Are you seeing someone?" he asked. "This whole school business aside, I'd really like to take you out, somewhere nice."

Korah's heart thumped as she shook her head. This was getting to be too much, which coincidentally described Brick to a T. He was *too much* – of everything, both good and bad. Her internal warning system was blaring. But at the same time, her clitoris was starting to tingle. She had to get away from this man, ASAP.

"I don't think that would be a good idea," she told him.

"Why not? Because of the school thing? Look, we don't have to work together on that. If you wanna take your chances with winning the bid, I understand. But I do want to see you again."

Korah couldn't stop herself from asking, "Why?"

"Because I've never been attracted to a woman in jeans and a hardhat," Brick confided. "But when I saw you this morning, I felt like you walked right out of a fantasy I didn't even know I had. I can't explain it any better than that. I've had female electricians and carpenters on my sites before, but not one of them ever affected me the way you did today. That's the God-honest truth."

Korah had been hoping for some honesty from this man for the past twenty minutes. Now that she finally had it, she found that she wasn't prepared to respond.

"We'll talk later," she managed and hurried out of the restaurant.

She didn't start hating Brick again until she got to her car and considered how easily he took her confidence away. But then again, if what Brick told her was true, then she had no reason to be upset about the meeting. He wanted to guarantee her a piece of the school job, and he was infatuated with her – both of which translated to an advantage for her company.

But of course that was a big IF. Could she trust anything that man had to say?

That remained to be seen.

• • • • • •

Korah told her son she'd return to his site after the meeting, but she decided against it. Not only would Devin be adamantly against Brick's strange proposal, but he'd be upset with his mother for even considering it. He might even notice that she was hot and bothered all of a sudden.

No. She didn't want that at all.

Instead Korah called Yolanda and told her about both of Brick's offers as she headed back to the office.

Her assistant surprised her by saying, "You should take that deal. And you should go out with him, too."

"Why would I do that?" Korah wondered.

"Well, he is fine," Yolanda said. "And he's rich. And you're both contractors. I'm sure you two have a lot in common."

"I'm not talking about dating him," Korah said with a frown. "I mean the school deal."

"Oh, well you should do that too, because I don't think we're gonna win the bid," Yolanda said. "I just got off phone with Mr. Harden. He says he's going to file a lawsuit against us and Clark Construction, if somebody doesn't start repairing that shopping center this week."

"*What?*" Korah was immediately livid. "I talked to him a couple of weeks ago! He said he was going to work with us on that."

"Yeah, but shingles are starting to fall off the roof now," Yolanda told her. "He had to block off some areas, because he's afraid they're going to fall on one of the customers. He said, and I quote, '*Everybody's talking about what they're gonna do, but nobody's doing a goddamned thing, and this shit's getting worse and worse.*'"

Korah gritted her teeth. She saw red behind her pupils. She couldn't very well fault Mr. Harden for any of this, because he paid for a job, and they didn't deliver the excellence they promised. She could, however, fault the hell out of Clark Construction. She intended to fault them all the way to the courthouse, if need be.

"Did you talk to Herschel?" she asked Yolanda. "You told him I wanted to meet with him this morning?"

"Yes," Yolanda said. "He'll be here at noon."

Korah checked the clock on her dashboard. It was a little after eleven.

"I'm on my way," she growled.

"He probably won't show up," Yolanda predicted. "Mr. Harden says Herschel won't even answer the phone when he tries to get in touch with him."

"If he doesn't show, you and I are hitting the streets this afternoon," Korah said. "I don't care what rock he's hiding under. We're not giving up until I see him face to face."

"Yes, Ms. Stewart. I'll be ready."

CHAPTER SIX
CONSTRUCTION WOES

The trouble with Frederick Harden started eight years ago, when he began taking bids for a shopping center he wanted built in the upscale Cedar Lake neighborhood. Korah's company had never constructed anything that large and expensive, but Priscilla submitted a proposal, just in case. She told Korah it was a long shot, which made their celebration that much sweeter when Mr. Harden called and told them the job was theirs.

Back then Devin Jr. was a freshman in college, and Texas Builders didn't have their own construction company. After considerable research, they hired Clark Construction to erect the shopping center. Herschel Clark, the owner, was confident about the project, and he was competent – or so they thought. He didn't have any complaints filed against him with the BBC, and all of the building owners Korah contacted had good things to say about him.

As fate would have it, this would be Korah's first bad business deal. Clark Construction had a long history of shoddy work, corners cut and overall unscrupulous work ethics. They didn't build anything to last forever; they just needed it to last for five years or so. After that they could blame their poor craftsmanship on any number of things and put off repairs until people were hopping made and lawsuits were being filed.

The problems at the Harden Shopping Center began to manifest one by one over the next eight years. They currently had foundation concerns, "organic" shingles that were inferior and were starting to fall off the roof, cheap materials used just about everywhere and even leaking toilets and other plumbing problems.

When contacted about these issues, Herschel and Korah's business relationship quickly began to deteriorate. Herschel did all he could to avoid fessing up to his evil deeds and taking responsibility for the repairs. At first he outright denied that the problems existed. Later he would promise to send a crew to the shopping center, but the crew never showed up. Towards the end he did send a few trucks to the Harden complex, but it was all for show. His workers repaired the obvious problems with the same half-ass craftsmanship they used when they originally built it. It didn't take long before their repairs needed to be repaired.

Korah was now at her wits' end because, as the contractor, she was ultimately responsible for everything that went wrong at the shopping center. Mr. Harden called frequently and threatened her, and she in turn called Mr. Clark and threatened him. In the meantime nothing was getting fixed, and her brand was getting dragged through the mud.

This fiasco was one of the main reasons Korah decided to assemble a construction company of her own. Unfortunately, for the Harden Shopping Center at least, this change came much too late.

● ● ● ● ● ●

When she got to the office, Korah had only a few minutes to discuss the legal ramifications with Priscilla before Herschel Clark showed up. He was a large man with long, oily hair and a reddish nose and face, which was indicative of an alcoholic. His golf shirt was not big enough to stretch comfortably over his belly, and his pants were slightly soiled.

It was hard to believe how far he had fallen. When Korah hired him eight years ago, he was clean cut and at least thirty pounds lighter. She knew he was a drinker back then, but that was acceptable because he never hit the bars before closing time on Friday. Now it looked like he rolled out of bed each morning and reached for the half empty bottle of booze on his nightstand. Korah was extremely upset with him, but she also felt compassion for his disheveled appearance.

Mr. Clark plopped down in the seat across from her desk and sighed loudly. His shoulders slumped in exasperation.

"Listen," he said, his voice deep and raspy. "I already know what you're gonna say, and you're right. I fucked that job up. Alright? I know it. You ain't gotta jump down my throat."

Korah didn't expect this level of honesty – or hostility. His comment, along with his unsightliness, temporarily left her at a loss for words. She wished she had audio on the security cameras strategically mounted throughout her office. His admission of guilt was something she could use in court.

"Mr. Harden has been calling me, too," Herschel went on. "I don't take his calls no more. I wasn't gonna take yours either, but I hope this will be the last time you drag me down here."

"I highly doubt this will be the last time you hear from us," Korah said, finding her voice. "You took our money and ran, and now everything you built is falling apart. You gotta fix this."

Herschel actually laughed at that, which made Korah's lips purse in anger.

"This is funny to you?"

The man patted his pockets. "What I'ma fix it with? My construction company is gone, Ms. Stewart. Went belly-up. I've already filed for bankruptcy. You know what I do for a living now?"

Korah could actually care less.

"I drive a *cab*," Mr. Clark said. "Got it parked right out front. That's my life now. I drive people around, take people to the airport, hope I don't get shot or robbed one day. My wife had to get a job at the mall. She'll leave me soon," he said honestly. "I know she's fucking her first husband again."

Korah was both shocked and disgusted by everything that came out of his filthy mouth. It didn't seem possible that she ever considered this troll competent. It's amazing what one bad decade could do to a person.

"Everybody I ever worked with is suing me," he continued. "So if you wanna add your name to the list, go right ahead. I don't have anything against you personally, ma'am. But I don't have shit. I got nothing to give you folks."

"You got a house," Korah said. "I'm sure you have cars as well. The courts can take all of that."

"And I'm sure they'll liquidate my assets and divide it amongst *everyone*," Herschel countered. "So if you wanna wait three years for them to drag this out in court, be my guest. You can have one-twentieth of my house and car. Congratulations."

"I'm getting sick of your attitude," Korah snapped.

"And I'm getting sick of all of you trying to squeeze blood from a turnip. I don't have any money! What do you want me do? You want what's in my pockets?"

He stood and began emptying his dingy pockets onto her desk. His outburst brought Stephanie and Yolanda to the doorway. There were no men in the office, but Korah wasn't worried about this pathetic loser. He didn't look like he could jog up one flight of stairs without becoming winded.

He produced three dollars, one quarter and three pennies. Korah had never been disrespected in this manner in her own office. She was glad Devin wasn't there to see this. He would've gone to jail today for sure.

She stood, the veins in her neck bulging. "Get the hell out of my office," she growled.

"Gladly!" Mr. Clark said. He turned and waited for Stephanie and Yolanda to back up before he stormed out of the building.

Korah slowly returned to her seat, her nerves shot, her heart knocking. Her coworkers tried to enter the office, but she told them, "Give me a minute. Close the door, please."

Yolanda did as she was told.

Korah took a few minutes to calm herself and assess the situation before she picked up the phone. She called Frederick Harden. He answered after a couple of rings.

"Howdy."

"Good afternoon," Korah said, completely composed. "This is Korah Stewart, from Texas Builders."

"Ms. Stewart. Thanks for returning my call."

"I understand the problems at your shopping center are getting worse by the day."

"You understand right," he said. "Did Priscilla tell you I got shingles falling off the roof now? I had to block off an area of the sidewalk and some parking spots. Some of my vendors are pissed, saying they're not gonna renew their lease. We need help over here. Pronto. This is absolutely unacceptable."

"I understand," Korah said. "I'm going to send a crew to start working on your property tomorrow morning."

"I hope you're not talking about Clark's people again," he grunted. "They never show. At this point, I wouldn't want their sorry asses at my shopping center, even if they did show up."

"No, sir. I have my own construction company now. They do excellent work, and they will come as many days as necessary, until they complete every single one of your repairs. I apologize for the problems you've had thus far, and I assure you everything will be taken care of as expeditiously as possible."

"Oh, well that sounds great," Mr. Harden said. "When I talked to Priscilla this morning, I did tell her I was going to file paperwork with the courts. But I can hold off on that – if you're gonna make good on the work."

Korah's heart was thudding again. Just the thought of a lawsuit was very unsettling. Her company had an excellent track record and outstanding ratings as well. She would do anything within her power to keep it that way.

"I appreciate that, sir. I talked to Herschel Clark a few minutes ago."

"That asshole."

"Yes, he is," Korah agreed. "And he already filed for bankruptcy. His construction company is gone. He has nothing left."

"I should sue him anyway," Mr. Harden said. "I've never met a more incompetent piece of shit."

Korah closed her eyes. Her knee bounced under her desk. She didn't want Mr. Harden to sue Herschel Clark, either. Korah's company would be mentioned in that lawsuit, even if they weren't directly responsible. But then again, Texas Builders was responsible. It was Korah who hired the incompetent piece of shit to begin with.

"I told him the same thing," Korah said. "But trust me, he's already hit rock bottom. He's driving a cab, and his wife is working at the mall. He's getting sued by so many contractors and property owners, any additional lawsuits would be a waste of time. I doubt if you would even get your attorney fees back. I've washed my hands of him, and I'm ready to move on."

And I hope you are too...

"I wouldn't let that sonofabitch drive me anywhere," Mr. Harden mumbled. "If you say there's no point in it, I won't waste my time. What time will your crew be here tomorrow?"

"Bright and early," Korah said. "Will you be there to unlock everything?"

"I'll be here at eight a.m."

Damn. Korah knew Devin wasn't going to like that at all.

"They'll be there waiting on you," she said.

"Okay, that's great," Mr. Harden said. "Thanks a lot, Ms. Stewart. Sorry it had to go this far."

"No, it's me who owes you an apology," Korah said. "You have a nice day, sir."

"I sure will. Bye."

• • • • • •

Korah left her office and called her staff to the break room for a brainstorming session. This was by far the worst trouble Texas Builders had ever been in. Korah knew they could only dig themselves out of this hole with honesty and integrity. She knew her late husband would make the same moves she was making, if he was there to call the shots.

"How are we going to pay for all of this?" Priscilla asked after Korah told them of her plans.

"We have to go in the red," Korah said simply.

"With just the repairs he told us about so far, it'll cost us fifty thousand or more," Priscilla replied.

Korah sighed and swallowed down the huge number. "We don't have a choice."

"We're not suing Clark Construction?"

"There is no Clark Construction," Korah replied. "That loser's being sued by everyone he's ever worked for. I don't have time to wait in that line. The only way he could pay me back is if he hit the lottery or something."

"That might happen," Priscilla said. "You never know when someone will get a financial windfall."

"Well, maybe we can sue him after this school deal goes through," Korah said. "But I don't want to do anything right now that might jeopardize our bid."

"Do you think we still have a shot, with all of this stuff going on?" Stephanie asked.

"That remains to be seen," Korah acknowledged. "I think we do, if we keep it under the radar. We only have three weeks before the school district picks a contractor. If they don't catch wind of Harden, I'd say we have as much of a shot as we did before."

"So he's not going to file a lawsuit either?" Priscilla asked.

"No, Mr. Harden said he wouldn't. Not as long as we make all of the repairs – and foot the bill for it, of course."

"Devin's not gonna like that," Yolanda predicted.

"No, he's not," Korah agreed. She didn't look forward to telling him.

"So, what happened with that guy you met with today?" Stephanie asked, switching gears.

The smile that spread across Korah's face pulled everyone to the edge of their seats.

"Hmmm..." Stephanie said, grinning mischievously. "Mama, what's that smile for?"

"That wasn't some random customer," Korah told them. "That was Mr. Brock Avery. I'm sorry – *Brick*. He hates it when I call him Brock."

Now the ladies' mouths popped open in addition to their eyes.

"What does *that* mean?" Priscilla wanted to know.

"Well, he's a liar," Korah said. "Let's get that understood off the bat. Obviously he lied about needing some work done. And you already know he's arrogant and cocky and so full of himself it makes me wanna punch him. And apparently he wants to work with us. Oh, and he *says* he likes me. He wants to take me out on a date."

The girls couldn't take much more of her teasing.

"*Mama*! Tell us what happened. Start from the beginning," Stephanie demanded. "Wait, hold on."

She actually ran to the vending machine to get some chips first.

Korah told them everything about the strange meeting, and, not surprisingly, everyone had a different take on it.

"We should definitely work with him," Yolanda suggested. "He's bigger, and he's got a better chance of winning the bid – especially with this Clark and Harden mess. You should agree to no less than a third of the construction. That'll be worth at least three and a half million. We need that money."

"We don't *need it* need it," Korah argued. "We're doing just fine."

"But this would be our biggest job *ever*," Yolanda said, "even if we're only working under him."

"Now, hold on," Priscilla said, raising her finger. "If he came to you with this offer, then he must know something we don't know. He must have a good reason to think we're gonna *win*." Her words hung in the air, like the essence of hope. "If you're even *considering* working with him, you need to tell *him* to drop out, so you'd be the contractor. You can hire his company to do a third of the construction."

That made a lot of sense. Korah was thinking the same thing.

"But if he won't go for that, you should still be willing to do it the other way," Yolanda suggested.

"We have no idea if he's going to win the bid," Priscilla said. "What if you drop out and someone else wins? How bad would you feel then?"

Korah nodded. "You're right. We can't drop out of the running, no matter what."

Yolanda rubbed her lips slowly with a perfectly manicured finger but didn't offer any further arguments.

"I wanna know what you're gonna do as far as his date offer," Stephanie said, grinning again. "Are you gonna go out with him?"

Before Korah could respond, Priscilla said, "Don't even think about it. First he offers you a business deal, and then he flirts with you when you don't agree right away? Korah, he's obviously trying to use you. I know you're not gonna fall for that. It's like you said; he's arrogant and conceited. I'm sure he's used his looks to get him out of a tight spot on many occasions."

Korah's face burned. She wasn't silly enough to fall for that, was she? Brick was probably married with four kids, for all she knew.

"But *Mama*," Stephanie said. "If he does really like you, then maybe you could use that to get him to drop out of the running. Women use men way more than men use women. I say you should keep that fool wrapped around your pinkie finger."

Korah smiled at that. "We'll just see how this plays out," she decided. "I'm always going to put this company in a position of advantage," she promised. "That's one thing none of you have to worry about."

CHAPTER SEVEN
PLAYING FOR KEEPS

On Wednesday, September 10th everything was looking sweet at Brick House Construction's main office in Dallas. The man in charge sat casually behind his desk while his personal assistant, Ms. Persia Moore, went over his agenda for the day.

"You have a ten o'clock meeting with Butch from Oklahoma Remodeling, and Peter Fleming will be here after lunch to go over those projections for his new project," Persia said. "Other than that, we're wrapping up work on the Del Monte warehouse in Mansfield. Manning says they need 'til the end of the week to finish up. Are you going to stop by there today?"

Brick nodded. "I'll go after I talk to Mr. Fleming."

"Okay," Persia said and scribbled in her ledger. "The remodeling jobs in Frisco and Houston are going well. I'm going to finish up the bid for the new Kroger's in Arlington. I should be able to submit an offer to them today."

"Make sure you let Isaac look at those numbers," Brick told her.

"Of course," Persia said.

Rather than go over his schedule from the seat across from his desk, she sat on the corner of it, on his left side. Persia wore a charcoal colored skirt suit that was both professional and sexy. She had nice thighs and hips, and she damned sure knew how to use them. She was caramel-colored with a dash of burgundy.

She had her legs crossed daintily. The toe of her right pump brushed Brick's leg as she spoke. The contact was slight, but it was obvious, and it was alluring. Persia had the top three buttons of her blouse open, revealing quite a bit of her succulent cleavage. Brick saw that the top of her bra was black and it was lace.

Persia wore a pair of large, nerdy glasses that didn't detract from her beauty at all. In fact, the glasses, coupled with her long hair, mascara and pouty lips, contributed to a naughty school girl fetish that Brick had been trying to overcome for over a year. But of course Persia was not helping the matter at all. She always wore a seductive look for her boss. Her voice was always sultry, no matter how mundane the information she delivered.

She knew Brick appreciated her round ass, so she found cause to turn away from him at least once a day. When he approached her desk for the first time each morning, Persia always rose from her seat and presented her breasts as much as her beautiful smile.

Back in the day, when Brick would encounter her in the break room, and it was just the two of them, sometimes he would give in to temptation. When Persia would look over her shoulder to acknowledge his presence, while she kept the front of her body turned towards the microwave, Brick would approach and caress her ass, before continuing on his way. Sometimes he'd comment about how nice she looked and felt. Sometimes he'd just let his fingers do the talking and not speak at all.

Persia didn't care if he spoke or not, so long as he did give in to temptation. On the occasions he did not, she considered her attempt a failure.

Unfortunately Persia had been experiencing quite a few failures as of late, thus the extra button opened on her blouse today and the flirtatious posture she took on the corner of his desk. She hoped Brick would touch her bare thigh, and in turn she would smile and spread her legs slowly. Maybe he would notice that she wasn't wearing panties this morning. But the possibility wouldn't come up at all if Brick didn't make the first move.

Today he did not. His hands remained firmly clasped in his lap.

Persia wasn't above throwing herself at him even more blatantly, but she wouldn't attempt it while Isaac was somewhere in the building. Brick always seemed to be on his best behavior when his partner was around, and Persia took that as her cue to do the same.

After a few moments of silence, she slowly rose to her feet and made peace with the fact that she had failed yet again.

Jesus, what is it with him? she wondered as she backed away from her boss' desk. She assumed he was in a new relationship and was attempting to be faithful. Persia hated to think about Brick's hard dick sliding deep inside another woman, so she quickly pushed the thought from her mind.

"Is there anything else I can get for you?" she asked.

Anything, her eyes pleaded.

Any Thing At All.

He smiled and shook his head. "No, thank you, Persia. You've done a great job."

She turned and kept her head high as she exited the office, though her shoulders were itching to slump in defeat. She knew Brick was watching her ass as she stepped, but she didn't look back to confirm this. What good was watching, if he wasn't touching? And what good was no panties, if there was no one there to stare or care?

Persia forced a smile when she passed Isaac in the hallway.

"Good morning, Mr. Kennedy."

"Morning," Isaac said and continued to Brick's office. He walked in without knocking and promptly closed the door behind him.

● ● ● ● ● ●

"You've got to fire that girl."

Brick laughed as his friend took a seat. "Good morning to you too, sir."

Isaac made a *hmph* sound and looked back to make sure he closed the door securely. "Are you still fucking her?"

Brick shook his head, but his smile remained. "I haven't had relations with her in nearly six months. Scouts honor," he said, raising a hand in the air.

Isaac sighed and shook his head. "You still need to fire her."

"I know," Brick conceded. "But she does an excellent job."

"An excellent job at what?" Isaac countered. "Getting your dick hard?"

"Well, yeah, she's good at that," Brick acknowledged. "But she's also a great assistant. You know she is. Never calls in. Never forgets a message. And nobody looks better filing papers."

Isaac didn't find too much humor in the situation. "We can get Alice the Goon in here to file papers," he said. "And that would be a lot better in the long run."

"Better for who?" Brick asked with a chuckle. "I'm not the only person who appreciates our secretary. Do you ever wonder how many clients Persia has won for us single-handedly?"

"I'm not saying she doesn't add a certain flair to our office," Isaac said. "I just think it's foolish of you to think you can start something with that woman and then back away completely with no repercussions. I've seen it blow up in people's faces too many times."

"It's been six months," Brick reiterated. "If she was gonna key my car, she would've done it by now. I know she still flirts with me, but I haven't reacted to any of it. I think it'll blow over."

"So you don't plan on firing her?"

Brick rolled his eyes. "Fine. Start looking for a replacement."

"Great," Isaac said. "It's for the best."

Brick grumbled something. Isaac smiled and didn't bother asking him to repeat it.

"How's everything else looking?" Brick asked after a few moments.

"Excellent," Isaac said. "This is gonna be another great quarter for us. I'm gonna get Fred to update our website this afternoon; add some of the new properties."

Brick nodded. "Sounds good."

"I've got some news about the school bid," Isaac said. "Despite your efforts to sabotage us earlier this week, we're still looking very good."

Brick laughed. "Sabotage?"

"Yes, when you went to meet that woman, Korah Stewart."

"I didn't sabotage anything," Brick said. "As a matter of fact, I'm having dinner with Korah tonight."

Isaac's mouth fell open. "Brick! What the hell, man? I just told you: You gotta stop thinking with your dick."

"Why do you assume it's me?"

"What, you mean besides the fact that you wasted half a day Monday chasing that woman down, so you could offer her some asinine proposal she would never accept?"

"Well, I hate to burst your bubble," Brick said, though it was clear he enjoyed it very much, "but she called me. I was at home last night minding my own business."

Isaac frowned. "She called you?"

Brick nodded. "Yepper."

"Did she say she was interested in your offer?"

"Not exactly," Brick said. "But she did say she wanted to meet with me again."

"Is it business?"

"I'm not sure," Brick said with a shrug. "Maybe. Maybe not."

"Hmmm. That actually makes sense," Isaac told him.

"How so?"

"Just got word from some of the school board members. Texas Builders has got some serious problems."

Brick raised an eyebrow.

"Yeah, one of their jobs from eight years ago is falling apart," Isaac reported. "Apparently this was before they had their own construction company. They hired Clark Construction for the job, and those assholes screwed everything up. They went belly-up last year. Their owner is ducking everybody he ever worked for – Korah included.

"Apparently Korah's doing everything she can to make things right – and keep it quiet. And the school district is giving them a little leeway, since it was almost ten years ago. But, as you can imagine, they're not taking this news lightly. We were already on top of them in the bidding race. Now we're looking like the obvious choice."

Brick wasn't as pleased as that news should've made him. Years ago his company was in the same situation; required to outsource their construction and other major tasks. As a contractor, you have to make it a priority to bring qualified, upstanding talent to your worksites. But in the end, no amount of oversight can stop a construction company from screwing up a job – especially if they're being purposefully deceitful.

"I take it Korah didn't tell you about that, huh?" Isaac said.

Brick shook his head. "No, she didn't."

"And now your offer probably sounds really good to them," Isaac surmised. "I hate to say it, but you might be getting played, my brother."

Brick frowned. That would be a first.

"She didn't actually say she wanted to discuss the deal," he said.

"So your dinner tonight is strictly for pleasure?" Isaac asked. "You think she likes you?"

Brick's frown intensified. "You make it sound like that's unlikely."

"No, of course it isn't," Isaac replied. "But with you two competing for the same job and this new news about their legal troubles, I wouldn't put manipulation past either one of you. What's your incentive for wanting to see her again? Surely you don't still want to give her a piece of the school."

"I'm attracted to her," Brick said honestly. "That's the main reason I want to see her. I didn't realize we had such a big advantage over them when I offered her that deal..."

"But the deal is still on the table?"

"I'm not sure what I'll say, if she brings it up tonight," Brick admitted.

"Why do I feel like I'm always warning you to be careful?"

"I wonder about that as well," Brick replied. "No matter how much money we make each year, you think I don't know what I'm doing."

"Only as far as females are concerned," Isaac said. "I'm confident with your business decisions, for the most part. I just don't want you to get weak behind this woman and give away half of a job we could have all to ourselves."

"I'll never get played," Brick assured him. "You don't have to worry about that."

"I don't know why I bother," Isaac said with a defeated tone. "Every day that I come to work and see your secretary sitting there, I'm reminded that you like playing with fire."

"She's *your* secretary, too," Brick said with a grin. "And I've never been burned by any of these *supposed* fires, so calm down. Let me do what I do. We keep growing bigger and stronger, don't we?"

Isaac couldn't argue with that. Brick's methods were sometimes unconventional, but he was by no means reckless when it came to money. Few people could turn a dime into a dollar as quickly as he could.

"Well, I'll still feel a lot better when you fire *our* secretary," he grumbled. "And if you don't come in here tomorrow and tell me Korah's our new partner, that would be great, too."

Brick laughed. "Maybe I'll come in here tomorrow and tell you we just acquired *her* company. What would you think about that?"

"I would gladly eat my words. I'll drop to one knee and beg your forgiveness."

Brick smiled smugly, though he would much rather see Ms. Korah Stewart groveling. If her straits were as dire as Isaac described, then it may not take too much persuasion to get her in that position.

● ● ● ● ● ●

Korah lived in an 8,000 square feet, two story masterpiece on the east side of Overbrook Meadows. Among other highlights, she had an elegant spiral staircase, granite countertops in the kitchen, lighted tennis and basketball courts, and a resort style pool and spa; complete with decorative fountains. She also had three acres of beautifully manicured lawn out back. It was moderately populated with healthy oak, maple and mesquite trees.

Brick pulled another one of his toys, a tuxedo black Lincoln Navigator, into her circular drive at six p.m. sharp. He stepped out wearing a black suit with a tan shirt and no tie. His shoes were square-toed, shined to perfection. His only jewelry was a platinum Movado that hung loosely on his left wrist.

He mounted the doorsteps and rang the doorbell. He had a few moments to admire Korah's home before she answered and took his breath away.

For her date with the CEO of Brick House Construction, Korah wore a midnight blue dress that was both daring and elegant. It featured a cinched waist with a halter V-neckline that showed off oodles and oodles of chocolaty cleavage. It was floor-length and sleeveless with a slit that climbed well above her knees.

Korah wore her hair down and layered. Her lipstick and mascara further removed her from the boyish, construction outfit she had on when Brick first laid eyes on her.

He stared at her appreciatively for several seconds before reaching for her hand. Korah watched him curiously and allowed him to bring her dainty hand to his face and kiss it softly. Everything about Brick was hard and rugged, but his lips were quite the opposite. They were soft and pink and warm and electrifying against her flesh. Goose bumps sprouted on her forearms as she watched him. She thought her heart might have skipped a beat.

She didn't want to acknowledge the effect Brick's touch had on her body. But there was no denying that the intensity of his eyes was hypnotizing. The raw power of his gaze made her knees weak.

"You look lovely tonight," he said, just above a whisper.

He still had her hand in his, still close to his face. The sensation of his breath on her skin made the hairs stand on the back of Korah's neck. She withdrew her hand politely yet desperately. Brick grinned and took another moment to admire her attire before he filled his lungs with air and blew it slowly from his nostrils.

"I was about to comment on how nice your home is," he said, "but it pales in comparison to you."

"Thank you," Korah said, her face flushing with heat.

"Did you build this house?" he asked.

Korah nodded. "Eight years ago."

"It's breathtaking," he said. "I would love to see more of it."

He was so smooth, Korah almost invited him inside. But there were so many warning signs blaring, she could barely see straight.

"Maybe one day," she told him.

Brick nodded. His smile was both cunning and disarming, reminding Korah that she had to remain on her guard at all time. This was the first time she'd ever encountered a man she would describe as *too* handsome. Brick was too smooth. Too alluring.

"Well then, shall we go?" he asked.

Korah nodded, wondering what the hell she was getting herself into.

● ● ● ● ● ●

Brick took her to an upscale Arlington restaurant called the Reata. The building was an architectural work of genius with a traditional western flair that attracted diners from all over the city. Brick made reservations, so they bypassed a long line of walk-ins and were ushered to a cozy table next to a large window that offered an excellent view of Lake Arlington and one of the picturesque golf courses along the bank.

The Reata specialized in steaks, but Korah ordered grilled chicken breast with tomato bleu cheese salad. Brick requested the most expensive plate on the menu; a steak and lobster dish that made Korah's mouth water when the waitress finally placed their dinner before them. Brick also ordered wine and urged Korah to save room for desert. She told him she might try the west Texas pecan pie.

Brick told her, "That's my favorite," and then dug into his meal, as if he hadn't eaten all day.

"So, what made you decide to call me?" he asked as Korah cut into her chicken.

"I'm not sure," she said honestly.

"Did you agree to my proposal?" Brick prompted.

Korah shook her head. "No. I don't think so."

He grinned. "Really?"

"Your proposal is silly," she told him. "Why should I drop my bid, when we don't know for sure if you're going to win or not?"

"Oh, I'm going to win," Brick assured her. "Well, either me or you. One of us will."

Korah shook her head, but her smile remained. "You don't know that."

"I know a little something," Brick said and took a manly bite of his steak.

He chewed with his mouth closed, but there was something altogether fierce and fearsome about the way he tore into the medium rare flesh. Korah was reminded that he was an apex predator. Interestingly, she knew that she wouldn't mind if Brick knocked her over the head and dragged her to his cave and ravished her thoroughly.

"So, you'd be willing to drop your bid and let us win?" Korah proposed.

He began shaking his head before she finished the sentence.

"That was Monday's deal. Today it's all about me. I'm more likely to win, so you should drop *your* bid and let me give you a piece of the pie when I'm the contractor. Come on. You know you wanna get down with the team."

Too damned cocky.

"I think I'll take my chances without your bizarre offer," Korah told him.

He raised an eyebrow. "Why would you do that?"

"Because I think our chances are just as good as yours?"

Not with that shopping center coming back to haunt you, Brick thought. He would've brought it up himself, but he thought Korah should be the one to divulge.

"Are you sure?" he asked.

"I'm sure for now," she said. "I may change my mind later."

Brick's smile widened. He cut into his steak again.

"What makes you think my offer will be good later?"

Korah shrugged. "If not, I won't have lost anything."

Brick watched her eat for a few moments and then asked, "So if you're not interested in my *bizarre* offer, why'd you call me? Could it be that you enjoy my company?"

"I don't think anyone enjoys you more than you enjoy yourself."

He laughed. It was a hearty chortle that made Korah's chest flutter with amusement.

"Is it that hard for you to admit that you like me?" he finally replied. "I don't have a problem admitting that I like you."

Korah ignored his compliment and asked, "Are you married?"

He looked stunned by the question.

"No. Of course not. Why would you ask that?"

"I don't think it's totally out of the realm of possibilities," she said.

"I've never been married," Brick said with a frown. "Nope. Not for me."

Korah suspected as much.

"Why is that?" she asked. "Not much for commitment?"

"No. I mean, a little," Brick acknowledged. "Marriage means forever, and I think it would put me in a bind at some point. If I was married when I met you, I'd have quite a dilemma."

Korah rolled her eyes at the flattery. "How so?"

"You're beautiful, and you're a contractor," Brick explained. "I find you very intriguing. I don't think I would've been able to go on about my business, like we never met."

"If you truly loved your wife, you wouldn't have given me a second thought," Korah said.

"What do you think of this restaurant?" Brick asked.

That was one of the most blatant change-of-subjects Korah had ever witnessed, but she didn't call him on it.

"I know you built this restaurant," she said flatly.

He laughed. "Really? Why didn't you say anything?"

"I figured I'd wait until you started bragging about it."

"Oh," he said. His eyes twinkled. "Well, you didn't let me get started yet."

Korah laughed. She couldn't help it. "You are so full of yourself. I know you do great work, Brick. You don't have to throw it in my face every chance you get."

"I don't know about that," he said. "That's like asking a peacock not to strut. Goes against my nature."

God, he's such an arrogant asshole, Korah thought.

What exactly was she doing here? Initially her goal was to take him up on his offer to give her a piece of the construction work for the new school. But Korah's pride took over in response to Brick's continuous boasting. She couldn't bear to see the snooty look of satisfaction in his eyes if she conceded defeat.

But if they weren't doing business, then what did she want from him? Why was she so attracted to a man who admitted to preferring a love 'em and leave 'em lifestyle over the much more fulfilling aspect of a committed relationship? Korah didn't want to think about how many broken hearts Brick left in his wake over the years. Was she seriously considering being the next in line?

"You never said why you wanted to see me tonight," Brick said, reading her mind.

"I don't know," Korah said honestly. "Surely nothing good can come of this."

Rather than respond, he grinned and returned his attention to his meal, this time cutting into his lobster tail.

Flustered, Korah downed the rest of the wine in her glass and told him, "I want some."

Brick looked up at her. "Some of... what? My lobster?"

"Yes."

"I told you not to order chicken here."

"I don't want to take advice from you," she pouted.

He chuckled as he cut a portion of the seafood for her.

"Anything you tell me to do, I'll probably do the opposite," Korah said as she watched him.

"Well, in that case *don't* go out with me again," Brick said. "*Don't* invite me into your home, and certainly *don't ever* come to my home – or my ranch."

He offered his fork with a juicy bite of lobster speared. Rather than lean over the table and allow him to feed her, Korah took the fork from him and fed herself. She returned his utensil as she chewed the delicious morsel.

"Is that really your ranch?" she asked, "on your website?"

He nodded. "It's been in the family for years. It's all mine now."

"And I guess you have horses and cows and stuff?"

"No cows," he said, hypnotizing her with his intense gaze again. "But I do have horses. Would you like to go one day? You wanna ride my horse?"

Korah did not miss the innuendo, nor did she back down. "Where is it located?"

"Lewisville. I have a ranch hand who lives there full-time. He takes care of things while I'm away."

"What else you got on your ranch?" Korah asked.

"Actually, I could show you better than I could tell you," Brick said. "Are you saying you *do* wanna ride my horse?"

His boldness made Korah's clit quiver.

"I haven't ridden a horse in years," she replied. "I'm worried I might fall off."

"You gotta hold the reigns tight," Brick advised. "You gotta wrap your legs around him and squeeze a little, with your thighs. And if you do fall off, you gotta get right back on, and we'll take it a little slower."

Korah grinned. "I don't know what you're thinking about, but I'm only talking about riding a horse."

"Oh, well here, have some more wine," Brick said and commenced to fill her glass.

Korah couldn't help but laugh at that.

● ● ● ● ● ●

On the ride back to her place, Brick asked, "So, how does it feel to be a woman in this male-dominated industry?"

"Sometimes it works to my advantage," Korah said as she lounged on his soft, leather seat. "Sometimes it doesn't."

The fire was completely gone from the sky by then. The moon was full. The lamps on the freeway dimly illuminated Brick's face every quarter mile.

"Do you ever get funny looks from old-timers, who don't wanna trust a woman and will probably refer to you as *colored* when they get home?" he asked.

Korah giggled. "Of course I do."

"I won't lie," Brick said. "That was the first thing that came to mind when I saw you in your hardhat the other day."

"You were surprised that I was *colored*?"

He laughed. "No. I was thinking, well, outside of how beautiful you are, I was thinking, 'This woman probably doesn't know the difference between a sander and a power drill.'"

"Oh yeah? Is that what you thought?"

"Lemme see your hand," he said.

Korah offered her left hand. Brick pulled it into his lap as he drove. He turned it upwards, caressing her palm with his thumb.

Korah was perplexed by how his touch caused a heat wave to envelope her body every single time – even more so now because she was pretty sure the back of her hand was resting directly on his manhood. She had only to flip her hand over and give a squeeze to know for sure.

She wondered if that was what Brick wanted her to do, or if he was so much in control of his sexual prowess that having a woman's hand on his dick was no big deal.

"That's what I thought," he said, releasing her hand. "Not one blister or callous. You may know your power tools by name, but you've never used one."

Korah withdrew her hand, reluctantly. "Well, Mr. Know-It-All doesn't know everything," she replied. "Contrary to your chauvinistic suppositions, I've used every piece of equipment we own. I could probably use a sander better than you."

"Surely you'll forgive me for not believing you," he said without looking away from the road.

"Maybe I'll show you one day," Korah flirted.

"You already blew my mind when I saw you in a hardhat," Brick commented. "If I ever see you using a power tool, I'd have to take you, right then and there."

Korah didn't respond to that, partially because she had a sudden lump in her throat and also because Brick's southern twang and his relentless manliness made her pussy lips tingle unexpectedly. She knew her voice would be shaky, if she tried to offer a witty comeback. It was a struggle to keep from smiling, which would have further encouraged him.

They listened to the radio for the next five minutes, neither of them speaking.

When Brick rounded the corner onto her street, he turned the tunes off and asked, "Did I scare you?"

Korah shook her head. She didn't know why she was being so bold, but she couldn't help it.

"So you'll go out with me again?" he asked.

"Sure," Korah said and nodded. "What's the worst that can happen?"

That made Brick crack a smile. "Are you really this controlled?"

Korah found that amusing. Not only did her clitoris quiver each time he touched her, but her goal of securing a piece of the school job was all but dashed, her panties were wet, and for the life of her, she couldn't understand why she was pursuing something that was obviously bad for her.

She felt a lot of things at that moment, but *in control* was not among them.

"I'm the boss," she said. "I have to be controlled."

Brick nodded and kept his thoughts to himself. A few seconds later he pulled into her driveway, which was brightly lit by a multitude of lights leading to the doorway. He turned and smiled and cleared his throat.

Korah grinned but shook her head. "Uh-uhn."

"What?" he said.

"I'm sorry, go ahead."

"Well, now I don't wanna say," Brick complained.

"That's probably for the best," Korah said as she dug her keys from her purse.

"Just to be sure," Brick said, "we are talking about me asking to come inside for a tour of your home and you turning me down."

"Yes," Korah said. "That's what we're talking about. I had a really nice time, though. I appreciate you taking me to one of your marvelous constructions."

"You don't sound like you appreciate it. Come here."

He leaned in so smoothly, Korah had to catch herself from doing the same.

"Sorry," she said as she pulled away.

Brick's eyes were half closed by then. His perfect lips were puckered. He opened his eyes in disbelief.

"Wait, you don't kiss on the first date, either?"

"I have before," Korah said honestly.

His mouth fell open. "What? Why would you say that? Now it seems personal. You could've just told me no, you don't."

Korah chuckled. "Good night," she said as she opened the door.

Brick opened his, too. "Wait. At least let me walk you to the door."

"No," Korah said. The farther she kept him away from her home the better. She was already losing a bit of her resolve. If he hugged her or tried for another kiss in the doorway, she'd surely surrender to his charms.

"Okay," Brick said and closed his door. "As you wish."

He watched as she stepped out of his car and down the walkway. Her dress was loose-fitting from the waist down, but a blessed breeze made the fabric cling to her form for a few moments. Brick's chest rose and fell slowly as he admired her. Korah was a whirlwind of curiosities. Brick had to admit that he had never met a woman quite like her.

When she reached the front door, he saw Korah remove a small roll of paper that was wedged next to the doorknob. It appeared that she read the paper before opening the door and disappearing inside.

Brick waited a few more moments before he put his car in gear and drove away.

CHAPTER EIGHT
SEXY STUD CRIMPER

The date with Brick was surprisingly nice, but the note left on her door changed Korah's mood the moment she saw it. Her ex-boyfriend Quincy called her three times while she was with Brick. She sent him directly to voicemail the first time and turned her ringer off when he tried again.

At the time, Korah was annoyed with him, but seeing that he came to her home while she was away and left a note on her door pushed her annoyance to anger. She went to her bedroom and took off her shoes before she called him back. She looked at the note he left while she waited for him to answer. It simply read:

> *Call me when you get in*
> *- Quincy*

Korah shook her head in disappointment. She had no idea he wanted to take it to stalker level. Considering the effort he went through to reach her, she was surprised he let the phone ring four times before answering it.

"Hey, Korah. You just make it in?"

"What is your emergency?" she said flatly.

"I don't, I don't have an emergency," Quincy replied. "I wanted to see you tonight, is all."

"I got your calls," Korah said. "Why didn't you leave a message?"

"I'm sorry. I wanted to surprise you."

"Surprise me for what?"

"I'm, hey what's the matter? Did I do something wrong?"

"Yes," she said. "You're acting obsessed. If you call me, and I don't answer, what makes you think you should come to my house?"

"I told you it was a surprise," Quincy said. "I made dinner for you. I was hoping we could talk."

Korah scratched her head, wondering where she went wrong with this one. It had to be his birthday party. She agreed to be his date that night, and, after drinking way too much, she thought they could handle a night of passion with no strings attached. She hoped she shut him down sufficiently the next morning when Quincy tried to revive their relationship status, but apparently she wasn't firm enough.

"Quincy," she said with a sigh. "I appreciate your effort, but we're not getting back together. Never. You should not come to my house unannounced. What if I had a man over here?"

"Already?" he asked with a slight condescending tone.

"We broke up months ago," Korah said, not sure why she felt the need to explain herself to him. He didn't deserve half the respect she was giving him.

"Yeah, but we just made love last Sunday," Quincy countered. "Sorry. I assumed you didn't have another man so soon."

"No. We *fucked* last Sunday," Korah corrected. "And I've already apologized for that."

"You don't–"

"Listen," she said, raising her voice. "You need to give up all hope you have of us getting back together, Quincy. As a matter of fact, I'm starting to think we can't even be friends. If you don't respect me enough to wait until I call you bac–"

He hung up on her.

"You childish sonofabitch," Korah muttered as she set her phone aside and got ready for bed.

• • • • • •

On Friday morning Korah scheduled an early morning meeting in the break room of her main office. She stood at the head of the table offering her best solution for the new manpower shortage their construction team was experiencing. The head of the construction crew, Devin Jr., sat in front of her with his arms folded over his chest in an obvious defensive manner. He frowned and shook his head in disagreement as his mother spoke.

In general, Korah loved working with her family. But it was times like this that really tested her patience. If Devin was a *normal* employee, she would've berated him for his insolence. But this was her baby, so she kept her fangs retracted – for now.

When she was done speaking, Korah finally gave her oldest child the attention he was looking for.

"I take it you have a problem."

"I do," Devin said. "We have too much work to do already. We don't have enough people to fix that shopping center *and* do our other jobs."

"I was trying to let you figure it out on your own," Korah replied. "But if you need me to go through your staff one by one and send them where I think they're needed most, I can do that for you."

"No, I don't need you to do that," Devin said, again with more attitude than Korah would've tolerated from anyone else. "What I need to do is send my crews to the projects they already started and let that other man fix the mess he caused."

"And I already told you Clark Construction is out of business," Korah said. "So that other man can't fix the mess he caused."

"Then we need to sue him."

"And in the meantime we need to fix the Harden Shopping Center," Korah said patiently.

"No, Mama. They need to sue Clark Construction, too. When they get their money, they can hire somebody else to repair that place."

"That's our job," Korah said. "We're still responsible."

"I think that's a matter for the courts to decide," Devin insisted.

"No, that's a matter for *me* to decide," Korah countered. "And I've already made my decision. I don't care if you have to send every man we have to the shopping center and let our other properties sit for two weeks, Devin. The shopping center is our *number one priority*. If we don't do right by them, then we can kiss the school bid goodbye.

"But to be clear, this decision is not only about the school bid. It's about our brand. It's about integrity. I hired Clark Construction, so I'm responsible for everything they did. Period.

"You need to think about what your father would do, if he were here today. 'Cause he sure as hell wouldn't say, 'Screw those people. We already got paid.' And you shouldn't feel that way either." She shook her head slowly. "To be honest, your attitude right now is really disappointing."

"But, Mama—"

"This meeting is over," Korah said. "I need someone at that shopping center in thirty minutes."

Devin pushed away from the table and snatched the radio from his belt. As he exited the room, Korah heard him giving the appropriate instructions to his crew.

"That went well," Stephanie said after they heard him exit the building.

Korah wasn't in the mood for her daughter's mouth, either. "Shut up, girl. Don't you have school today?"

"Not 'til ten," Stephanie said. "You trying to get rid of me?"

"Don't tempt me," Korah said. She returned to her seat at the table with Priscilla, Yolanda and her youngest child. She sighed again as she worked the kinks out of her neck.

"He's just upset because he doesn't want to miss any of the other deadlines," Yolanda said in Devin's defense.

"I know that. But he needs to look at the big picture," Korah told her. "How am I supposed to feel comfortable with letting him take over the company one day when he's acting like that?"

"He's just a kid," Priscilla said with a soft, motherly smile. "He's taken on a lot of responsibilities, and he's done a great job, overall. But he is only 26. His maturity will deepen over time."

"Are you ready to step down, Mama?" Stephanie asked.

Korah shook her head. "No. I love my job. But I would like to let you guys have it in ten years or so."

"How are things going with Brick House?" Yolanda asked unexpectedly. "Are y'all still in negotiations?"

Korah's sudden smile let them know something had occurred.

"Hmmm. What's going on, Ms. Stewart?" Yolanda asked, a curious smirk lighting her features.

"I told Brick I wasn't interested in his deal," Korah announced.

"Why?" Stephanie asked. "Did he say he wouldn't back out and let us win the bid?"

"Actually we didn't get that far in the negotiations," Korah said. "Brick is such an asshole. He made me feel like we have no chance of winning, and I didn't want to give him the satisfaction of agreeing with him. I might bring it up again later, when he's not acting so arrogant. I'm seeing him again for lunch today."

That comment raised everyone's eyebrows.

"Seeing him for *business*?" Stephanie asked. "Or is this, like, a date or something?"

"I, um, I guess it's like a date, or something."

Her daughter's eyes lit up.

"But don't tell Devin," Korah quickly added. "I don't think he likes him."

"How come?" Stephanie asked.

"Because the first time Brick came looking for me, he lied about who he was, remember? He showed up at the site, and Devin was trying to figure out what work he needed done. When I told him who Brick really was, he didn't appreciate the deception."

"Mama, that man is *fine*," Stephanie exclaimed.

Korah had to smile at that. *So true.*

"I can't believe you guys are dating!"

"Me neither," Yolanda said. "All you ever talk about is what a jerk he is."

"I don't know what to say," Korah confided. She'd thought about this quite a bit, and it was somewhat exasperating that she couldn't figure it out, either. "In life, every now and then you'll meet a man like that; attractive to the point of ridiculousness but so arrogant you wanna punch him in the mouth – or kiss him, whatever will get him to shut up."

Priscilla laughed. "Oh, Ms. Korah..."

"I know he's a playboy," Korah went on. "He says he's never been married, but it's hard to believe he doesn't have a girlfriend, if not two or three. There's so much I don't like about him, and I know he's never going to be any different."

"It all sounds *bad*," Yolanda noticed. "What do you like about him?"

Korah's smile softened as she reflected. "He's tall, and he's handsome. He's southern. He's such a cowboy. He has a ranch, and he rides horses."

Korah blushed at the memory of him asking her to ride his horse.

"He's successful," she went on. "We're in the same business, and we have a lot in common. Brick seems exciting and adventurous. I never know what he'll say or do. Most of it is inappropriate, but even that's exciting. And despite being conceited, he is a perfect gentleman. He opens every door, every time, and he's very attentive. He definitely treats me like a lady."

Priscilla smiled knowingly.

"What happened to that other guy you were dating?" Stephanie asked. "What was his name? Quincy?"

"Oh, Jesus," Korah said, thinking of the stunt he pulled two nights ago. But then her eyes lit up. "Oh, wow. I think that's it!"

"What?" Yolanda asked.

"He was so *boring*," Korah told them. "Quincy is stale bread. Brick is cherries jubilee."

"What's that?" Stephanie asked. "Is that the one they set on fire?"

Korah nodded, still lost in her revelation.

"But aren't you worried about getting burned?" Yolanda asked.

"I guess that's part of the thrill," Korah acknowledged. "People who go bungee jumping may plummet to their death one day."

"I never took you as the thrill-seeking type," Yolanda said.

"Me neither," Korah said. "This may be something new."

"Well, whatever you do, make sure you don't let him con you into giving up any of our business," Priscilla teased.

"You don't have to worry about that," Korah told her.

She was pretty sure Brick was more interested in her giving up the panties anyway. That thought made a few beads of sweat blossom on her forehead.

"Alright, back to work," Korah said as she rose from her seat and returned to her office.

• • • • • •

She met with her cocky new friend at noon at the P.F. Chang's in Arlington. Across the street from the restaurant, there was another construction project underway. Korah was not surprised to see a huge **BRICK HOUSE** sign posted prominently near the entrance of the work site.

Korah did not get dolled up for her date that afternoon. Friday was still a workday, so she wore jeans with a Texas Builders' golf shirt. She did snag a pair of her tighter-fitting jeans with Brick in mind, but Korah didn't put on any more makeup than she would on a regular day.

It didn't matter.

When she entered the restaurant, Brick rose from the bench he'd been waiting at and regarded her in the same manner as he did when she wore a dress on Wednesday night.

"Good afternoon," he said, reaching for her hand. He brought it slowly to his mouth and kissed it softly, his eyes on hers the whole time.

His brief kiss sent tingles of heat from the back of Korah's hand, up her arm and through her chest. She had come to look forward to the way her body responded whenever he made contact with her. She hoped that wouldn't change.

Brick wore jeans, too. They were faded and well-worn, but not dirty at all. His work boots did have a bit of soil caked around the soles, but Korah didn't fault him for that. She knew he'd been checking on some of his worksites personally, and she appreciated a hard-working man.

Even with a long-sleeved, white collar shirt, Brick looked rugged, rather than preppy. The only thing that would've been better is if he'd worn his tool belt on the date. Korah assumed he'd wear it loosely, hanging lower on one hip, like the Texas cowboys of the days of yore.

Korah dined on lemongrass chicken spring rolls, while Brick opted for seared tuna with wasabi guacamole. He seemed very pleased to have another date with her, and Korah couldn't hide her interest in him, either. They eyed each other over their plates like teenagers, rather than a couple in their mid-forties.

"How are things at Texas Builders?" he asked her.

"Great," Korah lied. Apparently Brick didn't know about her troubles with the shopping center, and Korah didn't want to tell him. If he knew he had that sort of leverage, it would ruin any chance she had for a possible merger on the school deal – that was if she ever had the nerve to bring it up again.

"Did y'all finish that 7-11 yet?" he asked.

"We'll be done next week," Korah said. She hoped he wouldn't stop by her site to check on their progress, because, at Korah's request, Devin didn't send a crew there today at all.

"What about you?" she asked, eager to change the subject.

"Business is booming," Brick replied.

"I see that," Korah said, looking out of the window. "Is that why you asked me to meet you at this restaurant; so you could show off more of your work?"

Brick followed her gaze to the construction zone across the street. He didn't bother lying. "Yup."

Korah laughed briefly. "Why do you insist on showing off your work? Do you think that will impress me?"

"Hell, I hope so," Brick replied. "'Cause I don't have nothing else."

Korah looked into his beautiful brown eyes and chose to disagree with that statement.

No, Mr. Avery. You've got a lot more than that.

"If I was a painter, I'd show you my paintings," he went on. "The buildings I erect are much more beautiful. And it's rare that I meet a woman who can appreciate my projects as much as I do."

"But I've already seen your work," Korah stated. "You've got a million pictures on your website."

"But you've never seen a work *in progress*," Brick countered.

"I see works in progress every day."

"But you've never seen *mine*."

"Okay," Korah said, giving the site her full attention. "What are you building over there, sir?"

"A Barnes & Noble."

Korah frowned. "Really?" She studied the half built structure in more detail. "Two stories?"

He nodded. "Yeah, it'll be one of the biggest ones."

"I thought Barnes & Noble was going out of business. Why are they still building them?"

Brick shrugged. "I don't know. Not my business, really. I know their check cleared, so I'm building it."

Korah giggled. "It'll probably be closed down in five years."

"If so, I hope they call me for demolition."

"You do that, too?"

"Sure. Personally I would rather create, but I have a foreman who loves tearing shit down. Oh, excuse my French."

"It's fine," Korah said. She was actually surprised that he felt badly about cursing in front of her. She couldn't get over how refreshing his southern charm and chivalry was.

"So, you showed me your work. Is that it?"

"No," he said. "I haven't showed you anything. We have to take a tour."

Korah chuckled. "Brick, I've been on so many half-finished sites, I can't count them all. They're nothing new to me."

"But you haven't seen *mine*," he said.

Korah rolled her eyes in disinterest, but she was genuinely perplexed about something. "What do you want with me?" she asked suddenly.

"What do you mean?"

"You look like a model," she said.

"Really? Thanks?"

"You know you're handsome. And you're crazy successful. You can have any woman you want – and I'm pretty sure you have them as often as you'd like. I'm sitting over here in jeans and work boots. Do you think you can charm me into dropping my bid for the school?"

"No," Brick said, shaking his head. "I think you're too smart for that."

"Then what do I have to offer you?"

"You're kidding, right?"

"No," Korah said. "I'd really like to know."

"Woman, you are beautiful, regardless of what you're wearing. And you're crazy successful yourself. Yes, I could have some bimbo in high heels. I've met quite a few of those..."

Korah shook her head.

"Hey, I may be a womanizer, but I'm no liar," Brick said.

"You're a *womanizer*? And you're admitting it?" Korah couldn't believe it.

"Wait. Maybe I used the wrong word. What's a womanizer?"

"No, I think you used the perfect word," she said with a chuckle. "A womanizer is someone who sleeps with as many women as they can; someone who'll lie, cheat, steal and break hearts without a care in the world. A womanizer lives for the conquest, and they quickly forget the women they conquer afterwards."

"Is that what a womanizer is?" Brick asked.

"I'll bet your picture is in the dictionary," Korah said good-naturedly.

"Okay, I have been called that before," Brick admitted. "But that was by an angry woman. I assure you, Korah, I don't resort to any of those tactics when I'm interested in a woman. I don't lie, I don't cheat, and I don't steal. I don't run around trying to break hearts, and I've never pursued a woman, just so that I could sleep with her. *And* I don't break up with women after we've been intimate. So, no, I'm not a womanizer."

"Then what are you?" Korah wanted to know.

"I'm a single, heterosexual man," Brick said simply. "I appreciate women – a whole lot. But I don't hurt them, not intentionally."

"But they do get hurt..."

He shrugged. "I suppose every now and then... Are you saying you've never left a man brokenhearted?"

Korah thought about Quincy and said, "Touché. But I don't have flings. I have *relationships*."

"I have relationships, too," Brick said. "And I've had a few flings as well."

"Do you ever fall in love?"

Brick nodded. "Of course. I love being in love. It's a beautiful thing. Why are you so worried?" he asked. "Do you think it's my intention to hurt you – or use you?"

"I'd be a fool not to consider it," Korah replied.

Brick mulled that over. "I wish I could give you my assurances that I would never do anything that would cause you to feel hurt, but you know I can't do that. Neither of us knows where life is going to take us.

"But what I can do is promise that I have no intentions of hurting you, and I'm certainly not trying to use you. My interest in you is genuine. I've pursued a lot of bimbos with fake boobs and fake hair down their backs. But lately, all I can think about is you in your hardhat and work boots."

He's lying! Korah told herself. Surely he didn't expect her to believe that.

Or maybe she was overthinking this whole situation. She wasn't some teeny bopper with a crush on the star football player. Korah was a grown woman, with enough maturity to decide if she was willing to put her heart on the line for such a risky proposition.

But then again, why did she have to put her heart on the line? If Brick could have fun exploring the wonders of the opposite sex, why couldn't she? Maybe she could be a man-izer for once in her life – if that was even a word.

She was actually delighted with the prospect.

"So, will you let me show you around my project when we're done?" Brick asked.

Korah looked him in the eyes and said, "Sure. I'd be delighted."

● ● ● ● ● ●

When they got to his site, Korah snatched her hardhat from the passenger seat and barely had time to push it down on her head before Brick hopped out of his truck and approached her door. He opened it and took Korah's hand to help her out of her SUV.

His new development wasn't all that different from the many buildings Korah had built herself, but she was attentive as he gave her a tour of the outside before leading her into the structure.

Brick's crew was very professional. Korah didn't notice any goofing around, and even the usual jokes and banter among his men came to an abrupt halt when they noticed Brick was on the property. They all acknowledged him, with either a nod of the head or a hearty, "Hey boss!" as he and Korah passed.

Brick's foreman at the site, a Hispanic man in great physical shape, approached with dusty jeans, grubby work boots, and a faded tool belt wrapped around his waist that reminded Korah of the one she passed down to her son.

"Howdy," he said to Brick as he removed his work gloves so that he could wipe some of the dust off his face. "How was lunch?"

"Too good," Brick told him. "I think I could catch a nap right about now."

"You can check out if you want to," the foreman told him. "Got no problems here."

"How's it going upstairs?" Brick asked him.

"Everything's fine," the foreman told him. "I sent Bruce and his guys to lunch about an hour ago. Should be back any minute."

The worker eyed Korah curiously, especially the Texas Builders' logo on her hardhat.

"We outsourcing some of the work, boss?" He didn't look too fond of the idea.

"No," Brick told him. "But we might work with Ms. Stewart in the future. Korah, this is my foreman, Hector."

The worker quickly let go of his misgivings and got on board with whatever Brick had in mind. He stuck out a surprisingly clean hand for Korah to shake. "Nice to meet you, Ma'am."

"Hi," she said. "Nice to meet you, too."

"Come on," Brick told her. "Let's see what's going on upstairs."

"It's a mess up there," Hector warned them. "Be careful," he said, mostly for Korah's benefit.

"It's okay," Brick said with that sexy, southern grin of his. "Ms. Stewart's right at home on construction sites."

He led Korah to a corner of the building where a small room revealed a flight of unfinished stairs.

"The main stairway will be in the center of the building," Brick explained as he ascended. "This is the fire escape."

Korah followed, stealing glances at Brick's butt as she stepped. God, even his ass was perfect.

The stairway was dimly lit. When they reached the top, there was an explosion of dusty sunlight when Brick pushed open a metal door. The upper level was not nearly as complete as the first floor. Someone was in the process of erecting large cuts of sheetrock that would later be transformed into beautiful walls. But the floor was deserted at that moment. The workers had left most of their tools behind during their break, along with quite a bit of debris.

Korah loved the smell of fresh concrete and well-oiled machinery. She stepped over power cords as she explored the raw environment. The outer walls of the building were intact, but there was no glass in the large openings they cut for windows. Instead there were foggy tarps covering the apertures.

Korah picked up a screwdriver she almost stepped on and placed it on one of the window sills. She didn't realize how closely Brick was following her until he spoke.

"What do you think?"

She turned, and the hairs stood on the back of her neck when she nearly bumped into him.

"Huh, oh, sorry. Didn't know you were creeping on me."

He smiled. Korah did, too.

"Everything looks great," she said. "What do you expect me to say? You know I'm not gonna find fault in your work."

"If you see any, feel free to point it out," Brick countered. "That is, if you really know what you're talking about…"

Korah raised an eyebrow. "You don't think I know my stuff, do you?"

"I know you're a great contractor," Brick acknowledged. "But I still can't see you doing actual construction yourself. Not with those pretty hands of yours."

Korah's face flushed with heat. "I can put these walls up just as good as anybody you have working for you," she boasted. "With these pretty hands of mine."

"Is that right?"

"Yes," Korah said, though it was hard to maintain confidence while staring into his intense brown eyes. "I get the feeling I have to prove it to you somehow."

"No, I don't want you to get dirty," Brick said, but his grin made it clear that he did want something along those lines. He stepped away from her and picked up a random tool. He held it up to her and asked, "What's this."

Korah giggled. "You can't be serious."

"What's wrong? You said you knew your stuff."

"Maybe I don't like being called on it."

"Maybe you don't know what this tool is called," Brick ventured.

Korah decided to humor him. "A stud crimper."

"Hmmm," Brick muttered. He placed it on the floor and grabbed something else. "What about this?"

Korah yawned, feigning boredom. "A skate raker."

Brick sucked his bottom lip into his mouth and bit it slightly. "Damn. This is sexy as hell."

Korah giggled. "Me naming tools is sexy to you?"

He nodded. "Yep. You think that's weird, huh?"

"Kinda," she said.

However, Brick's reaction to her knowledge of tools was starting to turn her on as well. She sashayed to one of the walls and picked up another one. When she looked back, she saw that Brick was checking out her ass. He didn't try to hide it. His eyes gradually rolled up to her face and then to her hands.

"What's that you got there?" he asked as he took slow, purposeful steps in her direction.

"A joint knife."

"What's that next to your right foot?"

Korah looked down and said, "A drywall sander."

When she looked up again, Brick was closer, only a few feet away. Korah's heart was rattling in her chest. Her breaths came slow and hot. She kept talking, mostly out of nervousness.

"That's a loading pump," she said in reference to another fine piece of equipment.

When Brick was close enough to touch her, he reached and carefully removed her hardhat. Korah stared into his eyes, her shaky breaths pushing her breasts up and down. Brick lowered his hands until they settled on her hips. His touch ignited a wave of blue heat that was centralized right between her legs. Brick pulled her hips forward as his face inched closer to hers.

"I've never met a woman who knew how to put up a wall," he said when they were close enough to kiss.

Korah felt his warm breath on her mouth. It was sweet from the after dinner mint they delivered with the check from P.F. Chang's.

"And I can do it without that automatic taper your guys are using." Korah spoke softly now. It was a wonder her voice worked at all.

Brick grunted slightly as his lips pressed against hers. Korah's heart stopped beating completely and a tidal wave of emotions rushed through her. It was only four days ago that

Yolanda showed her Brick's website. Korah thought he was gorgeous but also arrogant and conceited. And he was the only thing standing between her and the contract of her dreams.

All of these things were still true, but now she added smart and gallant and insanely sexy to the pot. Not in her wildest dreams did Korah think she'd find herself lip-locked with this handsome contractor – on one of his worksites no less – but life always had a way of surprising her, especially when she threw caution to the wind and decided to live for the moment.

Brick backed her against the window opening as he deepened the kiss. He sucked Korah's lips into his mouth one at a time. He gripped her luscious hips harder. Somewhere, miles away it seemed, Korah heard her hardhat fall to the floor. The sound of the impact echoed loudly as it reverberated off of every one of the walls.

He jerked her hips away from the wall until there was no space between them at all. Korah moaned slightly when she felt the excitement building in his britches. With her lips parted, Brick wasted no time slipping his tongue between them and savoring the sweetness of her mouth. His hands roamed to the back of her jeans, and he palmed her ass as if he was reclaiming a treasure.

As if it had always been his.

Oh God.

Korah moaned again, and she felt her clit swell and yearn for his erection. The walls of her pussy quivered. A fresh coat of her essence lubricated them and made them slick and ready for him. She raised her hands to his sides and marveled at the sheer bulk of this man, this bronze god who had lost control of himself because of her knowledge of construction.

The feel of his body was mesmerizing.

He flicked his tongue inside her mouth. Korah sucked it gratefully as he backed her against the wall again. Korah felt her right leg rise on its own accord. Brick was in tune with every one of her movements. His hand slid down her leg and supported it with a strong grip under her thigh. He began to grind between her legs in earnest, and it wasn't long before Korah felt his dick anxiously stroking her clitoris through their clothes.

She threw her head back and moaned loudly, with barely a care for the workers downstairs or the ones who were expected to return to the second floor at any minute.

"Oh, Brick..."

He was insatiable. He took advantage of the newly exposed flesh, planting hot kisses up and down her jugular. He licked and sucked from her clavicle to her earlobe. Korah's hips pushed into him with urgency, craving his dick in the worst way.

If he stripped her naked right then and there, she thought she might have allowed and enjoyed it. But one of them had to have sense enough to know they would soon be found out. Brick pulled away from her and grudgingly released her leg. Korah thought she'd be more stable with two feet on the floor, but that was not the case. Her legs didn't have any strength at all. She took a wobbly step back and had to support herself against the wall.

Brick continued to stare at her, his breath's quick, his nostrils flaring slightly. His face was now a darker shade of tan. He reached down to adjust what Korah saw as a Humongous Boner. It bulged under his jeans, snaking down his left thigh.

Oh. My. God.

She wanted to touch it so badly, her teeth began to chatter. Her clitoris continued to throb with intensity. The visible girth of his dick made her walls contract again, which caused her knees to buckle slightly.

The look in Brick's eyes made it clear that this was not over.

No, not by a long shot.

"We will finish this," he confirmed.

Korah didn't respond. She slightly nibbled her bottom lip, savoring the taste he left behind.

"Until this goes down," Brick said, backing away from her, "do me a favor and don't say anything else about *tools*."

Korah giggled. She was so happy to be a woman. Men had to worry about people seeing their boners at inappropriate times. But no one but Brick would know how aroused Korah was.

She turned to retrieve her hardhat, which was a few feet behind them. When she turned back, she caught Brick staring at her ass again.

"I don't think that's gonna help your problem," she said teasingly.

"I know," Brick said. "I'm a glutton for punishment."

"Me, too," Korah replied. "If I keep talking about your tools, would you punish me?"

She couldn't believe she said that. She felt absolutely *naughty*!

Brick nodded, his eyes growing dark again. "If you want me to punish you, I certainly will."

Korah almost called his bluff, but she really didn't want to get caught in such a compromising situation. They'd gone too far as it was.

"Okay, I'll be good," she said. "Hurry and get your soldier at ease, so we can both get back to work."

"I'm working on it," Brick assured her, and he tried his best to think unsexy thoughts.

CHAPTER NINE
FUN, FAST AND FIERCE

On Saturday night, Brick pulled his black on black Lincoln Navigator into Korah's driveway at 7 pm and hopped out with a pep in his step. He ambled up the perfect walkway and admired her nearby shrubbery and floral arrangements after ringing the doorbell.

Korah answered wearing a new pair of denim jeans and a new pair of cowboy boots. She bought them yesterday from the Justin Boots store on Long Avenue specifically for this outing. Brick told her he wanted to take her to the historic Stockyards area of Overbrook Meadows for tonight's date, and she should dress appropriately. Also, he mentioned, it might be unsafe for her to wear heels on the cobblestone roads and squeaky, wooden sidewalks they had down there.

Korah was excited about the outing, and she was excited about seeing Brick again. She realized their whirlwind romance was spinning out of control, but she didn't want to hit the brakes on it. She wouldn't even allow worries about Brick's possible playboy lifestyle to spoil the fun.

The Brick House CEO stood on her doorstep wearing dark-colored jeans with a long-sleeved, black button-down. The shirt fit him perfectly; showing off his pronounced traps and shoulder muscles, while flowing loosely over his arms. He sported a black Stetson, similar to the one he wore in his website picture. His boots were top of the line as well.

"Is that ostrich?" Korah asked, checking out his fancy footwear.

"Yes'm," Brick said with a grin. He hooked his thumbs on his belt and did a quick two-step for her.

Korah laughed pleasantly. She looked him up and down, admiring his outfit and his beautiful bronze skin, his strong jawline and piercing brown eyes.

"Wow," she said. "A real-live cowboy. And you're not just playing dress up, like me."

Brick continued to grin affectionately. "You should see me ride a bull."

Korah shook her head in wonderment. "You're serious, aren't you?"

"I haven't done it in a while," he admitted. "But my uncle was in the official Cowboys of Color Rodeo. He taught me quite a few things, back in the day."

He reached for her hand and brought it to his mouth for what had become a wonderful custom for them. He kissed the back of her hand, but this time he drew her into his arms and kissed her lips as well. Korah wasn't prepared for the unexpected affection, but she wasn't opposed at all. Brick's touch gave her butterflies.

His kiss heated her whole body. The contact only lasted a couple of seconds, but that was long enough for Korah's clit to awaken with a bright smile. Her body definitely remembered the passion Brick bombarded her with when their lips locked yesterday afternoon. Certain parts of her were eager to resume the sultry scene and hopefully follow through to completion.

Korah inwardly laughed at herself. This wasn't like her at all. But that was part of the reason why it was so delightful.

"You look very beautiful tonight," Brick said when they separated. "And happy," he added, noticing her smile. "I love to see a smile on your face."

"You're pretty good at putting one there," Korah commented.

"I hope I can continue to do that for a long time," he responded casually.

A long time.

That could mean a lot of different things. What was *a long time* for Brick? Another week? A month? Surely not a year.

Her last tryst ended badly because Quincy wanted more than the no-strings-attached good time Korah was after. Was she now going to put herself in Quincy's shoes and look for something Brick wasn't offering – something that may not even be in his nature? Korah wasn't sure, and for now, she didn't want to think about it.

Brick turned and led her to his Navigator. He helped Korah into his car, like a proper gentleman. Her eyes were glued to him as he went around the front of the vehicle and climbed into the driver's seat.

"Would you like to eat anything in particular?" he asked as he buckled his safety belt.

"Anywhere you wanna take me is fine," Korah said as she did the same. "So far you can do no wrong."

He smiled and winked at her as he put his car in gear and rolled out of the driveway.

● ● ● ● ● ●

The Overbrook Meadows Stockyards was located on the north side of town. It was a rare treat in the middle of the bustling metropolis. Long ago, when cowboys led their cattle up the Chisholm Trail to the railheads, Overbrook Meadows was the last major stop for rest and supplies.

Today the streets in the district were still paved with cobblestones, reminiscent of the 1800's. The roads were lined with saloons, leather shops and a variety of western eateries. Most of the sidewalks in the district were wooden and creaky, which added to the overall old-timey appeal.

There were quite a few discrepancies nowadays, like the many gift shops that preyed on tourists' dollars and the Segway rental near the Texas Cowboys Hall of Fame. But for the most part, it was as authentic western as you could get in modern times. There were countless old west artifacts on display, and the Championship Rodeo attracted visitors from all over the world.

Brick mentioned taking Korah to the highly praised Cattleman's Steakhouse for supper that night, but he already enjoyed an awesome steak with her at the Reata earlier that week. Instead he took her to Billy Bob's, which had the fine distinction of being the "World's Largest Honky Tonk."

They dined on brisket and ribs and barbecue pinto beans with corn on the cob and coleslaw. Korah knew she'd avoid her bathroom scale for a week after such gluttony, but she even asked Brick to get her a mug of beer like his, rather than the glass of wine he was about to order.

"You drink beer?" he asked skeptically.

"Sometimes," Korah said with a smile.

"Alright, bring the lady a Bud Light as well," he told their waiter.

"Yes, sir," the young man said and left their table.

Brick leaned back in his chair and checked out Korah's physique openly. "You don't look like a beer drinker."

"Okay, I haven't had one in over a year," she admitted. "But when in Rome..."

"Are you having a good time?"

"I am. Thanks for bringing me."

"You didn't finish your plate," Brick noticed. "You full?"

"No. But I don't wanna get *stuffed*. What are you trying to do, put me to sleep?"

"No, I don't want that," Brick said. "Our night just started."

Korah found that interesting, considering he picked her up nearly two hours ago.

"What other plans do you have?"

"Are you gonna dance with me?" he asked.

Korah chuckled and began to shake her head. Billy Bob's had a live musical guest every Saturday night. Korah didn't know the country singer who was rocking the mic at that moment, but he was really good. A lot of folks in the crowd were singing along to the tunes.

There was a dance floor near the stage that was filled with couples; all of them wearing western attire like Brick and his date. But Korah was not familiar with any of their dance moves. They all looked like professionals to her.

"I don't know any western dances," she said. "Do you?"

Brick nodded. "Yup."

Of course he does.

Historically there was a surprisingly large number of black cowboys in the south. It was refreshing to know that a lot of their descendants kept the rich legacy alive.

"You can dance without me," Korah offered.

"I can't dance by myself."

"I'm sure you can find someone else to dance with. A strapping young buck like you..."

Brick chuckled. "I'm forty-five years old. Haven't been a young buck in some years."

Whew! Up until that moment, Korah thought Brick might be eight or nine years younger than her. He was so youthful and spirited. It was a relief to know that she was only one year older.

"There are a lot of ladies here who aren't with men," Korah noticed. "If you want to dance with one of them, feel free."

"Really?"

"I'm not your woman," Korah said. "I'm not tripping."

She didn't mean to say that. It just came out. She knew Brick would think she was testing the waters.

"Whenever you're with me, you *are* my woman," he said. "I wouldn't disrespect you by dancing with someone else."

Korah's heart started to squeeze with uncertainty, and she didn't like that. *Whenever you're with me* was just as vague as his *for a long time* comment earlier. Korah didn't know what was wrong with her. She hadn't known this man for a full week yet. It wasn't like her to be so sensitive.

"Brick, I wanna see you dance," she said honestly. "Just because you came with me doesn't mean you can't dance with another woman. I appreciate that you're such a gentleman, but come on. You don't have to take it that far."

His smile was adorable. Korah noticed, for the first time, that he had a few crow's feet in the corner of his eyes. Even they looked sexy on him.

Their waiter appeared at that moment with their frosty mugs. The sight of the ice cold beer made Korah's mouth water.

"Thank you," Brick told the waiter and then returned his attention to his date. "A girl that knows sheetrock and is willing to drink a beer..." he mused. "You're full of surprises, Ms. Stewart."

"Me? You're the one with all of the surprises, Brick. And you know it."

"I got a lot more surprises to come," he replied.

"Yeah, I'll bet you do," Korah said, smiling mischievously.

She took a sip of her beer. It was delicious – almost as delicious as the way Brick was eyeing her under the bill of his Stetson.

I am in cowboy heaven, she thought and giggled softly.

● ● ● ● ● ●

True to his word, Brick took her to the dance floor later and found a table for them with a great view of the band. With Korah's blessing, he left her when a new song came on and strutted toward the stage. Brick had no trouble finding a dance partner. He was one of few black cowboys in the building, and he was definitely the most handsome man, hands down. He looked around at the beautiful ladies watching him and then held his arms out in a *Who wants some?* gesture. Korah laughed when half a dozen hands flew up.

Brick pointed at one girl and motioned for her to join him. She jumped up with much a grin and giggle and met him on the dance floor. She was a beautiful Hispanic woman with long, black hair and tight blue jeans that had no pockets. The jeans stretched over her luscious hips and ass so brilliantly, Korah gave herself kudos for not becoming jealous.

The girl also had a nice rack, but Brick didn't ogle her in any obvious manner. He leaned forward and whispered something in her ear, and she nodded, still smiling brightly. He took her hands, and they embarked on a country swing dance that looked like they'd been practicing for months.

Korah couldn't believe it.

She stared at them in wide-eyed astonishment for the next four minutes. Brick's moves were smooth and fluid. His steps were sure and confident. He led his partner expertly, and she was fully in-tuned with his body.

The dance wasn't overtly sexual, but the way their bodies flowed together, and the way his partner stared into his eyes was nearly erotic. Brick spun the girl several times throughout the dance. Each time, her long, luxurious hair flowed like satin. He even dipped her seamlessly towards the end of the song.

Korah's eyes tried to catch everything, but there was so much to look at; Brick's feet, his legs, his arms and his *ass*. Korah was suddenly eager to take a western dance class, though she never had the slightest interest before.

When the song finally ended, a few people even applauded for them, Korah included. Brick gave his dance partner an appreciative hug before turning away from her and locking eyes with his date. Korah felt like a princess when he returned to her. Brick ignored all of the other southern belles who were damned near begging to cut a rug with him.

"That was freaking amazing," Korah said when they were closer.

Brick pulled her into his arms and hugged and then kissed her passionately. Korah thought she might melt into a puddle of nerves right then and there.

● ● ● ● ● ●

They toured the Stockyards for a while longer after they left Billy Bob's. Korah found a few souvenirs she wanted to give her kids, and Brick bought her a brand new Stetson that made her look and feel like a true cowgirl.

They stopped by Cattleman's Steakhouse, and Brick immediately dragged her to the mechanical bull ride. After watching a few country boys get tossed roughly onto the soft mats, Korah knew she wouldn't dare get on that contraption. But Brick could be very persuasive.

"You gotta ride that," he told her.

The bull ride had a short, padded wall encircling it. Korah stood facing the bucking machine while Brick stood very close behind her. His body was pressed against hers. He had his arms around her; his hands meeting at her waistline. The sexual tension between them was so thick, Korah wondered if everyone could see it. Brick spoke right next to her ear. The feel of his breath on her face and neck sent chills down Korah's spine.

"I am not getting on that thing," she assured him. "I'll break my neck!"

"No you won't," he said with a laugh.

"Did you not see what happened to those last three guys?"

"They take it easier with the girls," Brick assured her.

"Who is *they*?"

"The DJ's," Brick said and pointed to a nearby booth. "The machine's not automatic. That guy makes the bull buck and spin as much *or as little* as he wants to."

"How do you know he'll take it easy on me?" Korah wanted to know.

"They always do for the ladies. And if he does make you fall, I'll kick his ass and kiss you wherever it hurts when we leave here."

Dayum!

That was an offer she couldn't refuse.

Korah boldly threw her hand in the air when the DJ asked who was next. She hurried to the entrance of the ring when he waved her over.

Fear started to get the best of her when it was time to mount the clunky machine, but once again Brick knew what he was talking about. The DJ kept her ride slow and predictable. There were a few jerks and spins that made her new hat fly off her head, but overall the robotic beast was very manageable, even for a newbie.

When the ride ended, Korah climbed off the bull with a huge sense of accomplishment. Brick was waiting for her in the same spot she left him. Korah was gushing with excitement.

"Thank you so much! I can't remember the last time I've had as much fun as I've had tonight!"

"Me, too," Brick said. "But to be honest, I was kinda hoping you'd fall, so I could follow through with my promise to kiss you anywhere you're hurting."

"Oh, well, um, I may be hurting a little," Korah lied. "I think I must've fallen when I got off."

Brick grinned devilishly. "I know you did. I saw you. You should let me give you a massage," he suggested. "I know that saddle was uncomfortable. You might have some sore spots you don't even know about..."

Korah's mouth fell open. She stared up at him, thinking about all of the *sore spots* he had in mind. A lump caught in her throat, and she couldn't speak right away. Her clit began to swell again. That was definitely a sore spot that needed some attention.

"Yeah," she said vaguely. "Okay."

"You gotta let me take care of that," Brick stated.

Korah's eyes widened. Surely he was talking about her clit now!

"Do you wanna come home with me?" he asked.

Korah continued to nod, her heart thudding. She felt so heated all of a sudden. She thought she'd break into a sweat.

"Wh, where do you live?" she managed.

"Dallas."

"Oh, okay."

"Why do you look so nervous?" he asked. "Are you afraid to find out why they call me *Brick*?"

Korah's eyes widened even more. Her mind was suddenly filled with the image of his erection yesterday afternoon. That thing was big as hell! And, come to think of it, it had looked as hard as a brick.

Oh Lordy, what was she getting herself into?

Brick took her hand and led her out of the restaurant.

"Come on," he said, "before I throw you on that mat and take you right now."

Oh wow.

Korah almost dug in her heels, just to see if he'd really do it.

Wondrous vision of beauty, so lovely
Sweet goddess, caress me, come bless me, come love me
And rub me. Yes, I'm feeling feisty, girl. Take me
Taste me. Make me want much more of you. Tasty
Each morsel is sweet like molasses. How sticky
Like honey, each drop keeps me licking. You're glistening
I'm listening. The rise and the fall of your heartbeats
They quicken. I can't sleep. I can't eat. I can't breathe
Feed me. Allow me to suckle. I can't speak
Need me as much as I need you, girl, intensely
Immensely, so wonderfully perfect. So lovely
Caress me. Come bless me, sweet thing. Come love me

CHAPTER TEN
THE AVERY MANOR

Korah felt like she was leaving the city when Brick rolled his Navigator past the gated entry that led to his lavish estate. His home was red brick. The layering featured subtle, intricate design patterns that Korah immediately took a liking to. Two humungous circle top picture windows flanked double front doors that were so beautiful, they could have been mounted at a cathedral. Korah felt like a princess when Brick parked at the apex of his circular drive and turned to face her.

"Welcome to the Avery Manor."

Texas Builders had constructed quite a few homes and even a few mansions over the years, but Korah was still taken aback by the architectural feat she was about to encounter. She wished it was daylight, so that she could fully appreciate the mansion in all its glory.

"Manor?" she said with a wistful smile pushing her cheeks. "How very proper. Do you have a moat as well?"

"No, but I have a gorgeous creek out back," Brick replied. "There are several bridges that cross over it. It's breathtaking, really. Especially in the morning. You should check it out, before you go."

It did Korah's heart good to hear a man refer to a view as *breathtaking* – even if he was bragging again. She turned and eyed him coyly when she took in the rest of his comment.

Brick grinned, reading her mind. "Sorry. I was being presumptuous. If you decide to stay until morning, you should let me show you around a little."

He exited the vehicle and went around to help Korah out of her captain seat. He continued to hold her hand as he led her up his walkway. He unlocked the door and flipped a light switch as he stepped into a foyer that was nicer than many restaurants Korah had visited.

There was a sitting area with limestone flooring; it was nearly the size of the average living room. After entering his alarm code, Brick turned and grinned at her. He removed his hat and reached to remove Korah's as well. She brushed her hair down as she continued to admire his *manor*.

Brick sighed pleasantly and said, "There's no place like home. Would you like something to drink?"

Korah nodded slightly.

"Right this way," Brick said and motioned for her to follow him to the living room.

Without touching a light switch, the room was suddenly illuminated, as if it was a living thing, and its only mission was to please the lord of the land. Korah gasped slightly as her senses of sight and wonderment were bombarded with elegance. The living room had a 24 foot high ceiling with a massive chandelier that twinkled in the soft lighting. Now there was herringbone wood flooring with a marble mantle.

Brick tossed their hats onto the couch and headed for a fully stocked bar. Korah hadn't been this impressed in years. She felt giddy as she slowly followed him. Brick selected finely aged brandy for himself. He poured it over ice and handed Korah a drink menu when she took a seat on one of the barstools.

She thought he was joking, but the menu was professionally made, with a leather binding. The script at the top of it announced that she had just entered "Brick's Bar." Korah shook her head in amazement as she scanned the selections.

"You're a bartender as well?"

Brick took a sip of his drink and nodded as the liquor warmed his throat and then his chest.

"I'm not an expert," he admitted. "But I can make anything on the menu. Of course if you want a beer or a straight shot, I can definitely handle that."

Korah couldn't help but stare at him as he spoke. Not only was this man the owner of a very successful contracting and construction company, but he was *makes-no-damn-sense*-good-looking, he had a ranch, he was an excellent dancer, he lived in a mansion – a *manor*, that is – and he was a superb host.

Brick was also an incurable playboy who had no doubt brought many women to this very bar for the purpose of seduction. Korah didn't want to think about *the others*, but she knew she'd be a fool not to consider them, especially if she was about to become one of them.

But she didn't want to have that inner turmoil. Not here. Not now. Brick was who he was, and Korah knew who he was before she agreed to come home with him. Plus she liked the idea of being a free spirit and living for the moment. Her last child had recently left the nest, so this was her time to start really living. Wasn't it?

Surely it was.

She said, "I would like an Appletini," and placed her menu on the bar.

Brick nodded and reached for another glass. "Would you like it with apple juice or apple brandy?"

"Brandy," Korah said, fully aware that her drink would be much stronger.

Brick worked with the ease of someone who spent some time moonlighting as a bartender. He placed her drink before her and reached for a remote as she took a sip. Korah smiled as music from many unseen speakers filled the home with a contemporary jazz melody.

"Do you like it?" he asked as she drank a little more.

Korah nodded. "Yes. I do. Your home is beautiful."

"Thank you. I've been working on it for years. I'm remodeling the deck right now."

"Really? What are you doing to it?"

"Replacing the concrete with wood. I would've been done with it by now, if I brought a crew out here. But it's not a priority."

"Let me know if you need help," Korah offered.

Brick chuckled. "It's mostly demolition at this point. But I'll let you know if I run into something that requires your – expertise."

"No, you won't," Korah said with a giggle. "You don't think girls should do that kind of work."

"True," Brick said. He brought his drink to his lips and took a healthy swallow. "But you're changing my mind day by day."

They enjoyed the music and the atmosphere for a while as they finished their drinks. Korah declined a refill when she placed her empty glass on the bar. She left her host for a moment and took a leisurely stroll through the living room, admiring the furnishings and paintings he had on display. The music continued to titillate her senses as the alcohol coursed through her bloodstream, making her feel relaxed and worry free.

She didn't realize that Brick had left the bar until he approached from behind and wrapped his strong arms around her. Korah smiled as she leaned back into him. She closed her eyes and savored their closeness.

"If you don't mind, I'm going to take a quick shower," Brick said.

Korah had been thinking the same thing. The stockyards area was clean, and they didn't approach any of the actual livestock. But some of the attractions had a dusty feel to them, which was reminiscent of the old west.

Before she could inquire about herself, Brick said, "If you'd like to shower, one of the baths upstairs is fully stocked."

Korah turned with an appreciative smile. "That would be great."

Brick kissed her softly before guiding her to the marvels on the floor above.

• • • • • •

The guest bathroom he showed her to was larger than a mobile home. It was bright and cherry scented. And, in keeping with the rest of the home, it was immaculate and designed without a flaw. Brick's assertion that it was fully stocked was accurate. In addition to clean robes and linens, he opened two of the sink drawers to reveal a multitude of toothbrushes and deodorants that were still in the original packaging. He had also supplied the room with travel-size shampoos and razors and disposable bathroom slippers.

The music he turned on in the living room was still audible in the bath. Korah traced the soothing sound to a speaker mounted above the door.

"Is there anything else you need?" Brick asked before giving her some privacy.

Korah shook her head, her eyes bright and filled with merriment. He had truly thought of everything.

"I have lotions in this other drawer," he said. "But I'd like to give you a massage when you get out. So I'd prefer if you didn't use any."

Korah's eyes widened.

Was he serious?

Her back and neck muscles quivered in anticipation.

"Okay," she said simply.

"Would you prefer vanilla, coconut, garden strawberry, mango..."

Korah didn't think she could be more amazed. She had never been with a man who pampered her to this degree.

"Mango," she said and couldn't stifle a giggle.

"Great," he said and backed away. "When you get done, the master bedroom is all the way down the hall, on the left."

He stepped into the hallway and pointed in that direction.

"Okay," Korah said. "I'll see you in a few."

"Take your time," Brick encouraged her. "Sometimes I feel like I could stay in the tub for hours, if not days. I'm in no rush."

He gave her another fever-inducing stare before he closed the door and walked away.

● ● ● ● ● ●

Brick was right. Korah did not want to leave her shower. It was elegant and spacious with frameless, glass doors, mosaic tiles and brushed bronze faucets. The water was soft and warm, and the scented body wash smelled divinely. The continual jazz music coupled with the alcohol she consumed was exceedingly soothing. Korah had been in five-star hotels that weren't this comfortable.

It was the thought of Brick's massage that prompted her to turn the water off. She couldn't wait to feel his strong hands all over her body. His confidence gave her the impression that he was a skillful masseuse, but it didn't matter if he wasn't. By then Korah had come to believe that he could do no wrong.

She dried herself on one of his plush towels and wrapped her body with an even softer white robe. She checked her visage in the mirror and thought she still looked ravishing without any make up.

She began to feel anxious when she exited the bathroom and considered the fact that she was completely nude beneath the robe. She was comfortable in her skin, but her heart rate continued to rise as she stepped slowly towards the master bedroom.

Her pulse struck like lightening when she entered the room and took in the lavish surroundings. Her immediate attention was drawn to Brick's bed, which was enormous. Korah thought it was twice the size of a king-size mattress. The headboard was solid mahogany, as were the matching dressers and nightstands. The floor was carpeted. The walls and curtains had soft, earthy tones.

Brick sat in an offset office area with his back to her. As she inched closer, Korah saw that he was working on a spreadsheet of some sort. An intrigued smile parted her lips. It was interesting to see that despite all that had transpired tonight, he still had business on the back of his mind.

Korah also smiled because Brick was topless, and this was the first unabated glimpse she had of his upper body. His trapezius muscles were solid and defined, like two grapefruit halves positioned between his neck and shoulders. His hazelnut skin was slightly tanned. His back fanned out broadly, like a peacock's tail features.

He heard a sound behind him, and he swiveled his chair in her direction.

Oh my goodness.

Korah couldn't stop her lips from parting at the sight of his bare chest. She knew Brick was muscular, but not to this extent. His pecs had clear definition, even a perfect crease down the middle. His six-pack was equally distinct. His stomach muscles flexed slightly as he rose from his seat.

Brick wore black, satin boxers. That was all. It was a struggle for Korah to maintain eye contact, rather than stare at the bulge of his dick beneath the thin fabric. When she did meet his eyes, she was surprised to see that he also looked mesmerized.

"You look beautiful," he stated as he closed the distance between them.

Korah's brain turned to mush when he placed his huge hands on her waist and kissed her slowly. She emitted a soft moan. Her legs became weak when he deepened the kiss, sucking on her lips and then her tongue. Her robe suddenly felt very hot and cumbersome. She was not upset when Brick's hands moved up her body, and he pushed the fabric off her shoulders.

Standing fully nude before him, Korah's nerves started to make a comeback. Her hands subconsciously came together between her legs. But the look in Brick's eyes as he took his time indulging in her beauty gradually eased Korah's tension. She wondered if men knew that they could take away or restore a woman's confidence with just one look. The way Brick stared at her made Korah feel like she was the only woman he had ever wanted.

He offered to her help onto the bed and instructed her to, "Lay down, on your stomach."

His assistance was appreciated. Four sturdy, wooden feet held the bed a foot off the floor. The mattress and box spring increased its height another two feet. Brick went to his dresser to retrieve a bottle of lotion. He returned and joined her in the center of the mattress.

He positioned a goose down pillow beneath her head and wasted no time in straddling her, with a knee on either side of her thighs. The weight of his dick resting directly on her ass made Korah's heart stop.

He told her to, "Relax."

That was easier said than done. Korah felt him growing larger by the second.

The pillow was remarkably soft, as was the rest of the bed. But Brick was as hard as his moniker.

Korah turned her face to one side and told him, "I'm not really sore. You don't have to give me a massage."

Brick ignored her as he stared down at her nude physique. Korah's ass was delectable, her waist slim, her hips wide. He leaned down and hovered over her as he planted hot kisses down her spine. The feel of his soft lips titillated Korah thoroughly. Her pussy began to swell gradually.

"Why do you insist on denying yourself?" Brick asked as he opened the lotion and lubricated his hands. The scent of mango was immediate and delightful.

"I just don't want you to go through so much trouble," she said, speaking softly.

"You should always be treated in this manner," Brick insisted. "God made women to be beautiful, and He made men to admire a woman's beauty. I'm created to give you as much affection as possible. And you're created to enjoy and appreciate my affection."

Korah never expected to hear such words from someone who worked in construction. She didn't know how to respond.

Brick urged her to, "Relax and close your eyes."

Korah decided that she did deserve such affection, and she did as she was told.

"If you feel something brushing or poking you," Brick said, "and it's not either one of my hands, don't be alarmed. That's my dick."

Korah giggled but didn't open her eyes. Brick squirted warm lotion on her shoulders and down her back. He leaned over and started rubbing her neck and shoulders. His touch was surprisingly soft, even when he applied pressure. But his grip was strong. His hands swam across her skin slowly and soothingly. He worked out a kink on the lower side of her neck that Korah didn't even know she had. Her toes curled.

"Oh my God," she breathed. "I can't believe any of this."

"Why?" Brick asked, still kneading her muscles rhythmically.

"You can't be this good at *everything*," she muttered, a whimsical smile spread across her face.

"I'm not good at everything," he agreed. "I can't do cartwheels. Never could keep my legs straight enough."

Korah giggled and then moaned as his hands moved down her back. He caressed the muscles on both sides of her spine and squirted more lotion before massaging her sides.

"Oh, wow," she purred. "That feels so good."

Brick's hands were large, his finger's long and skillful. He rotated his thumbs in a circular pattern as he moved lower, to the top of her ass. Korah felt her pussy squeeze pleasantly. She shuddered involuntarily, which made her butt cheeks clench. She wondered what Brick was thinking. She wished she could see the look on his face, but from her vantage point, even if she opened her eyes he'd be out of her field of view.

She felt him scoot further down her legs. He squirted a little more lotion, this time on her ass. The lotion was warm, but Korah couldn't help but squirm a little.

"Ooh."

Brick chuckled, and then Korah felt both of his hands on her cheeks.

Wow. What am I doing?

Korah couldn't believe she was being so daring with him. She couldn't believe he was being so bold with her!

Brick rubbed her ass expertly, sending steady tendrils of pleasure straight to Korah's erogenous zone. She was so wet, she knew he could see it. Surely she was starting to leak on his beautiful sheets. Her mind was racing, wondering what he was thinking. Brick inhaled deeply before satisfying Korah's curiosity by speaking.

"You should commend me," he said with his deep southern accent.

"I do commend you," Korah managed. His voice made her heart throb. His hands made her whole body feel like a flowing mass of lava.

"Not for the massage," he said. "I should be commended for maintaining restraint, with this ass in my hands."

Korah's breath caught. She swallowed roughly.

"You have a perfect ass," Brick went on. "I've been staring at it all night. I love your jeans."

Korah continued to pant softly as Brick fondled the object of his desire.

"I want to prop this ass up," he continued, "and slide in from behind. I'm so hard right now. And you're so wet..."

She knew he could see it!

Her eyes flashed open, but she didn't attempt to look back at him.

Brick pulled her hips up midway.

Korah gasped and another shudder rolled down her frame, causing her labia to wink at him.

Brick palmed both of her cheeks and then slid a hand towards her pussy. One finger slipped in effortlessly, titillating her clitoris along the way. Her clit responded with a resounding **FINALLY!** and Korah's whole body convulsed as a powerful orgasm began to bubble deep within her.

"Oh!"

Brick marveled at the trembling beauty before him. His eyes narrowed and darkened with want. His nostrils flared, filling his lungs with the wonderful scent of her essence.

"Roll over," he growled, his voice deeper than before.

It didn't matter which way Korah went. There was no way she'd be in danger of falling off his massive bed.

The moment her back hit the mattress, she caught a fleeting glimpse of Brick as his head ducked and his face plunged into her wet center.

Korah's eyes flashed open fully, and she inhaled roughly. Her mouth hung open with a surprised scream trapped in her throat. Brick's tongue assaulted her pussy with malice. He went at her like he hadn't eaten in years, and her orgasm was the only thing that could satiate his powerful appetite. He gripped her thighs tightly and pushed them up, until her toes pointed towards the ceiling. His lips remained glued to her labia.

"Oh! Damn! Brick!"

Korah's hips jerked off the bed as her orgasm exploded from her, thundering through her pussy like a stampede of wild mustangs. Rather than try to hold her steady, Brick rode the wave with her. He continued to suck and lick her clit as it pulsated in his mouth, coating his tongue with her cum.

The jazz music still played coolly in the background. A saxophonist hit notes that could only be rivaled by the notes Brick was making Korah hit with his tongue.

He reached up and massaged her breasts with both hands. He tweaked her nipples between his fingers, sending pulses of electricity through her body that merged with the fiery flow of her orgasm. Korah's heart thundered as her hips slowly sank back to the mattress. The sweet scent of mango reminded her of where this orgasm had begun.

She was intoxicated with passion when Brick finally rose to his knees and crawled off of the bed. She panted slowly, her mouth half open, her eyes half closed. She sat up weakly when she heard him rummaging through one of the mahogany dressers. The muscles in Brick's back were primed. His bare ass was round and strong. Korah licked her parched lips. Her head swam when he turned towards her, his dick standing hard and engorged.

He opened the condom he retrieved and rolled it down his shaft before he noticed she was watching him. He kept his eyes glued on hers as he approached and climbed onto the bed. His gaze was intense and searing.

Korah surprised him by rolling onto her stomach and then pulling her knees up, until her ass was propped up perfectly. She gathered one of the soft pillows into her arms and lowered her face onto it. She knew Brick wanted to take her from behind, but he was too much of a gentleman to request it on their first time together. She grinned at his hesitance as he positioned himself behind her.

"I would've enjoyed missionary just as well," he said.

Korah chuckled and spoke into the pillow. "No you wouldn't."

"Maybe not, but–"

"After all you've done for me tonight," she said with a satisfied sigh. "The least I can do is let you hit it from the back."

Brick hummed and his voice seemed deeper when he spoke again. "You want me to hit it from the back?"

Korah inhaled sharply as she felt the head slightly pushing her opening.

"*Ooh*. Yeah. I do."

"Say it again," Brick urged her.

Korah grinned against the pillow. "Brick, please hit it from the back."

Her heart shot up in her throat when he started pushing again. He entered her slowly, encountering only mild resistance until the midway point. That's when her pussy began to grip him, squeezing pleasantly.

Brick moaned softly, loving her hot tightness. He pushed in all the way, and Korah cried out in pleasure. Her clitoris began to drum with each one of her heartbeats. She couldn't believe she was going to cum again so soon. Brick had her purring like a horny alley cat. Her clit was in absolute heaven.

He backed out and started pumping his hips slowly and deeply. He filled her completely with each stroke. Korah felt him everywhere; in her chest, the back of her throat. The continuous friction he provided made the hairs on the back of her head curl. She gripped the pillow as tightly as she could when he increased speed and rhythmically punched the back wall over and over again.

"Aww shit," Brick muttered. He squeezed her hips and drew her towards him as he slammed into her, making Korah wonder if she bit off more than she could chew. The sound of his hips smacking her ass filled the room. His dick was so hard and thick. Korah felt him stretching her, claiming her.

Owning her.

She mustered the strength to raise her head slightly and throw back at least half as much as she was getting. Brick was stunned that she did not yield to him. Her defiance broke down the last of his resistance, and his dick swelled even more as his orgasm gained momentum.

Korah's second climax peaked at the same time, and she threw her hips back even harder.

"Fuck me," she demanded. *"Fuck me, Brick!"*

He obliged, slamming in harder and faster. He squeezed her ass tightly enough to leave marks on fairer skin. He grunted loudly, and his dick jumped inside her. Korah's orgasm cascaded down her body, causing her pussy to grip him like a fist. Her climax coated his dick just as he squirted his seed.

Brick continued to pump his hips as Korah rode a wave of passion that made her feel like a ship lost at sea. His strokes slowed to a soothing rhythm as her body became weak from the release, and her arms and legs gave way to gravity.

When she lay flat on her stomach, Brick lay with her, still submerged deep within her folds. He kissed the back of her neck and buried his face in her hair. His breaths were warm and finally content. His body was hard and hot. Korah loved the feel of him all over her. She felt him flowing through her veins.

She had no way of knowing where their roller coaster love affair would take them next. But for tonight, she was happy to say that she didn't care.

The only thing that mattered was this moment.

CHAPTER ELEVEN
THE PANTY PROBLEM

On Monday morning, Brick sauntered into his office at nine a.m. sharp. He was well-rested and energetic. Unlike most of the American workforce, Brick loved the start of a new work week. He never partied too hard on Sunday nights, and he always preferred making money to staying home.

His secretary Persia followed him into his office before Brick had a chance to put his briefcase down. Today she wore a black skirt with a white blouse. Brick frowned at her as he settled in behind his desk. Persia always seemed to push the limits of what was acceptable attire at the workplace, but today she truly outdid herself. Her skirt was so short, Brick would have to classify it as a mini, and once again her blouse had enough buttons open to reveal the top portion of her bra.

Persia wore bright red lipstick with her nerdy glasses and long, press-on eye lashes. She was hot as hell, but that wasn't why Brick had trouble paying attention as she went over his schedule for the day. As she stood before his desk, trying her best to elicit some sort of acknowledgement of her sexiness, Brick cursed himself for giving in to temptation six months ago.

He and Persia had nothing in common, aside from the fact that she worked for him. If he met her under any other circumstances, Brick might have still tried to bed her, but not with the intention of developing something meaningful afterwards. He was pretty sure Persia would've agreed to those terms.

But having to interact with her every morning was like his own personal curse; a never-ending reminder of what can happen when you allow your dick to override professional boundaries. Isaac was right. He had to fire this woman.

But that was easier said than done. Brick felt like he was too close to the situation to handle it personally. Surely Isaac wouldn't mind giving her a pink slip. He was the one who wanted Persia gone so badly. Plus Brick had way too much on his plate, like running the business. He could make himself scarce for the next few hours, to give Isaac time to do the deed and give Persia enough time to clear the stuff out of her desk.

Unfortunately the matter came to a head before Persia left his office that morning. She finished her spiel and smiled at her boss. She was as bubbly as ever. She didn't notice that Brick hadn't heard much of what she said.

"Is there anything else I can do for you?" she asked. "I just made a pot of coffee. It's the dark, French roast. Just like you like it."

"Okay," Brick said and leaned back in his executive chair. "That would be nice."

"Very well," Persia said and nodded briskly. She turned and dropped her pen. "Oh, excuse me."

She bent to retrieve it, and Brick's eyes widened. Not only did the move cause Persia's skirt to rise halfway up her ass, but he saw that she didn't have on *any panties at all*. Not a stitch. He was absolutely astounded. He stared between her thighs and caught a partial glimpse of her kitty before she rose and said, "Excuse me," as she pulled her skirt down. She looked back at him, and Brick's eyes gradually rolled up to hers.

"Wait," he said. "Come back."

With her back to him, Persia's smile was from ear to ear. She managed to take it all the way down to a smirk as she turned to face him.

"Yes, Mr. Avery?"

"Close the door," Brick told her.

Persia couldn't hide her smile this time.

Mission accomplished.

She turned again to close the door.

"Have a seat," Brick instructed.

Persia sat across from him and crossed her legs. She seemed suddenly modest about going commando at the office.

"How are things going?" her boss asked.

"I'm doing fine," Persia said. "And yourself?"

"Not good," Brick replied with a sigh.

"Oh?" Persia's expression was now comforting. "I'm sorry to hear that. Is there anything I can do to make it better?"

"Um, actually no," he said. "I'm, uh, I'm afraid we have to let you go."

Brick cringed inwardly as her expression changed again. This time she looked shocked and hurt and unexpectedly betrayed.

"Wha, what? Why?" she whined.

"Listen," Brick said, leaning with his forearms on the desk. "I know some things happened between us in the past. It was my fault. I take full responsibility. I'm not blaming you at all. But because of those incidents, it's no longer possible for us to have a professional relationship..."

Persia's eyes quickly filled with tears. Brick hated to see a woman cry. He never relished the role of Heartbreaker, although he had to wear that hat many times throughout his life.

"What did I do?" Persia pleaded. "What'd I do wrong?"

"Well, as I said, it's not your fault," Brick told her. "The trouble started months ago, when we agreed to engage in a sexual relationship. I thought things could go back to normal afterwards, but that was foolish of me. I've since learned that things cannot go back to the way they were, and we – that is *I* was foolish to think they could."

"Yes we can," Persia cried. "We don't have to sleep together." Tears ran down her cheeks now. She was still beautiful, tragically so.

Brick didn't want to be a hard-ass, but being sweet on Persia is what got them in this sticky predicament in the first place. "You don't have on any panties today," he told her. "And even if you did, your attire is not appropriate for the workplace."

"I can, I can change clothes," she wailed. "I did, I didn't have any, any clean panties."

Brick didn't believe that for a minute. "Persia, you could come in here dressed like a nun, and it wouldn't change anything. I'm still going to remember certain things when I look at you, and you'll remember things about me. And *that's* the problem. That's why we can't work together anymore."

"But why do *I* have to get fired?"

Brick frowned at her. "Well, it's my company, Persia. I can't – what do you want me to do, fire myself?"

She didn't have a response for that, so Brick pressed on.

"I know this is sudden," he said. "So you can remain with us for two weeks, if you like. As a severance package, I'm willing to offer you one month's pay, you can keep your benefits during that month, and we'll pay for any of your unused vacation or sick time."

He thought that was pretty damned generous, but Persia didn't express any gratitude. She gathered her things roughly and yanked her skirt *way* down as she rose from the chair.

"This is bullshit," she muttered, and then she proceeded to vent even more. "I do a great job. I always come to work on time. It's not my fault you took me home a few times."

Brick didn't expect this level of hostility. He wondered if he was blinded by her curves for the past year, or if Persia had always been a bitch disguised as a bimbo.

"Um, does that mean you're not going to stay on for the next two weeks?" he dared to ask.

Her nostrils flared. She yanked her glasses off and wiped her eyes with the back of her hand. "So you want me gone now, just because I'm upset? You just fired me, *Brick.* I need this job. Can I at least be in my feelings for a few seconds, or is that too much to ask?"

"No, it's fine," he said. "Just, take it out of my office, if you don't mind. And I need you to go home and change into something appropriate. Pants would be nice. If you do wear a skirt, make sure it's to your knees and you have some underwear on."

If looks could kill, he would've turned into a pile of dust. She exited without another word, and Brick sighed loudly, burying his face in his hands. He looked up when he heard her reenter his office. But it wasn't Persia this time. It was his right hand man, Isaac.

Isaac eyed him peculiarly as he took a seat in the spot Persia just vacated. Brick rolled his eyes in preparation for the *I told you so* that was sure to come.

"What was that about?" Isaac asked. "Persia just stormed out of here, crying and snotting all over the place."

"I fired her," Brick said. "Just like you asked."

"Really? Well, don't blame me for that. Your dick's the one that got you in hot water with that woman."

"Yes, I know that," Brick said.

"I told you it was gonna be bad," Isaac went on. "You never should've slept with her. You should never sleep with *any* of your employees. Everybody knows that."

"Yes," Brick said. "You were absolutely right. But if you don't mind, I don't need a lecture right now. I did what had to be done, and I would really like to move forward."

Isaac nodded, though he didn't have too much pity for a playboy who couldn't keep his pants on. "So you flat-out fired her?" he asked. "She's gone for good?"

Brick inhaled and blew it out roughly. "I told her she could stay for two weeks. I offered her a month's severance pay. She'll be back soon – just went to get herself straightened up, and put on some panties..."

Isaac couldn't stop a smirk from curving his lips. "You got this girl coming to work with no panties?"

"I guess it was a last-ditch effort," Brick surmised. "All of her flirting hadn't been working, so she had to go all-out."

"All-out is right," Isaac said with a snicker.

"I'm glad you're amused," Brick said, "but this is actually very stressful for me. I made some mistakes, and now I'm dealing with it. I didn't want to hurt her."

His partner's expression said, *I told you so*, but thankfully he didn't say it again.

"I turned over a new leaf," Brick promised him.

"Alright," Isaac said. "I'm not going to harp on it. I saw the look on your face when Persia stormed out of here. I believe you have learned your lesson. If you haven't, I'm afraid you deserve whatever you get."

Brick nodded. That sounded fair enough.

"So what's on your agenda for today?" Isaac asked.

Brick chuckled. "I actually have no idea. Persia was going over my schedule for the day, but I was too busy wondering why the hell she was dressed like that and how soon you could fire her."

"*Me?*"

"That was before she bent over and gave me the full moon," Brick stated. "That's when I said fuck it and did it myself."

Isaac laughed. "Well, I've got good news and bad news about the school deal."

Brick was all ears.

"The good news is we're blowing our competition out of the water. According to my sources on the school board, we're still holding the number one spot in the bid. And our closest competition, your friends at Texas Builders, have slipped to number three."

Brick knew he should rejoice, but he wasn't happy to hear that. "Third? How'd that happen?"

"Another contractor is making a move," Isaac reported. "That's the bad news. Allied Construction and Remodeling is getting a lot of nods in the school board. From what I hear, they're the ones we need to be worried about."

"What?" Brick was incredulous. "I thought you said everyone was spoken for. Are they local?"

"They're based in Mansfield. They were spoken for. They withdrew their bid weeks ago, but they resubmitted it on Friday, right at the buzzer. And their new bid is much lower than the first."

"Lower than ours?"

Isaac nodded slowly.

Brick scratched his head. "And you looked at our numbers again? We can't go down any?"

Isaac shook his head. "Even if the bidding wasn't closed – *which it is*, we couldn't go any lower. As far as I can tell, Allied's gonna take a loss at that price. I can't see how they're gonna make any money."

"Maybe they just want it for the notoriety," Brick ventured.

"Or maybe they know something we don't," Isaac offered.

"Are they any good?"

"As good as anybody else," Isaac said.

"You don't have any dirt on them?"

Isaac shook his head. "Nothing obvious. But I'm still looking."

"They're getting serious consideration?" Brick asked. "You think they got a shot at taking it from us?"

"I'd say no, but you know how cheap school districts are. Honestly, I can't rule it out."

Brick felt a heavy sinking in his gut. He felt like his dreams were being snatched away, right before his eyes. Allied Construction and Remodeling just made his shit list.

"Can you grease the wheels?" he asked.

"Sure. But if we get caught, it's over. You know that, right? I'm talking about over with the school district *period*. Forever."

Brick inhaled and blew hot fumes from his nostrils. "Alright, hold off," he said. "What do we got, two weeks before they decide?"

Isaac nodded.

"I think our best bet is to find some dirt on Allied," Brick suggested. "If they're willing to take the job with virtually no profit margin, then something's up. They've got to be cutting corners."

"I'll let you know if I find something," Isaac said and rose to his feet.

"Could you get Persia's severance package written up?" Brick asked.

"Will do," Isaac said. "Do you think she'll come back?"

Brick shrugged. "I wouldn't, if I was her. I'd be too damned embarrassed. But if she's okay with coming to work with no panties on, I doubt if she has much shame."

Isaac grinned, shaking his head. "Don't worry too much about the school bid," he said on the way out. "We're still number one."

Brick drew some confidence from that, but they had a long two weeks to wait for the official decision. If Allied Construction could swoop in and push Korah's company out of the number two spot so easily, then no one's bid was safe.

● ● ● ● ● ●

Thirty miles away at the Texas Builders' headquarters in Overbrook Meadows, Korah sat behind her desk with a frown on her face while her son Devin gave his best arguments for not wanting to follow her instructions. Korah held the phone against her ear and was actually glad that he didn't try this mess in person.

"You're putting all of your eggs in one basket, Mama. We have three projects on hold now. There's no way we can fix all of the problems at that shopping center by the end of the week."

"Yes, we can," Korah said with as much calm as she could muster. "If you send every truck we have—"

"*Every truck*? That's ridiculous."

She sighed. "No, it's called a *sacrifice*. Did you talk to your sister yesterday?"

"What? No. What about her?"

"The school district knows about our trouble with that shopping center," Korah reported. "That news pushed us further away from winning the bid. Our *only hope* at this point is to make things right over there. If not, we can kiss that school goodbye."

"They said that?"

"That's what Stephanie told me."

"Okay, so you want to sacrifice *all* of our other projects, just so we'll have a chance to win *one bid* – even though our chances of winning are slim to none."

"The school is worth more than everything we have on our plate," Korah replied. "And our chances are better than *slim to none*."

"And in the meantime, you're okay with pissing off these other clients?"

"You know what, I just had an epiphany," Korah said, leaning back in her chair.

"What's that?" he grumbled.

"I just realized that if my head of construction was anyone but my son, I'd have to replace him for repeatedly undermining my authority."

After a pause Devin said, "So you wanna fire me for speaking my mind?"

"I want you to remember your role," Korah advised him. "When you come to work, maybe it would be best if you forget that I'm your mother for a little while and respect me like I'm your *boss*. Now, for the last time, your boss wants the repairs at the Harden Shopping Center completed within the next ten days. If you can't get that done, tell me now, and I'll find someone who can."

Devin made a show of breathing heavily into the phone for a few moments before saying, "I'll do it. But I—"

"Thank you, sir," Korah said and disconnected.

She looked at Yolanda, who was seated across from her desk, watching the conversation with wide, fretful eyes.

"Wow, Ms. Avery," she said after a few beats. "That was hardcore."

"The bad thing about a family business is dealing with *family*," Korah said. She sighed and shook her head in disdain.

"Would you really fire him?" Yolanda wanted to know.

Korah grinned at that. "Of course not. This company is as much his as it is mine."

"Oh." The girl was clearly relieved.

Korah knew that her assistant was often defensive of Devin, almost unnaturally so. She assumed there was a crush going on, and she hoped things never went any further than that. But Korah was pretty sure Devin liked Yolanda as well. For that reason, she was always on guard when the two of them had cause to be in the same room.

"So Stephanie says we're falling even further behind?" Yolanda asked.

Korah nodded. "I don't know how they found out about the shopping center, but it might just do us in. Fixing it really is our only hope. It would break my heart to know that we got this close to winning that school and then lost it because of a bad deal we did eight years ago."

"Is Brick House still the front runner?"

Korah's heart skipped a beat at the mention of Brick's name. She nodded. "Yeah."

"And... how's that going?" Yolanda ventured. "Are you two still dating?"

Korah's quick smile said it all.

Yolanda smiled, too. "Ms. Avery, if you don't mind me asking, what is your agenda?"

"With Brick?"

"Yeah."

Korah shook her head. "I don't have an agenda. We're just having fun."

"So, you like him?"

Her smile deepened. "Brick is exactly what I thought he was. But at the same time, he's different. He's a gentleman. Very respectful. He's chivalrous. He's exciting."

"Wow," Yolanda exclaimed. "That's a big turnaround. How many times have y'all gone out?"

"I think we went out three times last week. Everything's moving so fast."

"You sound like you really like him."

"I know," Korah said with a tinge of despair. "And I'm trying not to."

"Why?"

"Because I don't want to end up hating his guts. Brick is a ladies' man. I don't think he loves them too long before he leaves them."

"What about the subcontracting?" Yolanda asked. "Are y'all still talking about that?"

Korah shook her head. "No. He hasn't brought it up again."

"What about you? Why haven't you brought it up?"

Korah sighed. "I think it would be trouble. Too much could go wrong. Between us."

"Here's how I see it," her assistant said. "He initiated contact with you because he was worried that we might win the bid, and he wanted to work out a deal so that he would still get a piece of the job either way, right?"

Korah nodded.

"And now he probably knows he's ahead of you," Yolanda continued, "so he hasn't brought it up again. But I think Stephanie was right; two can play at that game. If you and Brick have something going on, now would be a good time to make a deal with him. If he'll guarantee to let you subcontract part of the project, I think you should take it."

"I'd have to drop out of the bidding," Korah reminded her. "And if Brick ends up losing...?"

"It's a gamble," Yolanda agreed, "but it would be your best business move at this point. Brick is more likely to win than we are. They've been saying that since day one. And if he's a playboy, then we don't know how long you'll have an opportunity to use him. You should strike while the iron's hot."

Korah shook her head. She'd never used sex for a business advantage before, and she didn't like the idea of starting now. However there was a slight chance that Brick was doing the same thing to her at that very moment.

Korah was sick of wondering if he really liked her, how long it would last and whether they would hate each other afterwards. Maybe it was time to stop waiting to see how things would go and do something proactive instead.

But using Brick in that manner still sounded too whorish for her tastes.

"I think it's too early to concede defeat," Korah said. "We still have two weeks to make a comeback. And it would be nice to maintain a bit of integrity when this is all said and done. He hasn't brought it up again, and I don't think I can be the one to do it."

"What if he does ask again," Yolanda pressed. "You could accept his offer then, right?"

Korah honestly didn't know what she would do. She'd be a fool to turn him down at this point, wouldn't she?

"I don't want to think about that right now," she replied.

"Of course," Yolanda said, her fair skin growing red about the cheeks. "You have an appointment at ten with Gregory Stearns," she said, switching gears.

"Is that the guy from the zoo?"

"Yes, that's him," Yolanda said.

Korah smiled. They recently won a contract to build a new tiger exhibit. Of course that wasn't as prestigious as the school, but it would be fun. And for Korah, it was confirmation that her company would continue to thrive despite the recent adversities.

"You got the designs ready?"

"Yes, Ma'am." Yolanda left the office to retrieve the paperwork.

CHAPTER TWELVE
JACKHAMMER

On Thursday Korah took a trip to Dallas for what Brick promised to be "an enjoyable experience." She arrived at the Avery Manor at sunset, just as Brick requested. His majestic estate looked even more grand with the fading sun dimming in the background, casting a beautiful orange glow across the earth as a parting kiss.

Brick answered the door wearing canvas shorts with a pristine white tee. His exposed legs were muscular with a sparse coat of hair that Korah didn't notice when she saw him butt-naked a few days ago. He invited her inside his home with a small kiss on the corner of her mouth.

"You look beautiful," he told her.

Korah wore a flirty sundress that had spaghetti straps and a cinched waist.

"Thank you," she said. "So, what's on the agenda?"

"It's out back," Brick said. "Are you in a rush, or do you mind if I stare at you for a few more seconds?"

Korah blushed, but she allowed him to make love to her with his eyes. In the background Luther Vandross crooned on the surround sound stereo system Korah had come to love.

"Okay," Brick said after a moment. "I'm ready." His smile was carefree and sincere.

He took her hand and led her through his home, most of which Korah had never seen before.

"Wait," she said as they passed the kitchen. "Do you mind...?"

She left his side so that she could inspect what had always been her favorite room of any home. Brick's kitchen was state of the art. It had a butler's pantry, granite countertops, two refrigerators, two built in ovens and a couple of dishwashers as well. The center island housed a sink, a covered grill and a deep fryer. Korah saw that there was an adjacent breakfast room, which had a beautiful view of the backyard.

"I can't believe you've never been married," she said as she slowly strolled through the room.

"Why do you say that?" Brick asked. Rather than follow her, he waited in the doorway, leaning on the doorframe.

"You have so much space," Korah said. "And if you don't have a cook, I can't imagine what you'd do with such a beautiful kitchen."

"That's rather sexist," he said with his sexy southern drawl.

Korah looked back at him and grinned. "Are you going to tell me you can cook, too?"

"Actually I can – and I did," he commented. "I cooked dinner for you tonight."

Korah had reason to narrow her eyes this time. The kitchen was immaculate, and she didn't see a meal prepared.

"It's out back," Brick said, shooting a thumb in that direction. "We might want to hurry. The sun is getting away from us."

"We're eating outside?" Korah asked, her smile bright and cheerful.

"Can't have a picnic inside," Brick said.

"A picnic? Really?" Korah was super excited.

"Yes, m'lady."

How wonderful! Korah thought as she hurried back to his side. She wasn't surprised that Brick wanted to go out with her in the middle of the work week, but she didn't expect anything as delightful as a picnic at sunset.

Who the hell invites a girl over for such a thing on a Thursday night? Korah giggled as she came up with the answer: Rich people, that's who.

● ● ● ● ● ●

Brick's backyard was so massive, he had to tool around in a golf cart. Korah hopped in the passenger seat and felt like a child visiting the mall for the first time as they rolled along a paved trail that offered an awesome view of his many acres.

Korah fell in love with the numerous trees along the trail, some of which had a huge canopy of branches and leaves that stretched over the sidewalk and engulfed them in shadows. And, as Brick mentioned during her first visit, he did in fact have an impressive creek that snaked through the property like a small river. There were three well-designed bridges that provided crossing points over the water at strategic locations.

After a short drive, Brick pulled up to a gazebo that had a solitary picnic basket waiting for them on the lone table inside. Korah thought it was the largest picnic basket she'd ever seen. When they got off the cart, she saw that he had a blanket folded next to the basket. The gazebo had a screen covering all of the openings. It was well-lit, but not too bright. Korah saw two similar gazebos in the distance.

Brick took her hand as he led her up the one step. In her lifetime Korah had been with a handful of men she would consider true gentleman, but no one took it as far as Brick did. What she experienced with him was almost surreal.

"Would you like to eat inside or out?" he asked before they took a seat.

Korah considered spreading the blanket out on the lawn, but she was a city girl at heart, and a chair sounded a lot better than sitting Indian-style for a prolonged period of time. Plus she wasn't a fan of insects at all.

"In here is fine."

"Great," Brick said. "Have a seat." He then proceeded to unload his basket, which was gourmet all the way. He announced each food item he removed.

"Ricotta, tomato and spinach frittata..."

"Herbed breadsticks..."

"Quinoa pizza bites..."

"Veggie wraps..."

"Potato salad..."

"And of course wine, cheese and grapes..."

Korah's mouth was watering by the time he finished laying out the delectable offering.

"Brick, everything looks awesome. But that is way too much food."

"That's what picnics are for," he replied. "You get to pick and choose. I'll take whatever we don't eat to one of my sites tomorrow. The guys will love it."

Korah giggled. "You're gonna take frittatas to a bunch of construction workers?"

"They'll look at me funny at first," he admitted. "But once they put it in their mouth, it'll be all over."

"Where did you get this food?" Korah asked.

"I told you I made it," Brick said. He placed an empty plate before her and himself.

"I know what you told me. And I'd still like to know where you bought it. There's no way you cooked all of this. I find that very hard to swallow."

He grinned. "You're not gonna swallow that?"

"There are a lot of things you could offer me that I would swallow," Korah said. "But you being a five-star chef ain't one of them. Besides, your kitchen didn't smell like you cooked at all today. And neither one of the ovens was warm."

"Okay. You got me," he said as he took a seat. "I had most of the food delivered – but I won't tell you where I ordered it. A guy's got to have some secrets. But I did cook the cheese and grapes."

Korah laughed. "You mean you pulled them out of your refrigerator?"

"And I cut the cheese."

Korah cracked up even more.

"What?" Brick asked. His smile was cute and totally oblivious to what he just said.

"You cut the cheese?" Korah said.

"Oh. Ha-ha."

"Well, whoever cooked this food did a wonderful job," she said. "Thank you very much."

"What would you like to start with?"

"I'll take a little of everything."

"So, um, there are a lot of things I could offer you that you would swallow...?" Brick said as he filled her plate.

Korah's smile was mischievous. "Why Mr. Avery, I do believe you're trying to proposition me..."

"No, not at all," he said. "I was referring to the wine, of course."

"Oh, well, yes," Korah said. "If you cram it in my mouth, I'll slurp down as much as you like."

Brick lost control of his tongs for a moment, and a pizza bite rolled onto the table and then to the floor.

"Need some help, there?" Korah teased.

"I do, but not with this," he said and continued serving food.

Korah was left to wonder what he might need help with. But, of course, she thought she had a pretty good idea.

● ● ● ● ● ●

They wined and dined without a care in the world as the sun left them for the day and the moon made its grand appearance. The food was divine, but the company was even better. Towards the end of the meal, Brick made his way to her side of the table so he could feed her grapes one by one.

Later Korah lay back in his arms and listened to the night life come alive. In addition to blue cichlids and spotted puffers, Brick had a multitude of horny frogs living near his creek who were looking for love that night.

Korah sensed it was probably a bad move to try to put some sort of label on their *situation*, but she couldn't control the drumming of her heart or the way her flesh singed whenever he touched her. She feared that she was falling in love with a man who may have no interest in her outside of the bedroom. But if that was the case, why was he being so damned romantic? A seasoned playboy like himself wouldn't go through all of this trouble just to get her panties off. Would he?

"Why do you treat me so good?" she had to know.

Brick reclined with his back against the cushioned bench seat. Korah lounged with the back of her head on his hard, broad chest. She was glad she couldn't see his face at that moment.

"Why do you ask me that?"

"I know a lot of women who have been with their husband or boyfriend for years, and they're still waiting for a picnic."

"I don't know those guys," Brick said, "so I don't want to call them losers. But personally, I would feel like a loser if I was unable to fulfill my woman's romantic needs. She shouldn't have to want for such simple things."

"You make it sound like this is run-of-the-mill. Every girl you date gets picnics and massages?"

"Of course not. She'd have to be really special."

But what makes me so special? Korah wondered. *And what's the expiration date for the special women in your life?*

She couldn't ask those questions, because they had only been dating for two weeks. Even regular guys don't like clingy women. Dreamboats like Brick were probably even more cautious. But Korah didn't think she was clingy. Just curious, that's all.

"How's work?" he asked.

She took that to mean he didn't like the path of their current conversation. She wasn't disappointed by that, because she expected as much.

"Everything's fine," she said.

"Got any new projects going on?"

"As a matter of fact we do. We're building a new tiger exhibit at the Overbrook Meadows' zoo."

"Really? We bid on that job, too."

Korah sat up so she could look at him. "I didn't know that."

"They called us last week and told us we didn't get the contract," he said. "But I didn't ask who beat us out."

"Well isn't that something? I guess the underdog does come out on top sometimes."

"Sometimes," Brick agreed. "Do you think you've got some of that magic left for the school bid?"

"I hope so," Korah said. "I take it you still think you'll win, hands down."

"I do," he said. "But I don't want to rain on your parade. I know that contract means just as much to us as it does to you guys."

Korah's heartbeats suddenly felt audible. She wondered if Brick could hear it. She thought this would be the moment when he brought up the idea of them working together again. Korah still didn't know if she would sacrifice her integrity and share the project with him – or if her integrity even had anything to do with it.

Competing businesses worked together all the time, and there was nothing wrong with that. If she had never seen Brick naked, this would be an easy decision. But sex complicated things considerably.

Fortunately (or maybe *un*fortunately) Brick changed the subject again without bringing up the subcontracting.

"Can you stay the night, or do you have to leave?"

"I have to leave," Korah said quickly. "I have to work tomorrow."

"Or we can have a three-day weekend," he offered. "I could take you down to my ranch. You said you wanted to ride my horse."

She smiled and eased back into his sweet embrace. Brick immediately wrapped his arms around her. His hands came together over her lower belly. The September evening was warm. The lights around the gazebo and the bridges that crossed the creek glowed in the moonlight.

"I would like to ride a horse," Korah said. "Hopefully it would be a lot smoother than that bull ride."

"Of course," Brick said.

He caressed her hands as their minds returned to that magical night. Korah thought of how he massaged her; his big, strong hands skating across her hot skin. She blushed as she recalled how she threw shame to the wind when she rolled over and presented her bare backside to him and allowed him to do as he pleased.

She had no doubt Brick would send their freefall love affair spiraling sinfully out of control if she accompanied him to his ranch. She was actually eager to be immersed in the rustic, dusty environment, where they could perhaps take a roll in the hay *literally*. But there was too much going on at the office.

"Sorry, but I have to take a rain check," she told him.

"I understand."

Korah checked her watch and was startled to see that it was after ten.

She sat up again. "Oh, wow. I didn't know it was this late. I have to go."

Brick stood and began gathering their picnic supplies.

"You've got an hour drive," he complained. "If you stay the night, you'll get to sleep sooner."

Korah grinned. "I doubt that very seriously. But even if I did get to sleep sooner, I'd have to wake up earlier, so I could go home to change for work."

"I have plenty of Brick House gear," he offered with a smile. "I can get you suited up perfectly, and you can go straight to work."

Korah wanted to stay so badly, she took a moment to consider the chaos that would ensue if she showed up for work tomorrow wearing a shirt with the Brick House emblem on it.

"You'd like that, wouldn't you?"

He stopped what he was doing and slowly looked her up and down. "Actually I would," he said with one of those sexy, southern winks that was nearly powerful enough to make her panties fall off all by themselves.

● ● ● ● ● ●

On the way back to the manor, Korah asked, "Hey, what's going on over there," in regard to a small work area she noticed on the way out to the gazebo.

"That's the deck I'm working on," Brick replied.

"Can I see it?"

He shrugged and steered his golf cart in that direction.

When they got to the back of the house, Korah hopped off the cart and stepped onto the concrete portion of the deck he planned to eradicate in favor of much more pleasing redwood. This was the only portion of the home Korah considered an imperfection, and she understood why Brick wanted to make it right.

"Hey, be careful," he said as he followed her off the cart.

Work had been started on the deck, but not much. Someone had already begun to break up the concrete that was attached to the home, and there was an open area between the remaining deck and the wall. There was a wheelbarrow there for hauling debris, some scraping tools, and Korah thought she saw a jackhammer lying on the grass.

Brick stepped past her and entered his home through the patio doors. A moment later two floodlights illuminated the area, temporarily blinding Korah. When her eyes adjusted, she saw that there was still much work to be done. There was exposed rebar in the area she was approaching, and she understood why Brick wanted her to be careful.

He exited the house and stood before her with his hands on his hips.

"This deck is going to extend twenty feet past the original one," he said. "I'm still not sure why the designer chose concrete. Made my stomach turned the moment I saw it, but it wasn't enough to keep me from buying this house."

"You're working on this by yourself?" Korah asked.

"I'll bring some guys out to haul the concrete and install the new deck," Brick said. "But I love demolition. Completely destroying something that was meant to last forever is a great stress-reliever."

Korah stepped over the exposed rebar on her way to the jackhammer.

"Hey, watch out," Brick said and made a move to stop her.

"I've been on plenty of construction sites," Korah reminded him.

"But you don't have a hardhat on, and you definitely don't have work boots," he said, glancing down at her leather sandals.

Korah ignored him. "Is this thing plugged in?" she asked as she bent and hefted the heavy machinery.

"Korah! Don't pick that up. You're gonna hurt yourself."

"Stop it," she said with an eager smile. "I wanna play with it. I never get to play with jackhammers anymore. Can I break up some of your concrete? I know it's late, but your neighbors aren't that close. Just give me thirty seconds – a minute, tops."

Brick was stunned by what he was hearing. Korah was correct about his closest neighbors being too far away to be bothered by the noise, but it wasn't his neighbors that concerned him.

"Do you even know how to use that thing?" He couldn't believe he was considering it.

"I'll tell you what..." She leaned over the machine with her forearm resting between the handles. "If I don't know what I'm doing, you can ban me from your tools for life."

Brick approached her, his eyes unreadable. He scooped up a pair of work gloves from the soft grass and snatched a pair of safety goggles from a nearby patio table.

"Well, if you're gonna do it, you have to wear some sort of safety gear."

Korah giggled. "You're gonna let me use it?"

"Why not? This should be interesting. Let me see your hands."

Korah offered them, and he slipped his oversize gloves over her dainty hands. The gloves were new, but Korah thought she could feel the contours of Brick's palms and knuckles that had already been molded into the cowhide.

He slipped the goggles onto her face, taking care to brush the hair away from her ears to ensure a snug fit.

"Is it plugged in?" she asked.

Brick shook his head. He was clearly bewildered by the sight of her in a sundress and sandals with a jack hammer, while the moon rose steadily above them.

He went behind her and followed the cord to the back of the house. He plugged the jackhammer in and retreated to the golf cart.

Korah waited until he was a safe distance away before she hefted the electric monster and lowered the tip onto an unbroken portion of the deck. She tilted it slightly and gripped both handles tightly before she turned it on.

The jackhammer immediately sprang to life, thrusting the heavy drill bit back and forth with such force the whole machine left the ground momentarily and skipped forward a whole foot from its own momentum. Brick immediately headed her way, but Korah brought her body weight over the jackhammer and managed to stabilize it after a few seconds.

It was hard work, but it required more technique than brawn. Korah chipped off a football-size chunk of concrete and then another. By then she felt comfortable enough to bring the hammer back to one of the chunks and break it into even smaller rocks for easier disposal. Her heart pounded just as fast as the piston in the drill.

Korah knew how to operate nearly every piece of equipment on her sites, but her son had only let her use a jackhammer exactly twice. She couldn't believe Brick gave her the okay – in the middle of the night, no less. This was more fun than the mechanical bull at Cattleman's!

Her minute was up long before her arms grew tired. After thirty more seconds, Korah was respectful enough to turn the drill off and lower it safely onto the grass. Her bones felt like jelly. The muscles in her arms and shoulders were tense, but her heart was soaring.

She had forgotten how her knowledge of tools affected Brick until she looked up at him and saw him approaching with slow, deliberate steps. His eyes were as dark as the night. His swollen pecs rose and fell under his tee shirt.

"That, that was one of the most impressive things I've ever seen," he managed.

The look in his eyes made Korah's throat catch. Her heart hitched as well. She didn't know how to respond.

"I'm not a breast man," Brick said, still walking. "But I've never seen breasts jiggle like that. And your ass..."

His nostrils flared as he inhaled deeply. He was within a few feet now. Korah's eyes were locked on his, but in her peripheral vision, she couldn't miss the fact that he was as hard as a rock.

He plucked the goggles from her face and kissed her deeply, intensely. His hands immediately clutched and began to slide across her body like butter on a hot skillet, making Korah sizzle all over.

Her hands were down to her sides, trapped beneath his arms. Her ears were still ringing from the sound of the drill. Now her head swam with the passion his touch and his tongue provided as he explored her mouth and tasted the wine that still lingered on her taste buds.

"*Whoa!*"

Korah cried out as he lifted her completely from the ground. He blindly stepped over tools and broken concrete on his way back to the patio. The gloves fell from Korah's hands, and she held on to him for dear life, not sure what to make of this sexual creature who was excited by her use of tools – apparently the bigger the better.

He deposited her on a patio sofa and lifted her legs in the air.

"*Brick!*"

He ignored her protest.

Korah's back was on the sofa. Her sundress fell to her waist, revealing lace, red panties that she wasn't expecting him to see tonight (but was prepared, just in case). Brick caressed her hips and then pulled the panties up and over her legs. Korah had never known him to be so aggressive, but she wouldn't say that she minded. She lay back as Brick tossed the panties over his shoulder and stared down at her. Her chest heaved. His eyes flamed.

He dropped to his knees unexpectedly and buried his face in her pussy, sucking her labia greedily as his tongue sought and found her hardening clit.

"Ahh! Oh Brick!"

The first lick set off a thunderous racket of tremors that rolled down Korah's legs and made her toes clench in her sandals. Brick's face was at the epicenter of the quake. His head bobbed up and down as he lapped her juices. He was ravenous. The sounds of his sucking and slurping gradually filled Korah's ears, as the ringing caused by the jackhammer started to subside.

Brick held her thighs up, squeezing them so tightly his fingers dug into her skin. Korah's ass squirmed on the soft cushion. She reached down and grabbed hold of his head and began to buck her pussy in his face as she gave in to the reality and pleasure he was providing her. Brick grunted and increased the whipping action of his tongue, which had become a taste bud-covered inferno.

"Oh! Oh, Brick! Oh, baby! Yesss!"

Her screams filled the night sky, which now had a pink, effervescent glow that Korah didn't realize was only in her mind. Brick thrashed his tongue in and out of her with such fury she lost her breath and couldn't immediately pull another one in.

Her eyes rolled to the back of her head, and then they squeezed closed. She didn't feel the tears squirting from her closed lids, but she did feel the earthquake Brick had set into motion. It rumbled down her chest and up her legs at the same moment, coming together at her wet center.

Her legs tried to snap closed, but Brick was having none of that. He forced her thighs apart, and she pulled his face deeper into her love, and her orgasm made her buck against him even faster. Her eyes snapped open, and she sucked in a breath of air hoarsely. She saw the lights from his house and the stars twinkling above them, and she realized this was not a dream.

Brick really did have her spread eagle, outside his beautiful home on a Thursday night.

She looked down at him. Her heart froze when she saw that he was staring up at her. Korah's chest rose and fell unevenly. Her dress was disheveled. Her expression was stuck somewhere between lust, confusion and extraordinary contentment.

Brick flattened his tongue and continued to lick her up and down as he watched her. Her clit twitched and her walls continued to contract around his tongue as her orgasm subsided. He backed away slowly, his mouth wet with her essence. He stood and rubbed his erection through his shorts as he stared down at her. Korah's blinked quickly as she watched him.

She didn't know what to say, nor could she speak if she was required to, but Brick did not want to spark up a conversation. His face was dark, and his dick grew steadily as he rubbed it. He growled at her and then turned and left her there. It took Korah thirty seconds to realize he told her, *"Don't move."*

Movement was not an option. Korah's body was numb, and her pussy continued to throb with pleasure. She closed her eyes and tried to get her breathing under control, and then she heard him again. She opened her eyes just as Brick returned to the patio. He yanked his shirt over his head with enough force to rip it, and then he pulled his shorts and boxers down his hips. Korah watched as he tore open a condom wrapper.

She was surprised that he didn't request that she come inside, but she didn't really care. She had never been so turned on by the sight of a man putting on a condom. She watched his dick steadily jump as he rolled the prophylactic towards the base. Her whole body trembled when he approached and took hold of her legs again. He turned her sideways, so that she lay fully on the sofa cushions, and then he climbed on top of her.

He positioned himself between her legs and kissed her softly, and then he eased his dick deep inside her.

"Ohhh."

Korah moaned against his mouth. She loved the smell and taste of herself on his lips. Brick went balls deep on the first stroke. Korah's body welcomed him like he'd been away fighting a war. Her pussy caressed him as he stroked her. His hips moved slowly at first.

"Oh, baby. Yes. Yes, baby. Give it to me."

Brick lowered his chest onto hers, and he moaned in her ear as he began to increase speed.

"You feel so good," he whispered. *"I'm gonna go deeper, baby. Is that alright?"*

Deeper?!

Korah's eyes flashed all the way open. She thought he was already as deep as he could go. She didn't respond, but she reached and dug her nails into his back in preparation for the pussy-pounding that was about to commence.

Her tight grip made Brick's flesh sting. He grunted again and began to thrust his hips harder and, yes, *deeper*.

"Oh, God! Oh, shit!"

Korah began to wail in earnest as he filled her completely and commenced to punish her box like he was mad at it. Brick raised his upper body and took hold of her thighs again, with a firm grip behind her knees. He threw his hips into her at the same rate as the jackhammer, and their thighs began to clap rhythmically – not with the smooth R&B strokes he displayed last time, but with a fast-paced techno beat that set Korah's clit on fire.

Clapclapclapclapclapclap!

"Fuuuck!"

She didn't try to keep pace with him or throw it back, because Brick was in the zone, and he needed no assistance. His face reddened as he looked down at her. Korah's pussy greedily gulped him down with each stroke. She didn't realize she was cumming again until her clit began to pulsate at the same erratic beat of her heart, and her walls closed tightly around his dick, sucking him down deeper and deeper.

"Damn, baby," he muttered.

Korah felt him grow even harder as the pleasure she gave him sapped the last of his strength and caused him to lower his body until they were chest to chest again. Brick gripped the cushion next to her head and continued to pound her box mercilessly as his dick exploded inside of her.

His baritone moans mingled perfectly with Korah's high-pitched screams, creating a symphony of eroticism that rolled through the night air and reverberated off every tree on Brick's estate.

Korah's second release was wonderfully mellow. She whimpered softly as Brick's hips slowed. He continued to push inside of her, with care and compassion now. He grinded soulfully between her legs, and he sucked from her earlobe to her collarbone. His climax made him lightheaded, to the point that he felt high.

When his movements finally came to a stop, and the air was thick with the scent of their love as well as the smell of freshly broken concrete (an aroma that would make Korah's clitoris harden for the next six months), Brick told her, "I think we should go to the bedroom."

Korah chuckled and spoke weakly. "Yeah right. A little late for that, don't you think?"

"It's never too late. What time do you have to leave?"

She hummed and sighed pleasantly. "About an hour ago."

"I don't want you driving," he replied.

Korah found that endearing. "I'll be alright." She swallowed and tried to moisten her lips. "Just need a few minutes, and some water."

"I'll get you some water," he said. "And I can take you home in your car and have a cab bring me back. I'll call them when we get ready to leave."

"You don't have to do that."

"I insist," he said with a grin. "But I don't think we should leave for a little while. You should let me take you to the bedroom."

Korah knew she was being conned, but a con never felt this good. "Okay," she said. "But I think I need a nap first." She closed her eyes, smiling dreamily.

"I'll go get your water," Brick said, finally sliding out of her. He rose to a sitting position. "If you can't make it upstairs when I get back, that's fine. Beds and a roof over your head are way overrated."

Korah's brain was foggy with passion. She didn't understand what he meant by that until he returned a minute later with a bottle of water *and* a new condom. At that point Korah doubted if she'd make it to Brick's mega-size bed upstairs – or to her own bed at home, for that matter.

Once again, it felt wonderful not to care one way or the other.

CHAPTER THIRTEEN
SWIMMING IN THE COMPANY POOL

While Korah did manage to make it home a little after one am on Thursday, her son Devin didn't even try. He woke up at seven am in a beautifully decorated bedroom that smelled of lavender and Christian Dior perfume. His girlfriend Yolanda (who also happened to be his mother's prized assistant) rolled over to catch a few more winks as Devin sat up in the bed.

His movement caused the sheets to uncover a portion of his woman, and he was greeted with a wonderful view of her bare-naked ass. He grinned and reached to squeeze it. Yolanda smiled but didn't open her eyes or otherwise acknowledge the affection. Devin covered her bottom half before rising to his feet and making his way to the bathroom.

Sleeping with one of his mom's employees was a big mistake – or so Devin was told many times in the past. But Yolanda was not the kind of girl you could pass up day by day. She was tall and brown-skinned with long hair she currently had styled in braids. Her teeth were perfect. Her smile. Devin thought her lips were beautiful. But it was her smarts that attracted him the most. He sat in countless meetings over the years staring in awe as Yolanda briefed the team on one project after another.

He dreamed of asking her out, but separating Yolanda from Korah seemed to be mission impossible. Devin only had cause to come to the main office for their morning meetings. *Sometimes* he was invited to those. But of course his mom attended them as well.

It wasn't until a company party last Christmas that Devin found himself alone at the punch bowl when Yolanda approached. He offered to pour a drink for her, and they talked for a few minutes before Devin noticed his mother stealing glances at them from across the room.

"I have to walk away now," he had told her. "My mom is watching, and I know she doesn't want us talking."

"Why not–"

"Don't look," Devin warned her. "That'll just make her more suspicious."

Yolanda brought a hand to her mouth as she giggled. Of course the giggle was a dead giveaway. Devin knew his mother would zero-in on that for sure.

For Yolanda, he was not only her boss' son. Devin was also the head of a very successful construction company, and he was tall and handsome, the quintessential hardworking man. Yolanda knew that he'd been watching her during their morning meetings, and she also knew that Korah didn't want them to date. But they were both young and naïve, with more hormones than good sense.

Devin had told her, "I know I shouldn't, but you're too damned sexy. I love the way you dress, and I love the way you talk, and I love the way you walk. Can I please have your number? I don't think I'll ever get another chance to ask."

That night he wore dark slacks with a button-down to the party. His shirt had three buttons open, revealing strong dark pecs. Yolanda had never seen him in anything but jeans and work shirts. She thought he looked equally sexy in both outfits.

She recited her number and walked away. Devin hurried to the hallway so he could program it into his phone, before it slipped from his memory. Later that night, Korah proved that she still knew her only son better than anyone else. As the party winded down, she took his hand and led him to the dance floor.

"Dance with your mama," she said.

Devin was happy to oblige. As they two-stepped to an old-school classic, Korah looked him in the eyes and asked, "What's going on with you and Yolanda?"

"Nothing," he said immediately. "Why you ask me that?"

"I know you like her."

He smiled nervously. "She's beautiful, Mama. Everybody likes her."

"I think you like her a little more than everybody else."

That wasn't a question, so Devin held his tongue.

"You can't date anyone who works in the front office," Korah warned. "It would be very *bad*."

"Who said we were dating?" he said with a chuckle. "All I said to her tonight was *Hi*."

"You said more than that."

Korah's expression remained cheerful, but Devin guessed that was for the benefit of whoever might be watching them.

"You didn't see us exchange numbers or anything like that," he said. "So why you tripping?"

"Because I know how it starts," she told him. "First you stare at her all goo-goo-eyed at the morning meetings. And then you talk to her at the Christmas party, and she says something that makes you think she likes you, too. Next thing you know, you're waking up in her bed, and you're both telling each other not to tell me about it."

Damn, Devin mused. Did she have a crystal ball?

"And two months after that," Korah continued, "you break her heart, and she hates you, and I can't have both of you at my morning meetings anymore because neither one of you can stay focused."

"Mama," Devin said, raising his eyebrows. "You're obviously reading way too much into whatever you think you saw."

"Don't go swimming in the company pool," Korah warned him.

"I won't, Mama. I promise."

It took exactly five weeks before Devin took a swim in the company pool. And it was *great*. Not only was Yolanda smart and funny, but she had a freaky side that only came out when she was in a committed relationship.

Eight months later, they were mutually in love, and Korah's warning had created an enormous dilemma. Devin had to keep coming up with excuses for why he wasn't dating anyone worthy enough to meet his mother. And Yolanda also had to lie to Korah about her relationship status.

Devin and Yolanda were both adults, so they knew there would be no deathly consequences if they came clean. But it was the principle of the matter. Devin gave his word, and he didn't want to tell his mother that he had lied to her face. And Yolanda worked by Korah's side five days a week. She didn't want to tell her boss that she betrayed her trust and had been doing so for such a long time.

● ● ● ● ● ●

Devin heard Yolanda enter the bathroom as he showered. When he turned the water off and peeked around the shower curtain, he saw his girlfriend standing over the sink, rinsing off her toothbrush. Yolanda wore panties and a bra now. Her hair was a little messy, and she didn't have on any makeup, but her body was well-toned, and her beautiful face consistently made his heart skip a beat. Devin thought he was completely satisfied from last night's lovemaking, but Yolanda's curves made him reconsider.

"Do you want me to make you some breakfast?" she asked without looking over at him.

Devin pulled a towel from the rack and began to dry himself.

"Thanks to Mama, today will be long, hard and frustrating," he replied. "I better eat something."

"Are you still upset with her?"

"Yes, I am," he said with a frown. "If I look a man in the eyes and tell him I'll be done with something by a certain date, I don't wanna come back later and tell him I was wrong. I don't want him calling me asking why no workers at his site. It pisses me off."

"You know this is a special situation," Yolanda said. "Sometimes you have to do the best you can for *everybody* – not just one person."

"But we're not doing our best for everybody," Devin countered. "The only thing Mama cares about is that shopping center."

"Baby, it's too early to stress yourself out," Yolanda said. She approached the shower and put the seat down on the toilet before sitting on it. Devin watched her with a confused expression.

"Come here," she told him.

He stepped out of the tub holding the towel in front of his body. Yolanda took the towel away from him when he was close enough. She tossed it onto the sink.

"Come here," she said again. "Lemme see your dick."

Devin didn't know what she had in mind, but that was an offer he couldn't refuse. He stepped closer. Yolanda reached and pulled his hips, until he was nearly standing between her knees.

"Why you acting funny?" she asked. "You don't want me to suck your dick?"

Devin's eyes widened, and his manhood swelled right before their eyes. Yolanda smiled and stared at it.

"I guess that means you *do* want me to suck your dick..."

Devin had a hard time responding. He loved it when she talked dirty to him, even though he couldn't reciprocate most of the time.

"I got an idea," Yolanda said. She held her chin up and brought both of her hands to her lap. "If you do want me to suck your dick, put it in my mouth."

Devin overcame his surprise and took another step towards her. He eased his hips forward until his manhood encountered her soft lips. She kissed the tip and then opened her mouth by degrees.

He continued to push forward, until she took in as much as she could. The warmth of her mouth made him shudder with pleasure. His chest and stomach muscles tightened, still glistening with beads of water. Yolanda's cheeks went concave and she began to suck and titillate his dick with her tongue.

"Mmmmm," she hummed.

Those were Devin's sentiments exactly. He reached and grabbed a handful of hair on the side of her head.

Yolanda closed her eyes and began to work her neck back and forth as she sucked.

● ● ● ● ● ●

The early morning fellatio led to an early morning romp that almost made both of them late for work. Yolanda did her best to ease her man's tensions, and she was disappointed when Devin continued to complain about his work assignments as he got dressed.

"Did you try to talk her out of it?" he asked. "Did you tell her how mad everyone's gonna be if we do all of this work on the shopping center and still don't get the school bid?"

"No, I didn't tell her that," Yolanda said as she fastened the leather strap on her sandals. "That's not my call to make, Devin. You know that."

"I know. I'm just asking if you tried to talk to her."

"No," Yolanda said. "If I keep trying to defend you, she'll know something's up."

"Do you think we have any chance of getting that school? Tell me the truth."

"I think your mom has things under control," Yolanda replied.

"How?"

"Well, this is only in the works right now, but we might have a possible deal with Brick House. That's what she's working on."

"What do you mean?" Devin asked.

Yolanda moved to fasten her other shoe, and she didn't notice that Devin had stopped getting dressed. He stared at her with a scowl that was growing by degrees.

"She didn't tell you she was dating that guy, Brick?"

"No," Devin said, fighting to keep his tone even.

"Well, don't tell her I told you," Yolanda said. "But Brick seems to like her. He offered to give us a piece of the construction work on the school, if we lose the bid."

"And what does he get if we win?"

"Well, I think we have to..." Yolanda trailed off when she finally looked up and saw the look on his face. "Uh, what's wrong with you?"

"Nothing," Devin snapped. "Tell me what that asshole is supposed to get from us if we win. And why is Mama making deals with him? Why hasn't she told me about any of this?"

Yolanda's mouth fell open – just about wide enough to shove her foot into it. "Hey, I, I mean, this is nothing definite. He did offer to work with us, but she didn't take him up on it. I was just saying the offer is on the table."

"How long has she been dating him?" Devin wanted to know. "And *why*? I met that dude. He's a jerk. Is Mama stupid enough to think he really likes her?"

"Devin, calm down," Yolanda said, her heart racing. "Forget I said anything. If she wants you to know about it, I'm sure she'll tell you."

"No, I'm gonna ask her," he said and continued to get dressed.

Yolanda's stomach twisted around something cold and hard as her whole career flashed before her eyes.

"What? You can't do that! You'll get me fired. Why would you do something like that?"

"You're not gonna get fired."

"Yes I am! You don't know what you're talking about."

"My mama loves you," he said. "She would never fire you. And if she does, you can come work for me."

"You work for Ms. Korah!"

"I can hire whoever I want," he assured her. "I need an assistant. I would love to work with you directly."

"You don't even have an office!" Yolanda exclaimed. "I'm not sitting in some stinky trailer on a worksite all day! Devin, if you care anything about me *at all*, do not tell your mother I told you that. What do you have against Brick anyway? You don't even know him."

She was right about that. But Devin did have a friend named Jason who worked for the police department. If Brick had any dirt under his nails, Jason could find it.

"I know she's your boss, but she's my mama," he said. "I don't want her to get played by that chump. We've been doing just fine without Brick House for over twenty years, and we don't need them in our business now."

"Okay. Whatever. Just promise me you won't tell her *I* told you any of this," Yolanda pleaded.

"I won't let anything bad happen to you," he said and left the room.

Yolanda was fully aware that that wasn't a promise, and she began to wonder if she should even bother showing up for work that day. She felt so sick, she thought she'd vomit.

Of course Devin had to look after his mother, but did he have to throw her under the bus in the process? She was a fool to tell him what was going on.

Damn that stubborn jackass!

• • • • • •

Devin left the house a few minutes later. He called his friend Jason before he backed out of Yolanda's driveway.

"Yo."

"Hey," Devin said. "You work today?"

"Nope," his friend replied. "I'm not even in the state. Thanks for waking me up early on my vacation."

"Sorry," Devin said. "I need your help."

"What's up?"

"I need you to look this cat up for me, see if he been locked up for anything."

"Who?"

"Brock Avery. He's a contractor. He has a website; it's Brick House Construction."

"You trying to get some dirt on the competition?"

"Worse," Devin said. "This fool's trying to date my moms. I think he's trying to weasel-in on our business."

"Oh shit. That ain't good."

"Nope," Devin agreed, his eyes dark. "Not good at all."

Jason called him back in less than ten minutes. Not surprisingly, he had unpleasant news about bad boy Brick.

Devin didn't have to attend the meeting that morning at Texas Builders' headquarters, but he couldn't avoid steering his work truck in that direction.

When he got there, he saw his mother's SUV and Priscilla's Cadillac in the parking lot. But thankfully Yolanda didn't manage to beat him there. And his little sister wasn't on the premises, either. Perfect.

Devin tried to keep his cool as he entered the building, but the unsettling news he learned about Brick had him fuming. Korah saw it in his eyes the moment he entered her office.

"Morning, son," she said without rising from her seat. "What can I do for you? And this better not have anything to do with you not wanting to work on that shopping center."

Devin didn't bother taking a seat, nor did he try to ease into the conversation.

"What's up with you and that Brick guy?"

Korah's nostrils flared slightly, and then she sighed. "What are you talking about?"

"You dating him?"

Korah looked past him but didn't see Yolanda at her desk. "Who told you that?"

"Stephanie." Devin knew the truth wouldn't hold up for long. His sister was at school that morning, but she'd show up later, when she was done with her classes for the day.

"What business is it of yours?" Korah asked.

She didn't look like she got much rest last night. Devin didn't want to cause her anymore additional stress. But this time he was right, and he could prove it.

"You offered him part of our business?" he spat.

"That's ridiculous," Korah said. "And I don't like your tone. You'd better–"

"You don't even know him, Mama. Why would you want to work with him?"

"*I'm not working with him*," she said sternly. "You got bad information."

"Just tell me the truth. How come everybody knows about this except me?"

Korah shook her head. Kids could be such a pain in the ass. You birth them, feed them, clothe them and raise them to be productive members of society. But that still wasn't enough. And when it was all said and done, they would get the last laugh by throwing your ass in a retirement home.

"Okay," she said. "I have gone out with Brick a few times. He did offer us a deal, where we could work together on the school job. But I didn't take him up on the offer. That's it. There's nothing more to it."

"And why do you think he offered you a deal?"

"I don't know," Korah said. "Are you in my face because you've got an answer to that, or are you just bitching for no reason?"

"Did you do any research on this man, Mama?"

"Either say what you got to say, or get out of my office, Devin! I don't have time for this."

The boy stood his ground. He folded his arms over his chest and continued to stare down at her, which pissed Korah off even more.

"He beat a woman," he said. "Her name is Vicki Espeland. She later tried to commit suicide. He got arrested for assault. I had my homeboy in the police department check. That man is a player and a woman-beater, and he don't want nothing from you but to con you out of the school job."

Korah was floored. She couldn't hide it at all. She was also hurt – and furious. A *woman-beater*? That was one of the lowest things a man could be. It was disgusting. Her heart seemed to shrivel up to the size of a walnut, taking all of the air in her lungs with it.

But she was also disgusted with herself, the way she'd been carrying on. Tears stung her eyes, but she wouldn't give her beloved son the satisfaction.

"What would dad think?" he asked.

Korah's eyes burned. She rose to her feet, her face hard and fierce.

"That's enough, Devin! Brick and I are not doing business together, so your worries about the company are invalid! And for the *last time*, you do not have a say in the direction *I* choose to take this company! I would never fire you, but I *will* put someone else over construction, until you get your act together.

"I appreciate you trying to look out for me, but I don't need your help with that either! Brick and I only went on a couple of dates, and he certainly never hit me. We're not in a relationship. We're barely even friends. You need to learn to stay out of my business!"

Devin surprised her by softening his stance. He sighed. "I'm sorry, Mama. I was just trying to help."

"If you wanna help me, then get those trucks out to the shopping center. That's all I need from you right now."

Korah's chest heaved.

Devin shrank beneath her gaze. He left the office without another word.

He passed Yolanda on his way out of the building. For her, he could do no more than lower his head and say, "Sorry."

It took five minutes for Yolanda to muster the courage to darken Ms. Korah's doorway. Her boss looked up at her and simply said, "Close the door, please."

With wide eyes and trembling fingers, Yolanda did as she was told.

CHAPTER FOURTEEN
MONEY TRAIL

While Korah was in her office reacting to the news of Brick's trouble with women, Brick had to contend with even more trouble with women at his place of business forty miles away.

Isaac sat across from his desk delivering the worrisome news. Brick sat up in his huge executive chair with his forearms resting on the desk. His eyebrows were bunched together in disbelief.

"Embezzlement?" he said. "Persia? Are you sure?"

"I'm positive," Isaac reported. "I checked the numbers three times. There's no doubt about it."

"How, how much?" Brick asked. "For how long?"

"It's been going on for over a year," his second in command replied. "But it got real blatant this week. I would assume she's trying to get all she can, before her last day with us. All in all, she took us for nearly fifty thousand."

Brick shook his head slowly. He knew this shouldn't be so shocking, but it was. This was the first time they ever caught an employee blatantly stealing from the company.

When he fired Persia on Monday and told her to go home and change clothes, Brick was surprised when she returned to the office a couple of hours later. Her new attire was definitely professional, and she didn't seem all that upset about the termination. Brick thought she recognized the folly of her ways and decided that her pink slip was just and the severance package was a good deal.

But apparently it was all a ruse. Persia wasn't happy with the one month's pay Brick offered her. She wanted a full year's pay, and she figured out a way to get it.

Aside from the impact this would have on their business, Brick was also hurt because he and Persia once had a semblance of a relationship. She had been to his home. He couldn't believe that he had been so comfortable around someone he obviously didn't know at all.

"How?" he asked. "How did she do it?"

"It wasn't all that ingenious," Isaac said. "If I had been paying closer attention, I would've caught this long ago. Persia inputted all of our payroll and the payments to anyone we contracted for glass, electrical, plumbing and what not.

"Every now and then she'd put in a bogus payment to a company we didn't hire, and she'd print a small check, usually around five or six hundred. She'd make the check out to an individual, complete with a business name and address, and we'd send them the payment, no questions asked.

"But after a little research, I saw that this person she was making the checks out to – his name is Damon Butler, by the way – has multiple checks written to him, and they're all for different companies. So I realized that either Mr. Butler works for A-1 Glass, Triple A Plumbing and B & C Electrical, *all at the same time*, or we had a rat.

"I searched Mr. Butler's criminal record this morning, and his rap sheet came back dirty as hell. He's done everything from dope dealing to assault and of course *check fraud*. And, here's the kicker, Mr. Butler has none other than *Persia Moore* listed as one of his next of kin in the police database.

"I'm not sure what their relationship is, but I'd assume he's a half-brother or boyfriend. Either way, I got a big enough paper trail to lock them both up. Just say the word, and I'll get the police over here to pick up Persia."

Brick's heart settled in the pit of his stomach. He was still more hurt than angry.

"How'd she get up to fifty thousand?"

"This week she clearly didn't give a damn," Isaac said bluntly. "She sent Butler eight thousand on Monday, nine thousand on Tuesday, eleven thousand on Wednesday and another nine thousand yesterday. I've already contacted the bank to put a stop payment on the last one, so we might be able to get our losses down to forty thousand."

He tossed a handful of papers onto the desk.

Now Brick was angry. The hairs stood on his forearms as he pressed a button on his phone.

"Yes, Mr. Avery?" a pleasant voice said over the speaker.

"Get in here," Brick growled.

"Yes, sir," Persia replied.

Isaac moved to one of the smaller chairs next to Brick's desk before she entered the office. Persia wore a gray pantsuit today. She was very attractive, but Brick saw nothing more than an ugly, lying thief standing before him. It took a great deal of will-power to remain seated as she grinned at him, like nothing at all was amiss.

"Who's Damon Butler?" he asked, and that changed her disposition entirely.

Persia's eyes widened, and she took a long, deep breath. She pursed her lips and then opened her mouth and closed it again without speaking. She put her hands on her hips and cleared her throat. Her eyes narrowed, and she finally spoke.

"What are you talking about?"

Brick snatched up the papers on his desk and threw them at her. Persia screamed and recoiled, like he threw a punch.

"You know what the fuck I'm talking about!" Brick's voice thundered like a lion's roar. His face was dark. The veins in his neck stood out like a hose spread across the lawn. *"Don't you stand there and lie to me!"*

"What do you want?" Persia shrieked as the papers fell to the floor around her. Her eyes were wet, her breaths quickened. She lowered her arms, and Brick saw that her hands were trembling.

"I wanna know who Damon Butler is," he repeated.

"What difference does it make?" his secretary asked defiantly.

"It makes a lot of difference, when you're sending this sonofabitch my money!" Brick barked. *"How dare you steal from me?"*

Persia folded her arms over her chest. A tear rolled down her cheek as she said, "I didn't steal anything."

"That's the way you wanna play it?" Brick said.

"The gig is up," Isaac added. "We know you've been sending this guy our money. We know where he lives. We know what bank he uses to cash the checks. And we know Mr. Butler listed *you* as a contact the last time he got arrested."

"Who is he?" Brick asked. "I know you're not stupid enough to involve a relative in this."

"I don't know what you're talking about," Persia repeated. "I don't know anything about that."

"Okay, missy," Brick said. "Let me tell you how this is gonna go: First I'm calling the police on your ass. And then I'm going to the address you're sending these checks to. And if someone answers the door who even *looks like* his name is Damon, I'm gonna whoop his ass until the police come and drag me off of him. And then *that* motherfucker is going to jail, too!"

He pushed a button on his phone, and a dial tone buzzed over the speaker. He pressed zero. Everyone watched him until an operator came to the line.

"Operator."

"Give me the non-emergent number for the police," Brick said, his eyes glued on Persia's.

"What city, please?"

"Dallas."

The operator rattled off a number. Brick didn't write it down. He had an excellent memory.

"Would you like for me to connect the call?" the operator asked.

"Yes, please."

Ten seconds later, a male voice came to the line.

"Dallas County Police Department. What can I do for you?"

"I would like to report a crime," Brick said. "Someone has been embezzling from my company; over fifty thousand dollars so far..."

Persia's composure finally snapped, but not in the way Brick expected. Although tears streamed from both of her eyes, she surprised him with even more defiance.

"Wait. If you, if you get me arrested, I'll sue you for sexual harassment."

Ha! That was laughable. Brick grinned at her. "That's the stupidest thing I've ever heard."

"Hold on a moment. Let me transfer your call," the cop said over the speaker.

"It's, it's not stupid," Persia said. Her heart was racing. She looked panicked, but she also looked conniving and somewhat prepared for this confrontation. "You fired me because I wouldn't sleep with you anymore," she said. "That's sexual harassment."

Brick thought she was a fool for thinking that would get her out of this jam, but when he looked over at Isaac, his partner shook his head slowly.

"Hello?" a new voice called over the speaker phone. "This is Detective Russett. How can I help you?"

"I'll call you back," Brick said and disconnected.

He stared at Persia for a few seconds before he spoke again. "Do you even know what sexual harassment means?"

"It means your sexual advances and requests for sexual favors has created a hostile work environment for me."

Brick's mouth fell open. He wondered how long she'd been waiting to pull this ruse.

"If anything, you've been sexually harassing *me*," he said. "You come in here, with your ass all out and then have the nerve to get offended when I fire you for it? You're out of your rabid-ass mind. I never sexually harassed anyone."

"I only slept with you in the past because I was worried about my job, and you gave me the impression that I would get fired if I didn't perform sexual favors for you," she stated. "But I've been going to church, and now that God is in my life, I realize what you were doing is wrong. When I told you I wouldn't sleep with you anymore on Monday, you fired me. That's my story. You can tell the judge whatever story you want to, when we get to court."

"That shit ain't gonna work," Brick told her.

"You can tell your story when we get to court," Persia repeated. "It's your word against mine."

"That has nothing to do with your stealing!" he said, growing more heated by the second. "You won't even be able to find a lawyer to take your lame-ass case after you get convicted of embezzlement. Everyone will know you're lying through your teeth."

"That's your *opinion*," Persia insisted. "I don't even want to argue anymore. Call the police on me if you want to. I'll file a lawsuit against your company the moment I make bail."

She turned and walked out with her head high, her heels clicking on the hardwood floor. Brick started to say something else to her, but Isaac held up a hand to stop him.

"Let her go," he said softly.

"But–"

"Let's talk it through," Isaac suggested.

It took every ounce of Brick's patience to remain seated and silent in the five minutes it took Persia to clean out her desk and officially leave the building for good.

● ● ● ● ● ●

"That's bullshit," Brick said when she was gone.

Isaac had moved back to the seat across from him. The papers Brick threw earlier were back on his desk in a neat pile.

"Of course it's bullshit," Isaac agreed. "But I've seen similar bullshit win lawsuits before."

"But she was coming on to me!" Brick was nearly exasperated.

"Towards the end, yes, she was," Isaac said. "But in the beginning, who initiated it?"

"She did!"

"And she'll say you did," Isaac countered. "So it really is your word against hers."

"Isaac, I know you're not going to sit there and tell me not to call the police on her."

"Brick, you fucked up. Can't you just take a moment to accept that?"

"How did I fuck up?!"

"Calm down," Isaac said. "Just, let's talk about it."

"Okay, talk."

"So we file charges against her, and she sues us for sexual harassment," Isaac ventured. "We will definitely win our case. But there's a chance she'll win hers, too."

Brick's mouth fell open.

Isaac kept talking, before he could interrupt. "I know she was trying her best to get you in the sack these past few months.

161

But I also know that you and her had a relationship. Once you tell a judge or a jury that – and Lord help you if there's a bunch of feminists on that jury – then you pretty much already lost.

"You can't prove that you didn't coerce her, so it's your word against hers. And since you're the boss, they're going to say you had no business sleeping with your damned secretary. I told you that shit time and time again."

"So we should let her steal from us?"

"How much do you think a sexual harassment lawsuit will cost us?" Isaac asked. "After attorney fees and a settlement – and trust me, we will end up settling out of court – we'll be in for at least fifty thousand. Right now we're only down forty thou'. So, yes, I say we leave well enough alone."

"So you are telling me I should let her steal from us..."

"Not to mention we'll probably get the school deal next week," Isaac continued. "How do you think the superintendent will feel when he finds out the guy he's paying to build the new high school is being sued for sexual harassment? They don't play that shit, Brick. We gotta be damned near squeaky clean.

"Obviously they won't be able to take the contract away from us, but they will sure as hell overlook us for the next project. That forty thousand is not gonna hurt us in the long run. But a lawsuit will."

"I don't believe this shit." Brick blew out a pent up breath. He couldn't accept that he was being outwitted by a bimbo.

"I can't believe you thought it was a good idea to screw your secretary!" Isaac said, his temper getting the best of him. "I relocated my family to help you with this business, Brick. I will not watch all of my hard work go down the drain, just because you're too immature to keep your goddamned dick in your goddamned pants! Jesus, man! Stop trying to blame people for your problems, and take a look in the mirror, 'cause that's the person who's gonna ruin you, if you keep it up."

Isaac stood and left Brick to stew in his own putrid juices.

● ● ● ● ● ●

Brick stopped by his office an hour later and told him, "I'm sorry, man. You're right. I fucked up. It will *never* happen again."

"I'm sorry, too," Isaac said. By then he was back to his usual mild-mannered self. "You gonna call the police?"

Brick shook his head and swallowed down a disgusting slice of humble pie. "No. You're right about that, too. She'll just bring more trouble to us in the long run."

"Okay," Isaac said. "Don't worry, man. I got that last check cancelled, so, you know, I guess that's good news."

Brick forced a smile. "I'll take it. I need some good news right about now. I'll be back in a couple of hours."

"Where you going?"

"Get some fresh air," Brick replied. "And get something to eat."

"Don't bring any food back," Isaac told him. "Wife's got me on Weight Watchers again. I gotta count points for everything I put in my mouth." He shook his head in dismay.

Brick smiled. "Lisa's a good woman. You're lucky to have her. I'll see you in a few."

"Alright. Take it easy, partner. Keep your head up."

● ● ● ● ● ●

After such a terrible morning, Brick was in desperate need of comfort. Unfortunately he didn't find it on the other end of the line when he called Korah. As a matter of fact, she sounded downright salty.

"I'm busy."

"Oh. I'm sorry. I didn't mean to disturb you. Just wanted you to know I was thinking about you."

She sighed, rather rudely, Brick thought.

"Is, is everything alright?" he asked.

"I'm great," she said, though she sounded anything but.

"What's wrong?" Brick was genuinely concerned. "Are you having trouble at work?"

"I don't... Listen," Korah said. "I don't think we should talk anymore."

Brick's eyes flashed open. He sat alone at a table in Starbucks. The Columbian blend he was nursing suddenly felt like slime in his stomach.

"Wuh, what?"

163

"This is a conflict of interests," Korah said. "We're both contractors competing for the same job. We're not friends, and we're not in a relationship. And this is getting to—"

"Whoa. What do you mean we're not friends? After the past couple of weeks, last night—"

"We're just having fun," Korah said. "Isn't that how you live? Wild and free?"

"What are you talking about? Who said anything about wild and free? I thought we were working on something real."

"Brick, you're forty-five years old, and you've never been married, and you have no kids. It's pretty obvious that you're not the type to settle down."

"Wait, okay, so you think I'm a player? Is that it?"

"You know you're a player. But that's beside the point."

"What is the point?" Brick rubbed his temple as he stared at the restaurant's cashier. The girl was trying her best not to get caught eavesdropping and failing miserably.

"The point is you and I need to go our separate ways, Brick. Now, I have to go."

She disconnected.

Brick was so confused, he held the phone to his face for five more seconds before he fully accepted that she was gone.

CHAPTER FIFTEEN
VANDALS

The weekend passed slowly and drearily. Korah didn't have any social plans, and her home began to feel very big and very empty as the slow ticks of her grandfather clock turned minutes into hours with no respite from her loneliness.

She missed Brick.

She knew she shouldn't care about him, but the short time they spent together in the past two weeks would forever reside in her memory as some of the best dates she'd ever had.

Korah couldn't get over the fact that he beat a woman. Every time she thought about what her son told her, she felt a heavy sinking in her chest. That wasn't the Brick she knew at all. She thought about how he massaged her body the first night they made love. She imagined those same strong hands balled into fists, his eyes mean and fiery as he used them to pummel a defenseless woman.

The thought made her shudder with unease. It made her nauseous. She understood that she didn't know him well enough to say that was out of character for him, and that bothered her, too. Why did she allow things to go so far with a man who was barely more than a stranger?

Korah began to second guess herself, and she came to the conclusion that she did compromise some of her morals and integrity for Brick. She let his good looks and southern charm taint what should've been an easy decision from the start.

Brick was no good for her. Everyone knew that. But Korah allowed herself to get caught up in a romantic fantasy that was destined for tragedy rather than them living happily ever after.

She wished she could chalk the whole episode up to youthful foolishness, but Korah would be forty-seven on her next birthday. She was much too seasoned to get swept off her feet so easily.

The only bright side was she never gave Brick cause to attack her, and she wasn't enamored enough to drop out of the race for the school contract or sign any potentially damaging contracts with Brick. Devin was right: If Korah had done that, her late husband would be rolling in his grave for sure.

●　●　●　●　●　●

On Sunday Korah met with her daughter Stephanie for lunch at Olive Garden. Korah didn't want to talk business, but the school contract was still the most important thing going on in their lives.

"How are things going with you and Anthony?" she asked around a mouthwatering bite of eggplant parmigiana.

"Not good," Stephanie revealed.

"Really?" Korah said. "Why? What happened?"

"I think he's sick of me asking about the school contract," Stephanie said. "He said he feels like a go-between for you and his mom. That fool thinks I'm using him."

Korah's expression was suddenly filled with concern. "Stephanie, I never wanted you to nag that boy. I never even asked you to talk to him about the contract."

"I know, Mama. But his mom is the superintendent's secretary. How am I supposed to be with him and *not* ask about the contract? We need that job, Mama. I don't care if he breaks up with me."

Stephanie sneered as she dug into her salmon bruschetta.

Korah was partly proud of her daughter's ambition and loyalty to the family business, but, "You shouldn't do that," she warned. "You and Anthony were happy before this job became our focus. You shouldn't let things go bad, just because his mom is the superintendent's secretary. She doesn't even have a vote in the matter."

"*I'm* not letting anything go bad," Stephanie said. "That's *him*. I just asked him a few questions, and he's acting like I'm a spy or something."

Korah grinned. "Sounds like you are spying to me. I hope you didn't ask him to put in a good word for us…"

"I did, but he wouldn't do it," Stephanie pouted. "That's when I got an attitude with him, and he started getting an attitude with me."

"So are y'all gonna break up?"

Stephanie shrugged.

Korah sighed. "Well, if you've already ruined the relationship, did you at least get any new news from him?"

Stephanie looked down at her plate as she spoke. "He said we dropped down to number three."

Korah's jaw dropped. "What? How'd that happen?"

"Another contractor offered a lower bid," Stephanie reported. "You ever heard of Allied Construction and Remodeling?"

Her mother shook her head.

"They're local," Stephanie informed her. "I don't think they're better than us, but right now they're cheaper."

"Damn," Korah muttered. The remaining food on her plate suddenly looked very unappetizing. "So we're definitely going to lose?"

"I don't know that for sure," Stephanie said. "We still have one more week. Anthony says they're looking at what's going on with our shopping center. He still thinks we have a chance, if we finish up over there before they vote."

"He thinks that?" Korah asked, a glimmer of hope lighting her eyes. "What is he basing that on? Did his mom say that?"

"I don't know. That's the problem. He'll tell me some things, but when I try to get more details, he says I'm using him. He's getting on my nerves, for real."

"What about Brick House?" Korah dared to ask. "Are they still number one?"

Stephanie nodded reluctantly.

Korah's heart thumped with both heartbreak and disappointment.

"I, uh, I heard about what happened with you and Devin," Stephanie said. "I'm sorry. I thought Brick was a good guy. I can't believe he goes around hitting women. I thought y'all were happy together."

"You never know who someone really is nowadays," Korah replied reflectively. And then she frowned. "Why'd you tell that boy Brick and I were dating anyway? You knew he would act a damned fool. And I never said I was gonna take Brick up on his offer to work together. You shouldn't have told Devin."

Stephanie frowned as well. "Mama, I didn't tell Devin that. I know he doesn't like the idea of you dating people. I would never tell him something like that."

"He said you told him."

Stephanie's mouth fell open. "No way, Mama. I want you to be happy. And I was the one who told you to take the deal Brick was offering. I don't know why he lied on me."

Korah was supremely confused, but Stephanie figured things out right away.

"It was probably Yolanda."

Korah considered that. "Why would she tell him? They hardly ever see each other."

"Because she likes him," Stephanie said. "They like each other."

Korah shook her head in dismay. She had her suspicions, but she never thought either one of them was stupid enough to act on their mutual attraction. "That's, do you think they're dating?"

"I don't know. But if she told him that, you know she didn't do it at work – which means they be talking *after* work."

"Aw hell," Korah muttered.

"I don't know that for sure," Stephanie added. "So don't start accusing nobody."

"I won't. But you've got to be right. If it wasn't you, then it had to be Yolanda. Priscilla's the only other person who knew about Brick, and she definitely wouldn't talk to Devin about it."

"Well, at least something good came out of it," Stephanie offered. "Devin found out about Brick beating on women. And you got out of that before it happened to you."

"Yeah, but Devin and I don't see eye-to-eye on a lot of work issues," Korah said. "If he's got an inside man – or *woman* – telling him all of my business, that's a huge problem."

"Oh, well, if you decide to fire Yolanda, you can give me her job," Stephanie said with a smirk. "You know I needs me a raise."

"No, you needs to worry about your grades," Korah said. "One of my kids has to take over this company one day. And at this point, I'm not too keen on leaving everything to Devin. But if you don't finish college, you can't have it either."

"I'm ahead of Devin?" Stephanie couldn't believe it. She rarely bested her big brother.

"No," Korah said honestly. "But I like your spunk. I don't agree with your decision to put the contract ahead of your relationship with Anthony. But I do appreciate the fact that you're willing to do so."

Stephanie smiled smugly. She knew that Devin was only ahead of her at the moment because of his age and gender. But if he kept up with his shenanigans, his little sis might swoop in and inherit the Texas Builders' CEO position.

Of course Devin would be less willing to take orders from Stephanie than he currently was with his mom, but she already had a solution in mind for that:

DEMOTION!

She'd send his feisty ass all the way back to the starting board. Devin would be fetching her coffee and sandwiches, until he got himself some act-right.

"What's so funny?" Korah asked, noticing the wicked grin on her daughter's face.

"Nothing," Stephanie said. "Just thinking about the future. I think everything's gonna be just fine..."

● ● ● ● ● ●

On Monday morning, Korah scheduled a brief meeting with her core team, which included Pricilla, Yolanda and Stephanie. She did not invite Devin to the meeting, nor did she bring up her suspicion that Yolanda was dating and leaking sensitive information to her son.

Korah didn't mention it because she still wasn't sure how she wanted to handle the situation if it turned out to be true. In the meantime she didn't see any harm in waiting to see if more evidence of their secret alliance emerged.

To Yolanda's credit, she did manage to keep a cool head in the face of adversity. Korah thought she looked a little apprehensive that day, but it wasn't enough to cast any serious doubt her way.

"So this week's goal is the same as last week," Korah said as she concluded the meeting. "We should hear from the school board by Friday – or Monday at the latest. Until then, our primary focus is the Harden Shopping Center. Hopefully we can finish up over there no later than Wednesday.

"From what I hear, we've been dropped to third in line for the school contract. But I'm not gonna let that deter us. Whether we get the school or not, we need to finish up that shopping center, so we can move on to other things."

Everyone agreed that was the best course of action, and they returned to their work stations a little dejected but certainly not ready to throw in the towel.

Rather than head for her office, Korah grabbed her purse and stopped at Yolanda's desk. Her assistant looked up at her expectantly.

"Yes, Ms. Avery?"

"Did you speak with Mr. Harden? Is he going to be at the site today?"

"Yes, Ms. Avery. He's expecting you."

"You wanna come with?"

Yolanda flipped through her planner rather than meet her boss' eyes. "Actually I have some stuff in the office I need to finish up."

Korah smiled inwardly. She knew her son was already at the shopping center. She was hoping to get a glimpse of how Yolanda and Devin behaved together, but Yolanda wouldn't allow herself to get busted so easily.

"I'm stopping by Starbucks on the way," Korah added, hoping to sweeten the deal. "You sure you don't want to go?"

Yolanda loved Starbucks like fat kids love cake. She looked up, and Korah thought she saw her eyes twinkle at the thought of a caramel macchiato.

But Yolanda bit her bottom lip and said, "I really need to get this paperwork done."

Korah didn't press the issue. She could've demanded Yolanda accompany her, but her presence wasn't needed, and Korah found amusement in her anxiety.

"Alright, suit yourself," she said and left the building with a smile on her face.

●●●●●●

At the shopping center, Mr. Harden was all smiles as well. He approached Korah and offered a hearty handshake the moment she got out of her SUV.

"Morning, Ms. Avery!"

"Good morning," she said. "You look like you're in a good mood."

"I am," Mr. Harden said, "because you're a woman of your word. Your guys have been here every day, and this place is finally looking like something I don't mind having my name on."

He stopped short of throwing his arms around her, but he did use both hands during their handshake.

Frederick Harden was an older man with piercing blue eyes and mostly silver hair. Korah knew that he grew up on a farm and was a self-made millionaire.

"I'm glad everything's working out," she said. "We should be finished here in a couple more days. Is Devin taking care of everything you need?"

"Your son's great," Mr. Harden said. "He's on top of it. I don't meet too many men like him. I'm sure you're very proud."

Hmph. You wouldn't be singing his praises, if you knew what it took to get Devin out here every day, Korah thought.

She was glad that her son was professional enough to keep his personal concerns to himself, but she couldn't say she was proud of him at that moment. They'd been doing nothing but arguing for the past couple of weeks. And at some point Korah had to confront him about what may or may not be going on with him and Yolanda.

"He is, something," she agreed.

There were three Texas Builders trucks on the scene. Korah spotted eight of Devin's workers walking about with their hardhats on and various tools in hand. She and the client spotted Devin in the crowd at the same moment.

"Here's our guy!" Mr. Harden said as the head of construction approached. He gave Devin a hearty slap on the back. "This man is a remodeling *genius*!" the property owner boasted. "He redid the floors in two of our stores. You got time to check them out?" he asked Korah.

She stared at her son, who either didn't feel comfortable about all of the praise or was still uneasy because of the recent fight he had with his mother.

"I'll check them out in a sec'," Korah told Mr. Harden. "I'm glad everything's working out for you."

"Did you stick it to that bastard at Clark Construction?" the older man asked. "I'd hate to think they're gonna get off the hook for all of the crummy work they did in the beginning..."

"We're still working on them," Korah said, her eyes returning to her son.

Devin looked strong and handsome in a long-sleeved button-down tucked into his jeans. His work boots were dusty, but it wasn't yet nine am, and the rest of his outfit was clean. His smile looked strained as he stepped to his mother and gave her a brief kiss on the cheek.

"I need to speak with you," he said.

"Okay." Korah nodded. "Could you give us a moment?" she asked Mr. Harden.

"Yes, of course," he said. "I'll be in the Donut Palace, if you need me."

In addition to the donut shop, the shopping center housed a cellphone store, a yoga studio and a dozen other businesses that were doing very well in the area.

Korah and Devin walked towards the cellphone store before he took a right and led her around to the back of the building.

"What's going on?" Korah asked him.

"I don't know," Devin said. "Vandals, I think."

Korah wore a mask of confusion as they reached the paved alleyway that ran behind the stores. It was large enough for the city garbage trucks to roll in and empty the eight dumpsters that were kept there for the shopkeepers' convenience. Behind the alley was a tall fence that offered a border between the property and an unattended field behind it.

"What do you mean, vandals?" Korah asked as they walked.

"You'll see," Devin said.

When they reached the area behind the yoga studio, Korah saw three more of Devin's crew collecting debris that was scattered nearly twenty feet in all directions. At the center of the mess was an eighteen foot equipment trailer that was owned by their company. It was mostly used for hauling and had been fortified with a metal cage on four sides to prevent cargo from falling off.

Korah was horrified to see that the trailer had sustained significant damage. Someone broke into the cage and looted some of the equipment they left there overnight. The heavy-duty chains that once secured two extension ladders had been cut cleanly with bolt cutters. The broken chains hung from the trailer like Christmas tinsel. The ladders were nowhere to be seen. All four tires on the trailer had been flattened as well.

"What the hell?" Korah gasped.

Devin shook his head. "This happened sometime last night. They stole our ladders and a small toolbox we kept on there. We had all of this trash collected," he said, referring to the old roofing tiles and other rubbish his workers were picking up.

"They scattered it all over the place," he said. "I don't think thieves would do all that. They would just get the tools and go. And thieves would have no reason to slash the tires..."

Korah agreed with him. It looked like the bandits had come there specifically to vandalize their equipment. The tool theft was most likely a crime of opportunity.

Korah's heart sank. She took a quick assessment of the damage and determined it would cost less than $2,000 to get everything back the way it was. But the manpower involved would hurt them more.

"Did you tell Mr. Harden yet?" she asked.

"No," Devin said. "I wanted to see what you had to say first. There's more over here..."

More?

Korah didn't see how things could get any worse, but she followed her son thirty more paces to where they had a huge Skytrak parked near one of the dumpsters. The heavy duty forklift was a rental. They used it to transport roofing materials from the ground up to the top of the shopping center. The $77,000 machine was a thing of beauty, but it looked sickly today because each one of its six-foot tall wheels was also on flat.

Most of the blood drained from Korah's face when she saw it. Her chest began to heave with hard, shallow breaths. Devin reached and placed a hand on her shoulder, thinking she might pass out.

"Wh, what the hell's going on?" she breathed.

"I don't know," he said. "But someone just cost us half a day's work. I gotta get the rental place to haul this one off and bring us another one. We can change the tires on the trailer ourselves, but right now we don't have our ladders *or* the Skytrak. We can't do any work on the roof at all."

Korah brought a hand to her mouth as she turned and surveyed the whole area. Devin's workers were staring at them, but they looked away quickly, as if they might be held responsible for the tragedy that had befallen them.

"Have you called the police?" Korah asked when her gaze returned to her son. Her eyes glistened with angry, bitter tears.

Devin shook his head. "I wanted to make sure you knew about it first. Mr. Harden isn't going to be happy when he finds out what happened back here. We were on a roll. Not only does this set us back on this job, but it's gonna set us back on our other projects, too. I'm so pissed... I swear to God, if I find out who did this..."

Korah looked into his eyes and noticed they were filled with rage. For her, this vandalism complicated dates and times and numbers. But for Devin, it was a matter of wasted manpower; blood, sweat and tears. Korah had never seen him so angry.

"I'll go talk to him," she said, just as Devin's cellphone rang.

He pulled it from his pocket and told his mother, "Hold on a minute," as he took the call.

Korah headed for the Skytrak, for a closer inspection.

But then she heard Devin say, "Man, you bullshitting!"

She turned and watched her son's scowl grow even deeper. He told the caller, "I'm on my way," and shoved the phone back into his pocket.

"Mama, they hit another one of our sites!" he announced as he marched quickly towards the front of the shopping center. "This is some bullshit!" he grumbled. "I can't believe this shit!"

Korah's heart rattled in her chest as she hurried to catch up with him.

"What? What are you talking about?"

"Somebody's messing with us," Devin growled, his fists balled, his eyebrows bunched together in a ferocious sneer.

"*What are you talking about?*"

Devin barely slowed down. "I gotta go, Mama. We got some more vandalism on Beach."

Korah knew that was the site for a pickle factory they were just getting started on.

"You gonna ride with me?" Devin asked.

"No," Korah managed. Her brain was racing. "I'll, I'll meet you there."

• • • • • •

Ten minutes later they pulled up to a construction site that was nothing more than five square acres of dirt that had been cleared of trees and grass and all other vegetation. There was only one Texas Builders truck on the premises, along with two rented backhoes that they used to move tons of soil each day.

This morning the backhoes were parked next to each other and both were idle. The three men Devin sent to the site were loitering hopelessly near the work truck with absolutely nothing to do because both of the backhoes were inoperable. Once again, someone had flattened all of the tires with what had to be a very sturdy knife.

Devin's lead man on the scene didn't have much of an explanation. He could only report that the vehicles were in this condition when they arrived that morning. After surveying the damage, Devin and his mother went to sit in his truck, rather than have a heated discussion in front of the workers.

"Someone's trying to sabotage us," he deduced.

"You don't know that," Korah said. "Until we talk to the police, we don't know if we're the only ones. It could just be some punk kids."

"These sites are twenty miles apart," Devin argued. "No one's gonna drive this far and do the exact same thing, unless they're targeting us *personally.*"

"You don't know that," Korah repeated.

"Well, just humor me, Mama." Devin had brought his temper down considerably, but Korah knew he was barely holding it together. "Who would want us to have problems with these jobs?"

She shook her head. "I don't know. No one I can think of."

"Who would want to delay us *period*?" Devin persisted. "There's got to be somebody who's pissed off at us. What about that dude you're dating, from Brick House?"

"I'm not dating him anymore. I haven't talked to him since last week."

"Well, if you broke up with him, maybe he wants to get back at you," Devin offered.

Korah couldn't imagine Brick doing anything this terrible. But then again, she never would've thought he was a woman beater, either.

"We weren't in a relationship," she said. "We only went out a few times. It wasn't that serious. I can't imagine him doing something like this. He's a millionaire, Devin. What would be the point?"

"Are you sure?"

Korah sighed and gave it more thought. Brick did sound upset when she told him that she didn't want to see him anymore. But he was a rich playboy, which meant she was easily replaceable. Try as she might, Korah couldn't picture him as a lovesick fool who was willing to resort to such treachery.

She shook her head. "Can't be him."

"What about that guy from Clark Construction?" Devin asked. "Isn't he upset about what's going on at the shopping center?"

Korah agreed that Herschel Clark was upset, but it was his own crummy life that had him in the dumps these days. He had filed for bankruptcy, and he said his wife was cheating on him. Korah wasn't one of the companies who was suing him, and neither was Mr. Harden, so Herschel had no reason to seek vengeance from them.

"He screwed up the shopping center," Korah acknowledged, "but we're the ones fixing it. And we're not even going after him for the money right now. If anything, he should be grateful for what we're doing."

"Did you break up with anyone else recently?" her son asked.

"No," Korah said with a frown. "Wait, what about you? Maybe one of your exes is trying to get back at you."

Even as she spoke, Korah knew that probably wasn't the case, either. She still thought Devin was dating her assistant, and this didn't seem like the type of damage a woman would be involved in.

Devin felt the same way. "Mama, I assure you no woman I've ever dated would do something like this. How many women do you know who are strong enough to use a pair of bolt cutters?"

Korah couldn't think of anyone offhand.

"What about that other guy you were with?" her son asked. "What was his name? Quincy?"

Korah didn't like how he was throwing this back in her lap. But these were drastic times, so she agreed that they shouldn't leave any stones unturned.

Quincy was very upset the last time she spoke to him. Korah could admit that she might have broken his heart, and she could also admit that she was a little rude in the process. But was Quincy distraught enough to stoop to this level of retribution?

She shook her head. "Quincy is too clean cut for something like this. I can't see him clomping around in this dirt. I honestly don't think he's strong enough to cut through those tires."

But Brick was.

Korah forced the thought from her mind.

"Call the police," she said. "That's the first thing we need to do. If they tell us we're the only ones who got hit, then we can go from there."

"If I find out it's someone we know," Devin said as he reached for his phone, "I'm gonna kick their ass personally." It wasn't like him to swear in front of his mother, and he quickly caught himself. "I'm sorry, Mama. But I'm pissed off."

"Me too," Korah muttered as she stared out of the passenger window at the wounded backhoes. She prayed that neither Brick nor Quincy had anything to do with this, because Devin wasn't kidding about the beat-down he wanted to deliver.

The last thing she needed was for her son to get arrested, on top of everything else.

Meekly, through bloodshot eyes I seek
Refuge, a love to take your place
I search in vain, for each embrace
Falls short. No substitute appears
No other love comes near. I fear
That with you all sunshine is gone
Away. I long to love. I moan
I'm wounded, girl. I simply want
You back. I want you to come home

CHAPTER SIXTEEN
WHODUNIT

Korah had to make a few calls of her own while her son talked to the police. Everyone at the office was completely floored. Yolanda even mentioned that she wished she had accompanied Korah that morning, but Korah was actually glad that she stayed behind. Whatever may or may not be going on between her son and her assistant was no longer a priority. They could elope right now, for all she cared.

Sitting in her SUV, Korah gritted her teeth as she placed her next call. She would almost be willing to bet money that Quincy was not involved with the troubles at her worksites, but that *almost* seemed very huge at the moment. Plus Devin wouldn't stop pointing the finger at him until Korah officially ruled him out as a suspect.

She didn't know what type of response she'd get when she called her ex-boyfriend at work. He surprised her with an upbeat and apologetic tone.

"Hey, Korah. Wow. Didn't think I'd hear from you again."

"Hi, Quincy. Is this a good time? I hope I'm not disturbing you."

"No, it's okay," he said. "What's going on? Hey, I'm sorry about coming to your house unannounced. I understand that I was wrong, and I hope you'll accept my apology."

Korah's eyes knitted together in confusion. That felt like such a long time ago. She'd nearly forgotten why their last conversation ended so badly. She did remember the note he left on her door after her first date with Brick and the multiple phone calls he made that night as well.

Memories of the subsequent argument and the spat they had the morning after his birthday party solidified Korah's thinking that Quincy might very well be angry enough to want to harm her business.

"Oh, that's fine," she said.

"No, I'm serious," Quincy insisted. "When we talked about it, I didn't really understand what you were saying. But I know I violated your privacy, and I want you to forgive me. I would like us to still be friends."

That comment gave Korah pause. Were these the words of a man who crept through two of her construction sites in the dead of night and stole equipment, ransacked her trailer and slashed tires wantonly? She shook her head. Couldn't be. But the stakes were too high not to find out for sure.

"I do forgive you," she said. Then, "Hey, do you think you could meet with me sometime today?"

"Really? Korah, I would love that. Would you like to go out tonight?"

"No," she said quickly. "How about lunch, or I could come to your office now, if you have time..."

"Oh. Um, what's up? What's going on?"

I need to confront you face to face, she thought. *There's no way you can look me in the eyes and lie about something this crazy.*

"It would be better if we talk about it in person," she said. "I'm sorry. I don't mean to sound cagey. This won't take but a minute..."

"Um, okay," Quincy said. "I don't have lunch until 12:30, but I can take a long morning break, if I want. There's a Dunkin' Donuts on Cooper & Matlock. Wanna meet there?"

"That's perfect," Korah said.

"Alright. I'll be there at ten."

"Okay," Korah said. "See you then."

She disconnected and got out of her SUV, so she could meet up with Devin, who was marching to his own vehicle at that moment. His face was hard, his eyes low and mean. He climbed into his work truck and lowered the window when he saw his mother approaching.

"What'd the police say?" she asked.

"They're on their way to the shopping center. I'ma meet them over there."

"Did they say whether anyone else's sites got vandalized last night?"

He shook his head. "No. They couldn't tell me yet. Did you talk to that guy, Quincy?"

"Yes. I'm going to meet him in about an hour."

"You didn't ask him over the phone?"

"I wanna see him face to face," Korah said. "He won't be able to lie to me in person. If he doesn't show up, I guess that'll tell us something, too."

"Want me to go?"

"Oh, hell no," Korah said. In her mind's eye, she saw her strapping, young son pummeling Quincy to a pulp while the Dunkin' Donuts' staff looked on in horror.

"Why not?" he said. "What if he tries something?"

"We're meeting in a public place. Plus I got my pepper spray."

She held up her keychain, which had the canister affixed to it. The pepper spray had never been used, but Korah was confident she could stop an attacker with it.

"That's not enough," Devin argued. "I wanna go with you."

"You have to meet with the police," Korah reminded him. "And you still have to get our equipment replaced and continue work at the shopping center when the new Skytrak gets there. Don't worry about me."

Devin sighed. "Alright, Mama. Where you going now?"

"I'll meet you back at the shopping center," she said. "I want to talk to Mr. Harden about what's going on. I don't want him to flip out when the police show up."

• • • • • •

Mr. Harden was surprisingly understanding.

"Shit happens," he told Korah. "I had a building built ten years ago. They brought in a boatload of sand, and over the weekend some neighborhood kids thought it'd be a good idea to play on it. Two of them climbed to the top and started sinking. Took half a day to dig them out. One of them almost didn't make it."

Korah thought she had heard about that incident.

"As soon as we get the new equipment here," she said, "we'll get a crew up on that roof. This might cost us a few hours of work, but we'll be done up there in a couple of days."

"No problem," the older man said. "They already got the shingles that were falling in the parking lot, so I'm good. Take your time."

Yeah right, Korah thought. Maybe it was no problem for him, but there was a chance the school board was still watching their progress at the shopping center. With less than a week before they made an announcement on who won the new contract, this was another delay Korah could hardly afford.

An hour later she pulled into the parking lot of Dunkin' Donuts and looked around for Quincy's car. As far as she could tell, he wasn't there yet. Korah checked her watch and saw that it was five minutes after ten. Either Quincy was late, or he knew what Korah wanted to ask him, and he decided to skip out on this meeting. She exited her vehicle with anxious tingles shooting up and down her legs. She ordered a coffee when she entered the restaurant.

Three minutes later, Quincy entered and spotted her sitting alone. He smiled as he approached her table and said, "Sorry I'm late," when he was close enough to speak. "I thought I'd have an easier time getting away."

"You're fine," Korah said. "Thanks for coming."

He saw the coffee she cradled in both hands but asked, "Can I get you something?" as a courtesy.

"No, thank you."

"I think I'll save my appetite for lunch," he said as he sat down with her.

Quincy wore a white collar shirt with dark slacks. His shoes were new and without a scuff. His shirt was equally pristine.

Korah felt like a fool as she noted that he didn't have any oil or dirt under his fingernails.

Quincy worked as an accountant for a legal firm. As far as Korah knew, he hadn't worked a job that required manual labor since mowing lawns as a child. That seemed to reinforce her notion that he didn't have anything to do with the vandalism, but maybe she was being naïve. There were plenty of people currently locked up for murder who would never ever *ever* think about killing someone – until their heart got broken by the love of their life.

"So, what's going on?" he asked.

"How have you been?" Korah replied.

"I've been okay," he said. "Not *great*, but not that bad, either."

"Really? What's been going on? Trouble at work?"

He looked confused. "No. I thought you were talking about what happened with us?"

"I do want to talk about that," Korah said. "I know we didn't end things on good terms..."

"I know. I was surprised you called me today. I thought I blew it for sure, with my last stunt."

Korah cleared her throat and casually wiped the perspiration from her forehead. She didn't think she'd be nervous about this, but being so close to him was starting to freak her out. What was she thinking? Either he'd deny her accusations altogether and get upset, or he'd admit to everything and get upset.

Either way, Korah only saw two employees behind the restaurant's counter. Both of them were female, and neither looked like they would physically intervene if Quincy snapped and decided to open up a can of whoop-ass that morning.

"What's going on?" he asked. "It seems like you have something you want to tell me..."

Korah took a deep breath. "I do. This is... I don't want you to get mad."

"There is nothing you could say that would upset me," he promised.

"I don't know about that," she said. She offered a weak smile.

Quincy did the same.

"I don't mean to accuse you," she said, "but I had some trouble at a couple of my sites last night, and my son asked me to contact anyone who might be angry with me – and your name came up..."

There. She said it. And Korah was smart enough to deflect responsibility to her son. Surely that would soften the blow.

If Quincy was responsible, he hid it well.

He shook his head slowly as he said, "Trouble? What kind of trouble? You know I would never do anything to hurt you."

"I know," Korah lied. "But Devin, he asked me to make sure..."

"Your son thinks I've done something to hurt you? Why would he think that?"

"At this point, we're grasping at straws," Korah admitted. "Someone went to a couple of my worksites last night and damaged some equipment. If it was just one site, we would chalk it up to vandals. But with it being similar damage at two different sites, it kinda feels like someone's after us *personally*. You know?"

Korah's blood froze as Quincy's confused expression quickly rolled to annoyance.

"What? You think I damaged some of your work equipment?"

"No," she said. "I don't think that."

"Yes you do," he said, becoming more upset. "That's why you wanted to meet with me – to accuse me of something like that?"

"We just needed to rule you out," she said. "Nothing like this has ever happened to us. We don't have any enemies, that I know of–"

"And I'm your enemy now? Is that what you think?"

His volume was steadily on the rise, causing Korah's face to flush with heat and embarrassment. There were no other customers in the restaurant at the moment, but out of the corner of her eye, Korah saw that both of the girls behind the counter had stopped what they were doing to watch the argument.

"I don't think you're my enemy, Quincy. I'm just saying you were upset with me the last time we talked."

"How upset would I have to be to commit a *crime*?" Quincy wondered. "That's what you're talking about, right? Vandalism? You think I'd commit a crime for you?"

As a matter of fact, Korah thought she was definitely worthy of a man who'd commit a crime for her. But that was beside the point.

"How would I even know where you're working?" Quincy continued. "What do you expect me to do, ride around the city until I see a construction site with your Texas Builders sign out front? You think I'm so obsessed I'd do that?"

"Actually all of our sites are in the public records," she said. "The city planner's office has a list of everyone's ongoing projects."

"Well, I didn't know that."

"Okay. So there's no harm done. You say you didn't do it, and I accept that. No need to make this more awkward than it already is. I apologize for offending you, and I'm sorry for pulling you away from work."

She hefted her purse as she rose from the table.

Quincy stood as well.

"You know, I thought when you called this morning, it was because you changed your mind about me," he told her. "I thought you were going to give me another chance."

Korah paused long enough to tell him, "I'm sorry."

"Yeah. I am too. I guess I'll always play the fool for you."

There was nothing she could say that would make him feel better about that, so she didn't bother. Korah felt his eyes burning the back of her head as she left the restaurant. She felt like she'd turn into a pillar of salt if she looked back at the bridge she just burned, so she kept her chin up and her eyes forward.

This was all Devin's fault. Korah knew Quincy didn't have anything to do with it, and she should've left it at that.

She was in the safe confines of her car before she realized that she left her coffee behind. That was okay. There was enough adrenaline rushing through her veins to keep her on her toes for at least eight more hours. Korah doubted if she'd be able to sleep when she finally crawled under her sheets and tried to put an end to this hectic day later on tonight.

● ● ● ● ● ●

"It wasn't him."

She sat at a red light at the corner of Cooper and Arkansas in Arlington. Devin was insistent that she call him the moment she concluded her meeting with Quincy, and Korah didn't want him to worry.

"You sure?"

"Yes, I'm sure. He was very angry with me for accusing him."

"Just because he got mad–"

"*I'm sure*," Korah insisted. "Quincy's not the guy."

"Then it must be Brick."

"What did the police say? Did anyone else get vandalized last night?"

"Nope. They said we're the only ones who reported anything."

That news made Korah's stomach twist up all over again. She didn't have ill-will for any other contractor, but misery does love company.

"It's still early," Devin said. "There's a chance something happened, and it didn't get reported yet..."

"I think we're gonna have to operate under the assumption that it was just us," Korah said. "What about the cameras at the shopping center?"

"They don't have any in the alley out back. No point in recording the dumpsters all night."

"Did you get the trailer fixed yet?"

"I got a guy bringing some new wheels for us, but they haven't made it yet. The rental company's bringing a new Skytrak right now, and they're sending a truck to pick up the other one. Neither one of them has made it, either."

"Do you think you can finish out there today?"

"No way. We had two days left before this happened. Now we might not finish 'til Thursday."

Korah sighed. The light turned green, and she got moving again.

"What about tonight?" she asked. "What if they come back?"

"I could set up some cameras, if you want. But I don't know if it's worth it, since we'll only be here a couple of days. I'll get someone to take our trailer back to the shop when we get done for the day, but I was gonna leave the new Skytrak here – unless you think we shouldn't..."

Korah didn't know what to think at this point. It was common practice for construction workers to leave bulldozers and cranes and other heavy-duty vehicles on the site overnight. But what if the vandals came back? The problem was there was no guarantee they could rent the Skytrak at eight am the next day. More than likely, they wouldn't be able to get one there until ten.

"I don't know what to do," she admitted.

"We might as well leave it here and hope for the best," Devin reasoned. "That way we're guaranteed to have it here in the morning, if nothing goes wrong."

Korah couldn't argue with that. "Okay. You're right."

"When are you gonna call that punk Brick?" he asked. "Mama, you know he is the most likely suspect at this point. He knows where we're working, he knows how to shut down a job. And he's mad at you. I didn't tell the police, but I can't think of anyone else who might be responsible."

"Devin, I don't think Brick had anything to do with this."

"Why? Because he was nice to you? You don't know that man, Mama. You need to–"

"I gotta go," she said. "I'll see you in a bit."

He blew out a hard sigh. "Alright. Fine. Bye."

Korah disconnected.

She knew that her reasons for trusting Brick were personal and possibly misguided, but she didn't have the heart to learn more disgusting news about him. Plus the recent encounter with Quincy left a very bad taste in her mouth. She was not willing to go through that again right away – especially not with a man she still had feelings for.

Her mind was so jumbled, Korah didn't realize she was approaching one of Brick's worksites until she stopped at another light, and she saw his humungous **BRICK HOUSE** sign planted firmly in the ground, no more than twenty feet from her SUV.

Across the street from the sign was the P.F. Chang's restaurant she and Brick once dined at. Korah smiled half-heartedly, thinking about how Brick told her he was a womanizer and then quickly backtracked, saying he didn't know the definition of the word.

I don't lie, I don't cheat, and I don't steal. I don't run around trying to break hearts, and I've never pursued a woman, just so that I could sleep with her. And I don't break up with women after we've been intimate. So, no, I'm not a womanizer.

The construction site Korah was parked next to was the two-story Barnes & Noble she teased Brick about. He had told her that he didn't care if it was foolhardy to build another store in the midst of Barnes & Nobles' financial woes. The only thing he cared about was their check clearing, which apparently it had.

Korah also remembered when Brick gave her a tour of the site. He was so excited because, unlike the women he normally dated, Korah could actually appreciate the hard work that went into creating a masterpiece from the ground up; utilizing sweat and muscle and equipment as huge as cranes that were ten stories high to itty bitty nuts and bolts that could fit in a soda cap.

As she waited at the light, Korah's eyes swam over Brick's bustling site. There were over a dozen workers there with BRICK HOUSE emblazoned on their shirts. There were three BRICK HOUSE trucks parked near the main entrance. Like a hornet's nest, everyone was moving with a purpose. Korah saw that the upstairs portion of the store was coming along nicely.

She felt a tug at her heart when she recalled her and Brick's special time up there. Wowed by her knowledge of sheetrock and the tools required to erect a wall, Brick had become erect himself.

A stud crimper.
What about this?
A skate raker.
Damn. This is sexy as hell.
Me naming tools is sexy to you?
Yep.

He had thrown caution and workplace etiquette to the wayside and assailed her with his mouth and tongue, his large hands and his grinding hips. The memory of how free she felt and how willing she was to lose herself when she was with Brick made Korah's eyes gloss over with tears.

When she wiped the moisture away, Korah thought she saw the man himself. Brick stood near the entrance of the building looking as handsome as ever in his jeans and collar shirt. Korah's heart froze as they locked eyes. Her windows were tinted, so there was no way he could see her, was there? If not, he seemed to recognize her car.

Korah didn't realize she was holding her breath until the sound of a car horn jarred her out of her reverie and caused her to cry out slightly. She glanced up and saw that the traffic light had turned green.

She looked back at Brick once more as she moved her foot from the brake to the gas pedal. He took a step in her direction and then stopped and watched as she pulled into the intersection.

By then Korah's heart was doing a drumroll in her chest. She wasn't sure why, but she felt guilty and apprehensive about him seeing her, as if she had been spying. Surely he would know that she was reminiscing about their interrupted love. He would know that she missed his touch and his smile and even his incessant boasting. He would think that she had come back to this location to remind herself of happier times.

Of course that line of thinking was foolish, just as it was foolish to assume he even noticed her. The tint on Korah's windows surely prevented him from seeing her face, let alone the longing in her woeful eyes. And Nissan Pathfinders were fairly common. Why would he assume she was in this one, just because–

Her cellphone rang loudly, causing her throat to catch.

Her breaths came in soft pants when she looked down and saw Brick's number on the Caller ID. She cringed. Her ringtone was set to sound like an old school telephone. She tried to ignore it, but each ring seemed to bleat for twice as long as normal, and the pause between them lasted an eternity. She knew her voicemail would pick up at some point, but after four rings it still hadn't done so.

The ringing became nerve-racking.

He was taunting her.

She picked the phone up slowly, giving the voicemail another shot, but the call was still active when she answered it.

"Hello?"

"Korah?" His deep voice made the hairs stand on her neck, as if he was standing right next to her.

"Brick," she replied tersely.

"Were you just at my site?"

No beating around the bush with this guy.

"No," she said.

"You, I thought I just saw you at my Barnes & Noble. You were stopped at a light. I could've sworn you were staring right at me."

"It wasn't me."

"Korah."

"It's a free country, Brick. I can drive down whatever street I want to."

"Okay. That's fine. I was hoping you stopped by because you wanted to talk."

"No. I was just in the area. Everything's not about you."

"You were just in the area?"

He clearly didn't believe her. His condescending tone bristled Korah enough to fight off the unnatural magnetism that continued to draw her to him, despite her common sense urging her to stay away.

"I gotta go. I'm very busy."

"*Fine,*" he snapped. "But we will talk about this. You're not gonna cut me off without an explanation."

That sounded like both a promise and a threat.

"Goodbye, Brick."

She disconnected and returned her attention to the road.

CHAPTER SEVENTEEN
SABOTAGE

Korah never considered herself lucky, but she wasn't prone to recurring bad luck either. Considering how poorly things had gone for Texas Builders on Monday, she knew that the construction gods would certainly show her favor the following day.

She was wrong about that.

On Tuesday Devin called bright and early, just as Korah was pulling into her parking spot at the main office. An uneasy feeling washed over her whole body when she saw his number on the Caller ID, so she kept her engine running as she took the call.

"Hey, what's up?"

"Mama, they got us again," her son reported. His voice was strained with anger and frustration. From the sound of his quickened breaths, Korah knew that he was pacing furiously.

"What are you talking about?"

"At the shopping center," Devin told her. "Our new Skytrak is sitting on four flats!"

"What?" Korah's eyes widened in disbelief.

"Mama, this is *personal*," Devin growled. "I swear to God, when I found out who's messing with us..."

Korah sat quietly for a few seconds, her mouth ajar, her head spinning.

Again?

She could hardly believe it. In the twenty-four years their company had been in operation, they endured setbacks from time to time. There was a powerful tornado in '94 that leveled a supermarket they were a few weeks away from completing. And

Korah would never forget the mega flood in 2010. That act of nature pushed four of their projects off course, and, next to Devin Sr.'s death, caused the biggest crisis the company had ever known.

But three acts of vandalism in less than twenty-four hours... This was a whole new threshold of stress, and it couldn't have come at a worse time. Korah's heart cracked in two as she finally forced herself to accept the obvious: The Overbrook Meadows school contract had gotten away from them. There was no way they could recover this time.

"Mama? Did you hear me?"

"Yeah," she said with a heavy slump of her shoulders. "Did you call the police?"

"Yes. Mama, you know somebody's trying to do us in. They wanna shut us down!"

"I'm on my way," Korah said as she backed out of her parking spot.

● ● ● ● ● ●

By the time she got to the shopping center, the police were there as well as the property owner. Korah let her son handle the police report, while she pulled the owner aside and tried to allay his concerns.

"What do you, what's going on?" he asked her. "This isn't good. The police have been out here two days in a row..."

It was not yet nine am, but the weather reports were all predicting today would be a scorcher. Mr. Harden dabbed the sweat from his face with an expensive hankie that didn't wipe away his look of distress.

"I understand this is a problem," she said. "And I wish I could tell you what's going on. But you know about as much as we do right now. It would appear that someone doesn't want us to complete our work over here. I have no idea who that could be or why they would want that. But I assure you we're not leaving until everything is perfect. You have nothing to worry about."

"I, I don't know if I'd agree with that," Mr. Harden said. "If they're coming at night to damage your equipment, what's to stop them from damaging other parts of the shopping center? My vendors don't like seeing the police out here. It makes them nervous, and it makes the customers nervous. It's bad for business."

You've got some nerve, Korah thought. It was a struggle to keep a straight face. They were working hard to fix a problem another construction crew caused, and it was their company who had the most to lose because of these incidents. The police presence wouldn't cost any of the vendors a dime. If anything, Korah thought they should feel more protected.

"We only have a couple of more days of work to do here," she said. "And whoever's doing this is clearly not after you, so I don't think you have anything to worry about."

"But, but you don't know that for sure. What's going on with you guys? Why would someone be out to get you?"

"We're trying to figure that out," Korah told him. "Texas Builders operates with compassion and integrity. We certainly haven't done anything to bring this upon ourselves."

"What about that Clark guy?" Mr. Harden asked. "You think he'd be out to get you?"

Korah already considered that. "I don't see why he would. I can't see what he'd have to gain from it, but I'll certainly mention him to the police."

"I'm really not comfortable with this kind of thing happening at my shopping center."

Korah's nerves were nearly shot. She had to get away from this geezer, before she told him what a pain in the ass he was becoming. She turned back towards Devin, who was standing near the new Skytrak with a uniformed officer. The vehicle was virtually identical to the one they had yesterday – flat tires included.

"I need to speak with the policeman," Korah said, walking away from the older man. "Don't worry. We will get to the bottom of this."

Mr. Harden looked plenty worried, but he made the right decision and didn't follow her.

Devin was finishing up his discussion when Korah approached. She inspected the new Skytrak while she waited. The vandal – who could be labeled a saboteur at this point – had punctured the heavy duty tires with a sharp object and cut a six inch hole horizontally, ensuring the tire could not be repaired.

Identical damage had been done to the other three wheels, which was a shame, because they appeared to be brand new.

The equipment rental store had plenty of insurance to cover the damage, and Korah's company wouldn't be penalized, as long as they provided a police report number. So these attacks wouldn't hurt them financially. At this point it was the principle of the matter – and the loss of labor for the six crew members who literally had nothing to do until a new lift could be delivered.

Devin's eyebrows were bunched together when he and the policeman parted ways. He shook his head at his mother and then headed for his company truck. Korah was thankful that he didn't voice his opinions until they were inside the cab; secluded from the eavesdropping workers who were desperate to know what the hell was going on.

"What'd the police say?" Korah asked as she settled into the seat and half-turned to face him.

"What can they say?" Devin said. "They'll open a case and look into it. But you see he didn't take any fingerprints or nothing. There's only so much they can do – especially since we're lying to them about not having a suspect."

"What do you mean, *we're lying to them*? We don't have a suspect, Devin. At least I don't."

He slowly rubbed his whole face with a rough, hard-working hand.

"I guess you're talking about Brick again," Korah said.

"Yes, I'm talking about Brick again! Mama I can't believe you're taking this so lightly."

"Lower your voice! And I'm not taking anything lightly, Devin. This crap is costing us a helluva lot more than some wasted work hours. I'm just as pissed as you are!"

"Then why won't you at least ask him? You know he had something to do with this."

"I don't think he did," Korah insisted. "And what good would it do to ask him? You think he'd just say, *Yeah, it was me?*"

"You're the one who's supposed to be able to cut through people's bull. You said if that other guy was lying, you would know it."

That was true. Throughout her life, Korah prided herself for having a built-in lie detector. It was really no more than paying close attention to the subconscious nuances people give off when they're under stress, but she was good pretty good at it.

"Brick would have nothing to gain from this," she said.

"Yes he would. He would get you back for breaking up with him – or whatever happened between y'all. Plus he would get the school contract, if we keep having trouble over here. You said so yourself: Fixing this shopping center is our *only* way to stay in the race."

Korah was surprised that despite all of his bitching about the Harden project, her son was actually paying attention to her.

"That school is pretty much guaranteed to Brick," she replied. "There's no way we can come back at this point."

"What did he do to you?" Devin asked. He stared deeply into her eyes.

"What do you mean?"

"What did he do that was so bad, you don't even want to ask him about this? Tell me, Mama. If he hurt you, I'll kill him. I swear before God."

Korah's pulse raced. This was getting out of hand. How could she tell Devin that *he* was the one who had actually hurt her? Everything was great with her and Brick until her overreaching son had a friend check his criminal record. But did that mean Korah was okay with a woman beater – just as long as she didn't know about it?

The truth of the matter was Korah was falling in love with Brick, and both he and Devin turned her world upside down. She didn't want to see Brick because she would feel like a fool. She would have to confront the fact that she let him take her way too far, way too fast. Whether it was for sex or a strategic advantage, Brick had played her for a fool. She would be forced to come to terms with that, if she saw him again.

But for her son, she would do that and more.

"Okay," she said. "I'll call him today."

"Alright," Devin said quickly. "Do you want me to come with you?"

Korah shook her head.

Her son didn't push it. "Okay," he said. "I gotta get back to work. Are you alright?"

She clearly wasn't, but Korah nodded. She reached and squeezed Devin's hand comfortingly. "We'll get through this."

"I know," he said. "I never stopped believing in you."

He gave her a reassuring smile and got out of the truck. When he closed the door, Korah summoned the courage it would take to face her demons. She called Brick and watched her son walk away while she waited for him to pick up.

"Korah?"

"I need to see you," she breathed.

"Where are you?"

"I'm on my way back to my office."

"You want me to come to your office?"

She didn't, but she hoped her home turf would give her a psychological advantage. Plus Yolanda and Priscilla and her daughter Stephanie were there, so there was no way Brick would assault her if their conversation took a bad turn.

"Yes," she said. "Do you have the address?"

"Of course. I'm on my way."

Korah exited the truck and gave her son a kiss on the cheek before she left the shopping center. He could be immature at times, but Korah was proud of the man Devin had become. She knew his father would be proud as well.

● ● ● ● ● ●

Brick showed up at the Texas Builders' headquarters an hour later, looking as dapper as ever in a straw-colored suit with a tan shirt and no tie. He managed to keep his confidence intact, despite the icy reception he received from Korah's daughter and her assistant Yolanda, who greeted him at the front desk.

"Ms. Stewart's office is right down the hall."

Yolanda gestured towards a door straight ahead that was wide open. Brick thought the girl was attractive, and he guessed the majority of people who visited this office loved her – when she wasn't shooting daggers at them, that is.

Brick entered the office and half-smiled when he laid eyes on a beauty he thought he'd never have the opportunity to see again. Korah wore a purple blouse today with her hair tied up in a tight bun. She didn't have on any makeup, and she didn't look well-rested.

Even still, she was certainly a sight for sore eyes. Brick's smile slipped when he saw that she wore the same look of guarded contempt as her staff members.

"Have a seat," she instructed. "Thanks for coming."

Brick sat casually across from her and took a moment to admire her office. He was surprised by the lack of feminine touch. The office was built for business, with no frills, flowers or pictures of smiling grandchildren. He returned his attention to Korah, who looked more uptight than he had ever seen her.

"Why do I feel like I've entered the danger zone?" he wondered.

"Someone's been damaging trucks and other equipment at my construction sites," Korah quipped, with no pretense. "Was it you?"

Brick's look of surprise was 100% genuine, as far as Korah could tell.

"Wha, why would you ask me something like that?"

"Answer the question."

"Hell no it wasn't me," he said. "Korah, this is outlandish. Is that why everybody's looking at me like that? You think I would do something to hurt you or your company?"

"I don't know what to believe," she said. "I have no idea what's going on right now."

"Who, when did this happen?"

"It's happened two days in a row. Twice on one site. Someone slashed the tires on two Skytraks and two backhoes."

"But why would you think it was me?"

"Because I don't know you," she said. "I have no idea what you would do to get your way."

"What would I have to gain? This doesn't make sense."

Korah shrugged. "Maybe you want to make sure you get the school job. Maybe you're mad because I haven't talked to you..."

Brick sat back in his seat and stared at her. After a few moments, his eyes brightened.

"Something strange happened on one of my sites yesterday..."

Korah was all ears, even though she wasn't sure if she'd believe him. "What are you talking about?"

"It was one of our scissor lifts," Brick said. "The cage came loose and nearly fell off completely, when a couple of my guys were on it. Luckily they weren't up that high, but it gave them a hell of a scare. They were about to head 30 feet up, to work on a ceiling. If the cage fell off when they were all the way..." He brought a fist to his mouth and sighed into it.

Safety was always the number one concern on any construction site, so Korah knew exactly what was going through his mind at that moment. A hardhat wouldn't have saved his workers, and their harnesses would've been fastened to the cage of the scissor lift, so that wouldn't have saved them either.

"The bolts..." Brick went on. "The ones holding the cage were all loose. Four of them were missing nuts altogether. Someone definitely wanted the cage to fall off while in use. We assumed it was some punk kids. We didn't even call the police, but I was livid. A prank is one thing, but a prank that could cost someone their life is something completely different."

The blood in Korah's veins suddenly ran cold. She was upset about a few flat tires, but if what Brick told her was true, then she had to consider herself grateful that her vandals didn't try to hurt anyone on her sites. She didn't even want to think about harm coming to her son.

Brick shook his head as he considered his and Korah's dilemmas, and then he asked, "What the hell is going on? And why do you think I'd resort to such tactics against you? I mean, seriously, Korah, you're talking like you don't know me at all. How could you feel that way about me – just because you cut me off? And I still wanna know what the hell that's about."

"Vicki Espeland," she said.

That caught him off guard. Brick was about to say something else, but instead his mouth just hung open for a few seconds. When he closed it, all of the bravado he was building up had suddenly left the room. He looked back and saw that Stephanie was watching them from her desk down the hall.

He cleared his throat and asked, "Can I close this door?"

Korah shook her head defiantly.

Brick rose to his feet anyway. "If you want to talk about Vicki, then I'm going to close this door," he said. "If I do something stupid, feel free to scream as loud as you want, and your guard dogs will come running. But I'm not that crazy, Korah. And I care too much about you. You gotta believe that."

He slowly closed the door without waiting for her to respond.

Korah's heart was racing when he returned to his seat. She tried her best not to let on how anxious she was.

Brick sighed and wiped his palms on his pants legs. He looked up at her and said, "Okay. What do you want to know about Vicki?"

Korah didn't think it would be this easy. It took a moment for her to recognize the power she suddenly had. "You beat her?"

"No," Brick said adamantly. *That is a lie.* I never laid a hand on her."

"That's not what the police say."

Brick's eyes flashed with anger for a moment, but it dissipated just as quickly. "Korah, I've been trying to get that off my record since the day it happened. I was arrested and charged with assault, but I was never convicted. I don't know what kind of half-ass detective you have checking up on me, but they dropped the ball. *Big time.*"

So far Korah didn't believe he had lied to her during this meeting, but she wasn't ready to let him off the hook just yet.

"Okay. Explain it to me then."

"Fine," Brick said with a hint of annoyance. "Back down that dark and ugly road we go..."

Korah didn't know if that comment was meant to dissuade her, but she kept quiet and let him talk.

"I dated Vicki nearly ten years ago. I won't lie to you, back then I wasn't the awesome guy you see today..."

Korah showed no amusement for that wannabe joke.

"Okay," Brick said, rubbing his hands together. "Tough crowd. Anyway, yes, I did treat Vicki unfairly. While we were dating, I had another girlfriend named Chantal Curley."

Korah frowned, shaking her head in disappointment.

"Come on," Brick said, noticing her expression. "This was ten years ago. You know I've never been married. Is it so much of a surprise, that I cheated on someone so long ago?"

"No," Korah said. "No surprise there."

"Look, I'm trying to be open and forthcoming with you. But I'm not gonna finish this story, if you keep condemning me at every step."

"Okay," Korah said. "Sorry. Please go on."

"Alright," Brick said, leaning forward in his seat. "So Vicki found out about Chantal. She went through my phone and got her number. She didn't call her when she was with me. She waited until she got home.

"Chantal told her, '*Yes, I am Brick's girlfriend.*' And, I don't know, I guess they got into a big argument. It ended with Chantal telling Vicki she'd kick her ass, Vicki saying she'd do the same, and Chantal giving Vicki her address, so she could come and take care of business."

Korah tried her best to keep a neutral expression, but it was impossible.

Brick lowered his head in shame. "I didn't know anything about it," he said. "I found out later that Vicki actually went over there. And Chantal, being the hood chick that she was, proceeded to beat the living shit out of her – excuse my French."

Korah pursed her lips but kept quiet.

"So then everything got weird," Brick said. "It turns out Vicki was truly in love with me – and she was crazy. She felt like I was responsible for what happened to her. So when she drove herself to the hospital, they asked who assaulted her, and the girl said *I* beat her up."

Korah must have looked skeptical, because Brick said, "I swear to God, Korah. That's what happened. The police came to my home and arrested me. I bonded out and rushed to the hospital to find out what was going on. Vicki had already been released, and by then Chantal was calling to tell me what happened.

"I was so pissed, I sicced all kinds of lawyers on Vicki, to make her recant her story. She eventually did, and my charges were dropped. But some background checks on me still show that I was arrested for beating a woman. And to make matters worse, Vicki cracked under all of the pressure I was putting on her. I mean, she was lovesick too, I guess. But most of all, she was crazy."

Brick sighed and became somber as he continued. "She tried to commit suicide. I think it was mostly a cry for attention, but I took it seriously at the time. I paid for her to get checked into a counseling center. The whole experience... It rocked my world, Korah. I vowed never to hurt a woman again. At least I'd try not to.

"I also began to evaluate my girlfriends a lot better. I had to ask myself: Why was I dating a crazy chick, and why was I dating another girl who was prone to violence? I knew that I couldn't go on with my life until I established some kind of standards. I couldn't let a woman's looks be the only determining factor. Vicki changed my life. That's the truth. And I never hit her. I never hit any woman."

Korah was surprised by how relieved she was to hear all of that. It didn't change anything between her and Brick — not right away at least — but it did make her feel a lot better about the decisions she made when they were together.

"Okay," she said. "Thank you, Brick. But if you've been a changed man since that incident, why do you still live such a playboy lifestyle?"

"Who said I do?" he asked with a grin.

"So you're telling me you haven't had any disgruntled girlfriends since Vicki?"

"Oh, well, uh..."

Korah sighed loudly and poignantly.

"I, um, I had an affair with my secretary six months ago," he said. "And she's threatening to sue me for sexual harassment."

"*Jesus.*"

"But it wasn't harassment! I swear."

"Your *secretary*, Brick? That's such a bone-headed move."

"I know," he said. "Korah, my partner has been kicking my ass about this for long enough. I learned my lesson. I promise."

"How can you say you learned your lesson with her when you just said you learned your lesson with Vicki?"

"I'm a flawed man," was all he could say. "But I assure you, I haven't had any relations with *anyone* since I've been with you. And I would never do anything to hurt you."

"Yeah, I'm sure you'd try your best."

"Korah, stop it. I know this is a lot to swallow. But if you think about it, my track record is pretty clean."

"A suicide attempt and a sexual harassment lawsuit. Mmm hmm. Sparkling."

"But I'm coming clean now," he said. "I'm single and rich and still in my forties. If you only knew how much temptation I turn away from, you'd actually be proud of me."

The look on her face made him backtrack.

"Okay, maybe not proud of me, but I did right by you, didn't I?"

Korah shrugged. "I guess."

"I never treated you bad, did I? I was always a gentleman. I treated you like a queen."

Korah thought about the massage and the picnic, and she couldn't stop a slight smile from curving her sweet lips.

"That's what I'm talking about," Brick said. "I love it when you smile at me, Korah. So what do you say? You ready to give me another chance? I got everything out in the open. You won't hear any more shocking stories about me that I haven't already told you."

"I don't know," she said. "I'm kinda having my own little crisis over here. Whoever's sabotaging my projects – and yours too, apparently – has probably cost me the school bid already."

"You lost that bid weeks ago," Brick said. "Sorry, baby, but that's *my* contract."

Korah was so stressed-out, she could do nothing but laugh. "I can't stand you."

"Don't say that," Brick said. "I'm the one who's gonna find out who's been screwing with our equipment. And when I find him, I'm gonna kick his ass."

"You promise?"

"Yes, I promise," he said as he rose to his feet. "Now, I hate to cut this short, but I have another meeting I need to get to. This one's actually gonna make me some more money, so I can't be late."

"I knew you were dressed up for something."

"Of course," Brick said as he brushed imaginary dust from his lapel. "Gotta look good for the ladies."

He laughed as Korah's mouth fell open.

"I'm just kidding, babe. The guy I'm meeting with is old and fat. And he's got *deep* pockets."

Korah didn't want to admit it, but she loved hearing him call her *baby* and *babe*.

"Goodbye, Brick."

He opened the door and had to squeeze past Yolanda and Stephanie, who were openly eavesdropping.

"Afternoon, ladies," he told them and strutted out of the office, like a true cowboy.

The girls grinned at each other and then turned and smirked at Korah. She rolled her eyes at them but couldn't wipe the smile off her face, either.

CHAPTER EIGHTEEN
HEROICS

Korah and Priscilla were the last to leave the office that day. After Korah locked up, she walked her vice president to her car.

"Got any plans tonight?" the older woman asked.

Korah shook her head. "No. What makes you think I might have plans on a Tuesday night?"

Priscilla shrugged and gave her a knowing smile. "I see that you and that Brick fellow have made up. I figured you two would pick up right where you left off..."

"Where do you think we left off?" Korah asked. She stood with her briefcase and purse in hand, while Priscilla unlocked her Honda and tossed her bag to the passenger seat.

"Oh, I don't know," Priscilla said. "I hear things."

Korah grinned coyly and then asked, "So what's your opinion? You think he's the big, bad wolf, too?"

"I think you're smart enough to make your own decisions. Even if he is the big, bad wolf, there's nothing wrong with getting nibbled on every now and again."

Korah raised an eyebrow and giggled. "Wow. That's an interesting take on it."

"You only live once," Priscilla told her. "You shouldn't let anyone – your son included – steal your joy. Do what makes you happy, Ms. Korah."

That was the best advice Korah had heard all week. "Thank you," she said. "I'll see you tomorrow, Priscilla."

"Bright and early," her vice president promised. "Good night, dearie."

"Good night," Korah said. "Be safe."

● ● ● ● ● ●

Rather than head straight home, Korah stopped at the Harden Shopping Center to meet with her son before he shut down work for the day. It was after six when she pulled into the parking lot. Most of Devin's crew was still there, packing up their tools and cleaning up the small amount of debris they accumulated throughout the day.

The construction workers were all soiled and tired and sweaty. Some of them stepped lightly, because their work boots started to hurt their bunions after a hard day's work.

Korah was by no means a slave-driver, but it did her heart good to see the men in that condition. It reminded her of her late husband, when he used to come home past sunset after a long day on a construction site.

Korah would make him sit down in his easy chair, so she could remove his boots and his dusty socks. She would give him a beer and rub his feet while he flipped through channels with the TV remote. She would reheat his dinner and sit with him while he ate, even if he didn't have anything to talk about.

Most of the time Devin Sr. would be so tired, he wouldn't have the energy to make love after he bathed, but Korah never held that against him. She understood that he was working his fingers down to the bone for the betterment of their family, and one day things wouldn't be so hard. And she was right about that. It didn't take long before Devin Sr. elevated himself to contractor, and he never had to push a wheelbarrow or power drill again – unless he wanted to.

Devin Jr. approached his mother when he saw her step out of her SUV. He was a lot less soiled, compared to his crew, but it was clear that he got his hands dirty that day, too.

"Hey," Korah told him.

"Hey, Mama." He kissed her on the jaw and then looked back to tell one of his team members to, "Pack everything up! The ladders too! We're not leaving anything behind today."

When he returned his attention to Korah, she asked, "Y'all through?"

"One more day," Devin said. He wiped the sweat from his brow and grinned. "I can't wait to put this place in my rear view mirror for good."

"Is the roof done?"

He nodded. "Yeah. We just have to fix up some of the floors that were damaged when the plumbing started to leak. We're gonna re-do the tiles in that tanning salon, and that'll be it. Mr. Harden should write you another check by the time we finish up, considering everything we went through to get this place up to par."

"Yeah, we know that's not gonna happen," Korah said.

"I know. I'm just saying…"

Korah reached and wiped a smudge of concrete dust from his cheek. "I'm proud of you. You know that?"

"Thanks," Devin said, then, "I heard that jackass Brick came by the office today."

"Watch your mouth," Korah said, rather than inquire about where he got that bit of information from.

"Sorry. So what happened," Devin asked. "I guess he said he didn't cut the tires on those Skytraks…"

"No. I mean, yes. He didn't do it. As a matter of fact, he had a strange thing happen at one of his sites yesterday. He said someone sabotaged a scissor lift, and a couple of his guys almost fell off. The whole cage was unbolted."

Devin frowned. "You believe him?"

"Yes. I do believe him."

"Why?"

"Come sit with me," Korah said.

She returned to her car and took a seat behind the steering wheel. After a few moments, Devin followed her.

"Close the door," she told him when he climbed into the passenger seat.

Devin did as he was told, though he was clearly not interested in her defending a cocky cowboy, who also happened to be their biggest competitor.

"For starters, Brick didn't beat up that woman," Korah said.

She explained the story just as Brick had explained it to her. Devin kept quiet until she finished.

"So," he said finally. "He still cheated on her. And she tried to commit suicide because of him. Are you saying that makes him a good person?"

"No," Korah said. "Well, he wasn't a good person when all of that happened. But that was ten years ago. And I'm sure you know there are crazy women out there. If one of them gets infatuated and goes a little kookoo, you can't always blame the man for that."

"Really? You're defending him now?"

"I'm not defending him. I'm just telling you what he told me."

"He's probably lying."

Korah took a deep breath. "Or maybe you only want to see him in a negative light."

Devin's expression hardened. "Mama, I don't like the idea of you seeing him. Does this mean you're still gonna go out with him?"

"I might," Korah said honestly.

Devin shook his head.

"Tell me why that really bothers you," Korah said.

"'Cause I think he's using you."

"He's not. We never made any deals that would affect our company. I told you that."

"But he's a player."

"He might be," Korah said. "But I like him, and he has never disrespected me."

"But what if he does?"

"Then I'll stop talking to him. You don't think I can take care of myself?"

"So you're saying you're gonna allow yourself to get played?"

"I'm not getting played, Devin. I have fun with Brick. What's wrong with that?"

"It's wrong because he's not gonna marry you or even keep you around for a long time. He'll move on and leave you heartbroken."

"Okay, maybe that will happen," Korah conceded. "Maybe he'll break my heart. I know the risks, and I'm still willing to see him. Why do you think that is?"

"I have no idea."

"Maybe it's because I like him, and we're having fun."

"*Fun?*"

"Yes, *fun*, Devin. Is that so wrong? Maybe it is a fling, but let's be honest: I'm forty-six years old. How many flings do you think I have left? At what age do you think I should stop having flings – 'cause if you wanna know the truth, Brick isn't the only man I've had a fling with."

"I don't need to know all that."

"It's okay," Korah assured him. "I always use protection."

"Mama! Damn! TMI!"

She laughed. "What the hell does that mean?"

"*Too much information,*" Devin said, scowling.

"Well, if you don't wanna know about my love life, why are you investing so much time in it?"

"I just don't want you to get hurt," he said sincerely.

"I appreciate that. But the truth is, you've hurt me a lot in the past few weeks."

Her son looked seriously troubled by that. "How?"

"Well, first you complained about doing this job *every day.*"

"I got it done, though."

"We argued at every step, boy. And then you made me break up with Brick for no good reason."

"My homeboy told me he got arrested."

"Your homeboy did a half-ass investigation. And then you brought up your father when you were mad about Brick. That was a low blow, Devin. That's about as low as you can go. Don't you ever do that to me again."

After a few moments of consideration, he said, "I'm sorry. You're right. I shouldn't have done that."

"Especially since I never get into *your* love live," Korah said knowingly.

Devin was dark-skinned, but he still managed to blush.

"Who are you seeing these days?" she asked. "Are you ever going to bring your mystery woman by the house?"

He looked down and then out of the passenger window as he said, "Just some girl. I don't like her that much."

Korah's eyes were narrowed when he turned to face her.

"Okay, Mama. I'm sorry. I give you and Brick my blessing."

She frowned. "I don't need your blessing, goofball. It's not like we're getting married. We're just hanging out."

"Well, I give you my blessing for that, too."

Korah laughed and rubbed the back of his head. "I accept your apology," she said. "When are you going home?"

"As soon as I get everything cleaned up over here."

"Did they already come get the Skytrak?"

"Yup. There's nothing left for them to tear up – whoever they are."

"Brick says he's gonna help us get to the bottom of this," Korah informed him. "Especially now that we know that they're coming after both of us."

Devin bristled slightly, but he recovered quickly. "That's great, Mama. We could sure use the help."

● ● ● ● ● ●

Korah made it all the way home before she realized she forgot a couple of ledgers she needed to look over before morning. She pulled into her driveway and cursed her forgetfulness before making an executive decision: She had to go back to the office. Being the CEO of her own company came with certain sacrifices, and this was one of them.

It was only seven pm at the time. She could run to the office and make it home again by eight-thirty, if she didn't take a moment to change her shoes or let down her hair or do anything else that might lead to her staying inside the comfort of her home for the rest of the night.

It took forty minutes to make it back to the Texas Builders' headquarters. The sun was completely gone by then, but the perimeter lights surrounding the building provided enough illumination for Korah to see that something was not right. As she pulled into the parking lot, Korah frowned as her foot moved from the gas pedal to the brakes, and she came to a slow stop.

There was a dark-colored car parked in the shadows on the right side of the building. It appeared to be a Buick LeSabre. It was an older model. It had a long front end and a huge grill that gleamed in the night like a big, metal smile.

Other than the curb, there was no gate or any other barrier around the building that would stop drivers from entering the parking lot for U-turns or legitimate business. But the Buick wasn't making a U-turn, and from Korah's vantage point, she didn't think the driver was still inside. The headlights were off, and she didn't see any dark shapes sitting or moving in the front seat.

A quick shower of fear washed over her, causing her eyes to widen as goose bumps sprouted on her arms. The hairs stood on every part of her body. Her office wasn't in a bad neighborhood, but that didn't mean they were immune to the criminal element that was prevalent throughout the city. Korah didn't have any weapons in her vehicle, other than a small canister of pepper spray that was attached to her keychain.

She knew that wouldn't help her in this situation, but that was fine, because she had no intention of approaching the vehicle. For all she knew there was a prostitute and her john getting busy in what they assumed was a safe place. Or worse, there might be a junkie getting high in that car.

Korah reached for her purse on the passenger seat and pulled her cellphone from it just as the main entrance of the building pushed open slightly.

She gasped, emitting a short scream that made her lose her grip on the phone. It fell back into her purse and out of the reach of her trembling fingers. Korah's eyes were glued to the door. As she watched, she saw it push open a little more. And then a head poked out.

Her heart drummed as the intruder looked around quickly before locking eyes with Korah — although she knew that couldn't be the case. Her car was idling more than twenty yards away, with the headlights beaming directly in his face. The man wouldn't be able to see anything past the blinding brightness. She could be a cop, for all he knew.

But still, it felt like he was looking right at her.

Korah was so dazed, she barely took a moment to try to identify the intruder before he bolted.

His sudden movement caused Korah to scream again. Her car was locked, and the man didn't run in her direction, but Korah felt completely vulnerable. Her pupils were dilated nearly to the size of buttons. Her fingers scrambled in her purse for the phone. The intruder sprinted away from the building, in the direction of the Buick, which Korah suddenly realized was his getaway vehicle.

As realization dawned that he had no intentions of harming her, she tried to get control of her harried breaths and get some sort of identifying information for the police. The man was tall and burly. He was black, with short hair and a pudgy face that might have been clean-shaven. He wore a dark shirt with dark pants. That was as far as she got before the intruder pulled his car door open and hopped inside.

Korah didn't hear him start the engine, but she did hear the tires squeal as the monstrous vehicle lurched forward, heading right for her.

"You sonofabitch."

Korah surprised herself when her fight-or-flight mechanisms made a drastic switch. Adrenaline raced through her veins like heroin, and suddenly this asshole bearing down on her brought her more anger than fear.

How dare he?

This was her office, her home away from home. This building had been the brain center of Texas Builders since her late husband purchased the property in 1990. The thief wasn't just breaking into some random office. He was soiling the sacredness of what Korah considered her family's sanctuary.

And then another thought struck her: Was this the man who had been damaging their equipment? He tried to injure, if not kill some of Brick's crew? She had no way of knowing for sure, but Korah did not believe all of these incidents were coincidental. Someone was clearly out to get them, and this darkly clad creep certainly fit the bill.

What the hell was he doing here? Was this another phase in his efforts to sabotage them?

"*You sonofabitch!*" she growled.

It was clear that the intruder wanted to flee rather than force a confrontation, but if she let him go, they might never catch him. As he barreled towards her, Korah took her foot off the brake and made a move to cut him off.

Later she would realize the folly of this decision.

But in the heat of the moment, this vandal needed to get caught. If Korah was the only one who could do it, then so be it.

The creep still hadn't turned his headlights on. He tried to slip by on her passenger side, but Korah was having none of that.

She jerked her wheel to the right and slammed her foot on the gas, engaging them in a hellish game of chicken.

As he got closer, Korah was able to pick up more details about his appearance, like the fact that he had big lips that were currently pulled back in a snarl. And he had bushy eyebrows that were in stark contrast to the short hair on his–

The two vehicles collided with a loud **CRUNCH**! of metal and a jarring jolt that propelled Korah forward before her seatbelt snagged and jerked her back. The strap dug painfully into the skin on her neck and collarbone.

Her SUV was powerful, but the old school Buick was built back in the days when auto makers used real steel in the bumper, rather than the fiberglass that was supposed to protect drivers nowadays. Korah thought she hit him head on, but the intruder managed to skirt past at the last second – but not before knocking out her headlight and smashing through her SUV's bumper like it wasn't even there.

Korah screamed again as her head slammed back against the headrest, causing a bright field of red and pink dots to momentarily obscure her vision. She stomped her foot on the brakes, and her car came to a screeching halt.

"Shit!"

It took a few seconds for her to regain control of her senses. By then, the assailant had made a smooth getaway. Korah checked her rearview mirror and got a glimpse of his brake lights before he turned and disappeared around the next corner.

Oh my God.

She was squeezing the steering wheel so hard her fingers were cold. Korah suddenly realized she had absolutely no plan in place for if she had managed to stop the creep. She knew her son wouldn't appreciate her half-ass heroics.

Nope. Not one bit.

She unbuckled her seatbelt and rubbed the back of her neck and then the sore spots on her chest and shoulder. She tried to calm her nerves as she reached for her purse, which was now on the floorboard. But it was impossible to slow her racing heart. She didn't know where the intruder was, what he was doing in her building in the first place, or if he was coming back to take care of the only witness to his crime.

When she finally got hold of her phone, she called 911 first. And then she called her son. Devin was panicked to hear her so shaken. He said he'd be right there.

While she waited for everyone to show up, Korah called Brick as well. Surprisingly, he was more upset about her antics than her son was.

"*You did what?*"

"I thought I could stop him," Korah said.

"Stop him? And then what?"

"I know. It was stupid."

"Not just stupid, it was *dangerous*. You could've been hurt. Are you hurt? How bad did he hit your car?"

"I don't know," she said. "I haven't gotten out to check yet. I'm scared."

"Are you in pain?"

"My neck hurts," she said as she rubbed the top portion of her spine. "My head hurts, too."

"I can't believe this shit," Brick muttered. "I'm very upset with you."

"*Me?* I'm the one who got attacked."

"I'm upset with that bastard, too. But right now it's you I'm worried about – and upset with. I'm on my way."

"I already called the police. And my son's coming, too."

"That's fine. I'll be there as well. If you end up going to the hospital before I make it, call me, so I can meet you there."

"Brick, I appreciate it, but–"

"But what? Are you telling me not to come?"

Korah thought of how her son would react if Brick showed up at the scene. Devin did give them his blessing – whatever that meant – but Korah sensed he only said that to appease her, and shut her up.

Devin saying that he accepted Brick didn't necessarily mean he could be cordial with him if they were face to face, especially in a time of crisis.

Brick took her lack of response to mean she had no objections. "Okay, I'm on my way," he said and disconnected before she could talk him out of it.

CHAPTER NINETEEN
TAKING CARE OF KORAH

The police arrived first, followed by a fire truck, another police cruiser and finally an ambulance. By the time Devin pulled into the parking lot, the property was awash with brightly colored emergency lights that swam in all directions. The chatter from all of the emergency personnel's radios was incessant.

Korah was lying on a stretcher, being attended to by two EMTs. As a precautionary measure, they had affixed a bulky cervical collar around her neck. Devin was alarmed to see so many people fussing over his mother. He rushed to her side, his mouth dry, his heart knocking against his sternum.

But Korah sat up and smiled. She gave him a hug and told him, "Don't worry. I'm fine."

She noticed that Yolanda had come as well, though she didn't call her. It didn't take too much figuring to determine that Yolanda and Devin arrived together. But with so much going on, Korah didn't bother to ask them. That confrontation was not something she wanted to initiate with so many strangers around. She didn't know how she would approach the situation once she got the two of them alone, either.

The EMTs believed Korah had a slight concussion, and they thought she should go to the hospital for X-rays and a CAT scan. Korah's neck was a little stiff, but the only significant pain she felt was from the abrasion her seatbelt caused when it dug into her skin.

She told the paramedics, "I don't think that's really necessary."

"Mama you should go," Devin insisted. He stood next to her stretcher. He reached to rub her shoulder and then the side of her face.

His touch was very tender. His eyes were as well. Yolanda stood next to him with the same measure of compassion, but she also looked unsure of herself. Korah knew she was waiting for the obvious question about how she came to know of the incident and who brought her to the office. Korah found her guilt amusing.

"Hey, Yolanda," she said.

"Hi, Ms. Avery," the girl replied and quickly diverted her attention to the policemen who were congregating near the office's main entrance, looking for signs of forced entry.

"So you're going, right?" Devin said.

"I'm not riding in an ambulance," Korah complained. "I'm okay, Devin. I promise."

"Mama–"

"I'm not really hurting," she insisted. "Please save that ambulance for someone who really needs it," she told one of the paramedics.

"That's fine," the EMT replied. "You do need to go to the hospital, to make sure you don't have anything going on that we can't see. But it would be alright, if you want to ride with a relative."

"I'll take her," Devin said.

Korah sighed. She was tired, upset and bruised. The last thing she wanted was to spend the next three hours or more at Jackson Memorial. But there was no way Devin was going to let her off the hook.

Her son still wore his work uniform, so Korah knew that he hadn't had a chance to unwind from his long day, either. Considering how much harder he worked, Korah decided that if he was willing to make the trip, the least she could do was allow him to dote on her.

"Okay," she said. "You can take me to the hospital."

Devin nodded. His dark eyes transitioned from concerned to angry. "You think this is the same person who's been messing with our sites?"

Korah nodded. "It has to be, right? I don't think all of this stuff happening to us in one week is a coincidence."

"Who the hell is it?" Devin growled, his eyebrows bunched.

No one had a clue, so they all speculated silently.

One of the policemen approached at that moment and said, "I notice you have security cameras. Is it possible to get access to the video tonight?"

Korah opened her mouth to respond, but Devin beat her to it.

"Yes. I can get that for you right now." Before he walked away he said, "I'll be right back, Mama. You sure you're okay?"

"Stop fussing over me, boy."

Devin rolled his eyes before walking away with the officer.

Yolanda waited a few beats before she approached the stretcher.

"Hi," she said again.

"Hello," Korah replied.

"He's, um, he's kinda upset with you, for trying to stop that guy," Yolanda informed her.

"Yes, I know," Korah said. "He's not the only one."

Yolanda looked confused, and then her attention was drawn to another vehicle that pulled swiftly into the parking lot, as if it had every right to be there. Korah sat up in time to see Brick emerge from his SUV. He looked in her direction and then rushed to the ambulance. He approached the stretcher on the side opposite Yolanda and looked down at Korah, his eyes filled with dread.

"How are you doing? You alright?"

"I'm fine," Korah said, for what felt like the hundredth time. "As a matter of fact, I don't even know why I'm still lying on this thing."

She tried to sit up, but Brick reached with both hands to stop her.

"Whoa. What are you doing?"

He wore a tee shirt with jeans and sneakers. His shirt wasn't tight, but it didn't have to be to show off his prominent pecs and his defined arm and shoulder muscles. His bronze skin seemed to glow under the fluorescent lights. His strong hands were gentle as he eased her back to a lying position.

"You need to stay right there," he said. "Are they taking you to the hospital?"

"No," Korah said. "My son said he'll take me."

"I can take you," Brick offered. "Are you sure you're okay to go without the ambulance?"

One of the EMTs approached them and said, "Yeah, she's okay to travel to the hospital in one of your vehicles. I'm going to lower the stretcher," he told Korah as he pressed one of the lower levers with his foot.

She descended a couple of feet, and then the paramedic helped her up to a sitting position. Korah swung her legs around and waited a moment, to see if she'd get dizzy. The EMT held her arm on one side. Brick steadied her on the left.

"You okay?" they asked simultaneously.

Korah shook her head and grinned. *"I promise I'm fine."*

She rose to feet and proved herself to be a liar when she took an unsteady step to the left.

"Oh, wait a minute," she muttered.

Brick was quick to grab hold of her, this time with an arm around her waist as well as a firm grip on her forearm.

"I knew it," he said as he pulled her closer to him.

Korah felt so safe in his arms, she almost wanted to fall out completely, just so he'd have a reason to hold her even tighter.

"I was just a little woozy," she said. "I'm okay now."

"Come here, get in my car," Brick said, and he led her in that direction.

He didn't have on any cologne, but Korah found his natural scent utterly intoxicating. She missed him so much. She never imagined she'd feel so comfortable with him and Devin within such close proximity. Thinking about her son, she looked back at Yolanda, who was following them.

"Um, I guess I'm going with Brick," she told her. "Could you let Devin know?"

Her assistant gave her a look, a quick one, and then she nodded dutifully. "Yes, Ms. Avery."

Korah noticed for the first time that Yolanda wore a small, pink tee shirt with denim shorts that barely extended past her butt. She'd never seen Yolanda dressed so casually, and Korah had to admit that she had an awesome figure. Her boobs were big and perky, and her thighs and hips were very voluptuous. It was clear to see why Devin, or any other man, would easily become enamored.

Brick walked her to the passenger side of his Navigator and kept one arm wrapped around her waist as he opened the door. He helped her into the seat with much more care than was necessary and even reached to buckle the safety belt for her. Korah was thankful for that, because the cervical collar made it difficult for her to look down.

"Brick, this is—"

"Shhh," he said sternly. "I don't wanna hear it. We'll let the doctors decide how well you're doing."

Before he closed the door, he leaned in unexpectedly and kissed her on the corner of the mouth. The brief contact made Korah's heart flutter. She smiled as he backed away.

"Damn," she said. "I need to get in more accidents."

Brick grinned too, but his smile faded when he looked over at the damage to the front end of her Pathfinder.

"No," he said. "I would not like that at all. As a matter of fact, I might have to punish you, when you're feeling better."

Punish me?

Korah's eyes widened as a mellow heat enveloped her whole body. What on earth did he mean by that? She didn't have a chance to ask before he closed the door and went to talk to the EMTs again before he took her to the hospital.

● ● ● ● ● ●

The video cameras in Korah's building didn't get a good look at the intruder's face. He sneaked in quietly after forcing the door open with a crowbar, and he did not turn the lights on once inside. He had a small flashlight he used to help navigate his way through the small office, but the light was not bright enough to illuminate his features.

The man was not inside the building long enough to reveal his motive. Apparently he was alerted to Korah's unexpected arrival, possibly due to her headlights shining through the office windows. The intruder had less than a minute to search for whatever he wanted, before he went back to the entrance and peeked out of the door and then decided it was time to flee the scene.

There was one camera on the outside of the headquarters that did get a satisfactory glimpse of the perpetrator's face, but it wasn't close enough to pick up a license plate number from the Buick as it fled. The police concluded that they could probably use the videos to convict the intruder if he was captured, but they probably wouldn't be able to locate the man based solely on that evidence.

The robbery detectives were informed about the vandalism Texas Builders had experienced this week, and they said they would look for connections between all of these incidents.

Korah was informed of this by Devin when he made it to the hospital, which was about two hours after she and Brick got there. To Korah's delight, they didn't leave her to languish in the ER *for days*, like some of the horror stories she'd read about in the papers.

A nurse took her to a triage area right away, where a beautiful Ethiopian doctor named Lola Dego performed a battery of tests and then sent her off for X-rays and a CAT scan. Brick stayed with her the whole time. He was at her bedside when Devin and Yolanda walked into the exam room to give her the latest news from the investigation.

Devin and Brick still had some bad blood between them, well Devin did, at least. But the two men in Korah's life didn't bicker at the hospital. Devin grudgingly shook Brick's hand and thanked him for being there in his mother's time of need.

Brick nodded and said, "No problem," and a rather awkward silence ensued.

Thankfully Korah's doctor returned a few seconds later with good news. Much to Korah's delight, she finally removed the cervical collar as she spoke.

"Okay, Ms. Avery. I got the results from the tests, and everything looks good. You don't have any fractures or swelling in your brain. You do have a mild concussion and a little neck strain, but that's nothing that will require hospitalization. I'm prescribing you some medication for pain, and I'm also referring you to a physical therapist, just in case.

"Your neck will probably get stiff and sore overnight. Make sure you apply dry, moist heat, rather than a cold pack. I know it's pretty late, so if you're not able to fill your prescription tonight, you can use Tylenol. And..." She looked down at her notes. "That's about it. Are you ready to go home?"

"Yes," Korah said. She was lying on another stretcher with her son, Brick and Yolanda gathered around her. "I would very much like to go home."

"Great," her doctor said. "I'll write up your discharge papers, and a nurse will be in to give them to you in a couple of minutes." She smiled brightly. "Good luck, Ms. Avery. Try not to get into any more car accidents."

"I won't," Korah promised her.

The doctor left the room, which kicked off an unexpected argument.

"I'm glad you're okay, but that was a crazy move, Mama," Devin said. "I hope you won't ever do anything like that again. I can take you home, when they let you out of here," he offered.

"Actually, I think she should come with me," Brick interjected. "We don't know who's out to get you guys, so I don't think it would be a good idea for Korah to be alone."

"Yeah, you're right," Devin said. But his eyes narrowed, like he still believed Brick was the one responsible for all of this. His *supposed* scissor lift incident never even got reported to the police. "I'll take her home with me then."

Korah smiled at that. If Devin took her home, he'd have to pile her in his car with Yolanda, which would force Korah to inquire about why the two of them arrived at the office together. Korah would have to condemn their relationship and chastise them for starting it in the first place.

And then what? She couldn't very well force them to end it. And she certainly didn't want to fire Yolanda.

With all of the other things going on, she wasn't eager to entertain more drama. She surprised everyone by saying, "It's okay, Devin. You two go ahead. I'll go with Brick."

Her son couldn't hide his look of surprise. He recovered quickly.

"Okay. I, um, I guess I'll take Yolanda back home, and, um, I'll call you later, to make sure you're alright."

Take Yolanda home my ass, Korah thought, and she grinned knowingly.

Yolanda's face reddened. She tried to disappear completely, to no avail.

"I'm glad you're alright, Ms. Avery," she said.

"Thank you," Korah replied. "I'll see you guys tomorrow."

Devin took a slow, deep breath that made his nostrils flare. "Okay, Mama. I love you." He approached her stretcher and gave her a kiss on the cheek. He looked up at Brick as he backed away. "Be careful," he said to Korah and then exited the room.

Yolanda followed closely behind.

Brick waited thirty seconds before he stepped forward and asked, "Is he still mad because I didn't want to get a house and a barn built?"

She laughed. "Are you saying he doesn't have the right to be upset about your lies?"

"I just wanted to meet you," Brick said. His grin was drenched with southern charm.

Too goddamned sexy.

Korah shook her head. "You could've just called the office and requested a meeting."

"I don't always move like regular folk," Brick informed her.

You got that right, Korah thought.

"You'd better be glad you're hurt," he said. "Because you deserve a sound spanking."

"A *spanking*?" she said and laughed again.

"You shouldn't have gone back to your office alone – not with so much shit going on," Brick said. "You know someone is out to get you. What were you thinking?"

"I was thinking I've been taking care of myself just fine, and I don't need some man to protect me," she said.

"Oh, is that so?"

"No," Korah admitted. She smiled. "To be honest, it does feel nice to have you here. But, I gotta say, I don't understand our situation at all. We've only been dating for a few weeks. Why do you care so much?"

"I told you," Brick said, returning her smile. "As long as you're with me, you're my woman. What kind of asshole wouldn't come running, if his woman was hurt?"

As long as you're with me...

Korah was sick of wondering what that meant.

"But how long will this last?" she asked directly.

The question gave Brick pause, but he was too cool to show it.

"Korah, I have been a love 'em and leave 'em type of guy. You know that, so there's no point in me lying. But I don't want to be that way with you."

Korah knew she was pushing it, but her heart was on the line, so she dared to ask, "Why not?"

He shrugged. "You're beautiful Korah. You touch my heart, like no one else has. And you intrigue me. I can honestly say I've never known a woman like you. No one understands what I do every day, like you do. You're my equal. I've never met a woman who could operate a jackhammer. *Never.* I know that sounds stupid, but it's not to me. This is probably way deeper than you could understand."

Korah's eyes filled with tears, and her heart swelled to the point of bursting. He was right about her not fully understanding his motives. But for the first time since he initially expressed interest in her, she decided that she didn't need to understand.

She reached for his hand, and Brick eagerly wrapped his big mitt around hers. He was still holding it when her nurse arrived to give them the discharge orders.

● ● ● ● ● ●

When they left the hospital, Brick took her to a 24 hour Walgreens to drop off her prescription. While they waited for it to be filled, he took her to a Waffle House restaurant down the street for a very late dinner.

Korah hadn't eaten there since she was in her thirties. Everything was as delightful as she remembered. While they dined, Brick fed a couple of dollars to an old-school jukebox, and the restaurant was filled with smooth tunes from the Isley Brothers' greatest hits.

After they picked up her medications, Brick took her to his home in Dallas, rather than to Korah's place. She took a couple of pills on the freeway and was feeling no pain by the time they arrived at *the manor*. She told him as much, but Brick insisted on pampering her. He ran her a hot bubble bath and stayed to help her undress and make sure she didn't slip and fall in the tub. Korah thought his attention was over-the-top, but Brick was genuinely concerned about her wellbeing, which she truly appreciated.

He dried her off when she finished her bath, and then he took her to his gigantic bed and gave her another massage, this time from head to toe. Korah became quite aroused as he rubbed her neck and back and every last one of her little piggies, but Brick remained fully dressed the whole time. Sex was clearly not his motivation that night. Korah didn't want to ruin the image of being his needy patient by demanding that he jump her bones.

When he was done, Korah's whole body felt loose and relaxed. Brick left her alone, so he could bathe and get ready for bed himself.

"I swear I'm gonna find out who's behind all of this," he said when he returned to the bedroom twenty minutes later.

By then, Korah was sleeping soundly. Brick turned off the lights and climbed into bed with her. She did not stir as he settled in behind her, so close that her spine was against his chest, and her backside fit perfectly between his hips.

He inhaled the sweet scent of her hair, until he too quickly drifted off to sleep.

CHAPTER TWENTY
SUSPECT

The next morning Brick was on the phone bright and early. He sat in a leather, swivel chair in his home office with a troubled look on his face as his partner Isaac gave him the results of his latest investigative endeavors.

"His name is Solomon Gundry."

"Solomon?" Brick said.

"Yeah. He's the head of Allied Construction."

"These are the guys who submitted a lower bid last week?"

"Yup," Isaac said. "They're the ones who pushed Texas Builders out of the top three."

"They're still behind us, though?"

"Barely," Isaac said. "Honestly, Brick, it could go either way."

"Tell me why you think they're behind all of this."

"I found out some disturbing news about Mr. Gundry," Isaac said. "His company has a long line of financial straits. A long line of cheap work. None of it has officially hit the radar yet, but a few people are starting to complain. Plus some of the higher ups there have been to prison for theft and fraud."

Brick sat up in his seat. "Really? If that's the case, why would the school district even consider them?"

"I'm sure they ran a background check on Solomon and his bookkeeper, but I doubt if they'd go as far as run every one of his employees through the system."

"But Solomon himself, he's clean?"

"I didn't say that. He has some problems of his own, just not legal ones – not yet anyway. I hear that he owes a whole lot of money to some not-so-nice people."

Brick frowned in confusion. "What does that mean?"

"My sources couldn't provide any details just yet," Isaac said. "But they're working on it."

"You and your sources," Brick grumbled, but he didn't bother asking his partner to disclose the identity of these anonymous people. Over the years he'd come to understand that Isaac's research was always accurate. And like a reporter, sometimes he wouldn't reveal exactly how he came about certain information.

"So you think Solomon is behind Korah's troubles and ours, too?"

"It makes sense," Isaac said. "Allied Construction is desperate right now. Solomon needs money badly, and this school job would save the day for him. Submitting a lower bid got him close, but making Korah look incompetent got them even closer.

"Texas Builders was already looking questionable, because of that shopping center. If Korah was unable to finish the repairs before the school board made a decision, then they definitely wouldn't pick her."

Brick seethed. "But what would hurting one of our workers get him?"

"Maybe it would've been the final piece of the puzzle," Isaac offered. "What if Craig and Mike had got up to 30 feet on that scissor lift before the cage fell off?"

Brick didn't want to consider how awful that would've been, but Isaac pushed ahead:

"If we had a serious injury or even worse, *a death*, right before the school board's decision, I'm sure the superintendent would've dropped us from the running at the last minute. By the time we proved that someone sabotaged the equipment, it would be too late. The school would already be awarded to someone else."

That made sense, and it also angered Brick immensely.

It was not uncommon for contractors to try to undercut their competition, sometimes with devious tactics. But Korah was a woman. Brick may have been old-fashioned, but he felt like attacking Korah's interests was a cowardly thing to do. Whoever ran into her car last night was lower than dirt. And if that happened to be the same person who sabotaged his scissor lift, then Brick had another reason to give the creep a hardy ass-whooping.

"I'm gonna kick his ass," he grunted. "What's their address?"

"Who? Allied Construction?"

"Yeah. Give it to me." The hair stood on Brick's arms. Scorching hot blood rushed through his veins.

"No, you need to let the police handle this," Isaac warned.

"It doesn't sound like you have enough evidence to go to the police," Brick said. "Just some speculations."

"True, but you don't have any evidence, either."

"Then maybe I'll just go and ask him directly."

"Brick, all kinds of hell will break loose, if you go over there with these accusations. And these people sound dangerous. If they're breaking into buildings and slashing tires, there's no telling how far they'll go."

"Then call the police," Brick suggested. "Tell them what you know, and tell them I'm on my way over there to confront them. Maybe they'll get there before I do."

"You are one stubborn SOB."

"Are you gonna give me the address, or do I have to hang up and google it my damned self?"

Isaac reluctantly gave him the address and then said, "I'm calling the police right now."

"They'd better hurry," Brick said and disconnected.

He pushed away from the desk and spun his chair in the other direction. He was surprised to see Korah standing in the doorway. Rather than the clothes she wore last night, she only had a sheet wrapped around her body.

Brick knew what was under that sheet, because she slept completely nude last night. There was a pleasant and warm sensation in his boxers as he looked her up and down. With her tousled hair and confused expression, Korah looked very sexy first thing in the morning.

Brick wished he had time to yank the sheet away and plant hot kisses on every inch of her dark, brown flesh.

"Morning," he said with a bright smile that belied his anxiety.

"Your house is huge," Korah said. "Took me forever to find you." She cocked her head slightly. "Is everything alright? I heard you on the phone."

"I think we know who's behind all of this mess," Brick said as he rose from his seat.

He approached and did spare a moment to wrap his strong arms around her. He kissed her briefly on the lips as he backed away. Korah barely kissed him back.

"Who?" she asked.

"I'll explain on the way," Brick said and ushered her out of the room.

"On the way *where*?" Korah asked.

By then he had hold of her hand as he led her down the hallway. She had to put a little pep in her step to keep up.

"Do you need something to wear?" Brick asked without stopping or answering her question.

"Yes," Korah said. "On the way where? What's going on?"

He took her to a bedroom she hadn't seen before. It was fully furnished, but it didn't look like anyone had ever actually slept there. He walked her into a huge closet that was filled with Brick House uniforms, tee shirts, jeans and work boots. It was stocked as well as an outlet store.

Finally he turned to face her.

"You don't mind wearing my gear, do you? I love seeing my logo on your body," he said with a wink.

"Brick," Korah said, her voice nearly exasperated. "I'm not going anywhere until you tell me what's going on."

"Okay. I'll explain while you get dressed."

He turned again and looked through a collection of jeans that were all on hangers. Most of them still had the tags on them. "What waist size do you think you wear in men's?"

"Honestly, I have no idea," Korah said, not sure why she was going along with this.

Brick looked her way again. His eyes twinkled. "Okay. Drop that sheet, and let's have a look."

"I will not. If you want me to get dressed in here, the least you could do is give me some privacy."

"Okay," he said with a chuckle. "But I didn't have time to wash your clothes from last night. Are you okay with going commando – just for a little while?"

Korah rolled her eyes and said, "Just get out of here. And close the door behind you."

She didn't know her bum was exposed until Brick gave it a playful slap on his way out of the closet.

"That is one nice ass," he muttered in his sexy southern drawl.

Korah blushed and found herself grinning when he closed the closet door.

● ● ● ● ● ●

While she dressed in a Brick House tee shirt, jeans, socks and work boots, Brick stood outside of the door giving her the lowdown on Allied Construction and their shady CEO, Mr. Solomon Gundry. Korah knew the stakes were high for some of the companies bidding for the school contract, but she never suspected a fellow contractor would stoop this low.

By the time she emerged from the closet, she was very upset and a little fearful of the men who allegedly chose to target her family business and Brick's as well. She didn't realize that she and Brick were dressed identically, until she saw the smile that spread across his face when she stepped out of the closet.

"Baby, you gotta come work for me," he said.

He closed the distance between them and placed both of his hands on her waist. Korah had her shirt tucked in, and the jeans fit her well. She appreciated Brick's affection and his ceaseless attraction to her.

But surely this wasn't the time.

"We need to call the police," she told him.

"My partner already has. I'm sure they'll be there before us."

"Then why do we have to go?" Korah wondered.

"Because you can identify the guy who broke into your office last night – that is if he's stupid enough to show up for work this morning."

"You think it was a construction worker?"

"I think it was someone who works close to Solomon. Hell, it might have been Solomon himself."

"The police have the surveillance video," Korah reminded him. "They can make an identification based on that."

"No," Brick said. He took hold of her hand, and they were on the move again. "If the police tell them what we think they've been up to, they'll just deny it. And they'll have time to get rid of the evidence while the police investigate.

"But if you're standing right there saying, 'That's the guy who broke into my office and hit my car yesterday,' they can make an arrest on the spot. Trust me on this."

Korah did trust him, but there was no denying Brick's plan left a lot to be desired.

But it was hard to say no to someone who was so confident and cocky. All of the questions Korah had swirling in her head got stuck in her throat as they raced to the front door and out of the house, to his awaiting truck.

● ● ● ● ● ●

Allied Construction and Remodeling was based in Mansfield. It was a forty minute drive from the Avery Manor. On the way there, Korah did manage to voice her concern on several points. But she was unable to deter her dashing beau.

She watched him closely as he drove. She wouldn't say he was particularly *angry*, and that was the strange thing. He was certainly irritated, but Brick chuckled at times and even smiled when he referred to Allied's CEO as a *dastardly coward*.

None of that amusement reached his eyes though. Brick was extremely focused on the ensuing confrontation. Nothing could change his mind – not even the call he got, from who Korah assumed was his business partner.

"Where are you?"

"I'm on the road," Brick said. "On my way to see a man."

"The police said they're gonna go check it out," Isaac told him. "And they agreed that you shouldn't go over there."

"Free country," Brick said.

"And tell me again what your plan is, when you get there."

"I'm just gonna sit back and wait for the police," Brick said, glancing briefly at his passenger. "If Korah can make an identification at that point, then we'll point him out."

"That's it?"

"Sure. You know I don't want any trouble..."

When they reached their destination, Korah was appalled to see that the police had not arrived yet.

Allied Construction was a sprawling complex with a one story, 6,000 square feet central building and half a dozen construction trailers lined up near the main office. The parking lot was densely populated, with approximately twenty cars, a collection of medium to large construction vehicles and a group of men who had sun-beaten skin and calloused hands and were ready to get their long day started.

"Do you see him?" Brick asked as he entered the property, as boldly as a lion navigating his own territory.

"The police aren't here," Korah said, her heart thudding, her eyes wide.

"They'll be here," Brick said.

"You told your friend we would wait for them."

"We can look and wait," Brick replied. "Do you see him?"

"No," Korah said, her voice laced with dread.

"You're not even looking," Brick said.

Korah frowned and looked away from his brown eyes and into the faces of the men outside. By then Brick was fully on their property. He drove past vehicles in the parking lot, looking everywhere, all at once, as if he could make the ID himself.

A lot of the workers stopped to watch Brick as well. He and Korah weren't in his company truck, but Brick's Navigator was instantly the best car on the lot.

"Do you see him?"

"No," Korah said. She really was looking this time. "Brick, this is—"

"What about that car?" he asked, looking out of his window. He slowed and then stopped completely. "You said it was a Buick, right? An old one? About an '87?"

Korah did tell him and the police that, but she didn't see the car he was referring to. She sat up in her seat and tried to look through his window.

"Hold on," Brick said, and they got moving again. He turned right at the end of the row of cars and then went down the adjacent row. He made another set of turns until they were headed down the first row again, this time in the opposite direction. He slowed down and stopped. He lowered Korah's window.

"Is that the car?"

Korah saw it now. All of the air left her lungs as she eyed the dark-colored Buick. It was facing them, and she'd recognize that big, mean grill anywhere. Plus there was damage to the front bumper on the driver's side.

"I'm betting there's some of your paint on that there bumper," Brick said.

That there bumper?

Even in the midst of her apprehension, Korah noticed how goddamned *country* Brick was. She found him inexplicably *hot*. All he needed was a toothpick poking out of his mouth to complete the effect.

"Ye, yes, I think it is," Korah stammered. Her mouth was completely dry. All of the horror she felt last night when she went head to head with this vehicle was back with a vengeance.

The Buick's damage was rather minimal, compared to the destruction it dealt to Korah's SUV. The LeSabre's headlight wasn't even broken, which was probably why the driver felt comfortable enough to drive it to work that morning. It was clear that Allied Construction never thought anyone would suspect them.

"Are you gonna call the police?" Korah asked, her eyes glued on the Buick.

"They're on their way," Brick repeated. "We can–"

"Can I help you?"

The voice startled Korah, but Brick merely looked to the left, where one of the construction workers was approaching. It was a black man with a wide nose and a noticeable gap between his front teeth.

Brick looked back at Korah. "Is that him?"

Korah's eyes grew even wider. She couldn't believe he would ask her that right in front of the man! When the stranger stepped closer to the truck, she shook her head, or shivered in fear, she wasn't sure which.

"Whose car is that?" Brick asked, addressing the man again.

"Who wants to know?" the guy asked.

"I'm Brick."

Either that was an acceptable answer, or the man didn't know how to respond to Brick's straightforwardness, because he paused for a moment and then said, "Mack's."

"Where's Mack?" Brick asked.

The worker did look a little wary this time, but he still gave up the info.

"In the office."

Brick looked towards the main building and then told the worker, "Thanks," before heading in that direction.

Korah was at her wits' end. "*What are you doing?*"

"I'm solving a crime," he said matter-of-factly.

"You said we were waiting for the police."

"Why are you so worried? Do you think I would let something happen to you?"

As crazy as it was, Korah had to shake her head. They had literally entered the enemy's camp, and they were greatly outnumbered. But Korah totally believed Brick would protect her. It was a wonderful feeling, but it didn't make any sense.

He pulled to a stop in front of the office and got out of the car. When he went around to help Korah out, she had to put her foot down.

"I am not going in there."

"Why not?"

"Wha, what do you mean why not? You have no idea what kind of people those are!"

"That's not true. I know exactly what kind of people they are," he replied, his face darkening.

"Brick, I don't want you to get hurt," Korah pleaded. "We have to wait for the police."

His eyes left hers then. His attention was drawn to the parking lot. "Here they come."

Korah checked her side view mirror and was happy to see a police cruiser entering the property. She sighed, a cool wave of relief washing over her.

But at that moment, the front door of the building swung open, and a man stepped out onto the elevated porch. He wore jeans and a golf shirt with sneakers, rather than work boots. He was tall and powerfully built. He had a pudgy face that was clean-shaven. His hair was short. But the thing that stood out the most was his bushy eyebrows.

"Is that him?" Brick asked, looking from the suspect to Korah. Brick's teeth were clenched, making the muscles in his jaws flex.

The man standing in the doorway looked first to the police car and then to Brick and finally at Korah, who still had her eyes glued on him. That was definitely the face she saw behind the wheel of the Buick last night. Seeing him again made her blood run cold, and she couldn't help but nod slightly, her breaths coming in quick pants.

The burglar's eyes widened as he put all of the pieces of this terrible puzzle together, and he turned to run. But Brick was already on his way after him.

Brick, no!" Korah screamed as her boyfriend bounded up the few steps in one stride and chased the man inside the building.

Her hands flew to her face. Her mouth hung open. She watched the open doorway with bulging eyes that peered through trembling fingers.

What the hell was wrong with this man – not the burglar, but *Brick*?! They had no idea what lie behind that door. If Brick managed to avoid getting pummeled by the suspect's cronies, then surely he'd get arrested for attacking the man. And for what – some misguided attempt to defend Korah's honor?

It was definitely not worth it!

But even as she cursed him in her mind, Korah's heart exploded with exhilaration thirty seconds later when Brick emerged from the building with her assailant firmly in the grips of his big, bear claws. Brick nearly dragged the villain from the building with one fist wrapped around the back of his collar and the other hand gripping the man's belt.

The burglar's face was slightly bruised from whatever scuffled ensued when Brick chased him into the building. The man scrambled to get to his feet but was unable to free himself before Brick tossed him headfirst off the porch.

Korah yelped in surprise, but she had to admit that it did her heart good to see the Buick's driver rolling in the dust. Brick hopped down and hovered over him – just as the policemen emerged from their vehicle and rushed to get control of the situation.

"I'm making a citizen's arrest!" Brick boasted, his fists balled, his broad chest swelling.

"What the hell's going on here?" another man yelled.

Everyone followed the voice to a portly gentleman who had emerged from the building. He was completely bald on top, but he held on to the hair on the sides and back of his head. He looked just as exasperated as Korah felt.

"If you're Solomon Gundry, then you're next!" Brick yelled, and then he nearly made Korah pass out when he turned and headed towards the building again.

"Alright, hold on!" one of the cops shouted. "Everybody stay right where you are!"

"Oh, Jesus," Korah muttered. Surely she was going to have a heart attack.

She locked eyes with Brick, who did have sense enough to keep his feet planted, as the cop instructed. He winked at her, and Korah frowned, not wanting to encourage him.

But the cocky look in his eyes made her shake her head. Her lips subconsciously curved into a grin.

And of course, Brick was plenty encouraged by that.

> *Passionate rivulets cascade*
> *Auburn hazes of sun sweet rays*
> *Through fragrant jasmine scents I gaze*
> *I'm awestruck by your loveliness*
>
> *The forest painted. The autumn leaves*
> *Crinkle beneath your steps. I breathe*
> *But slightly, though my heartbeats peak*
> *I'm smitten by your loveliness*
>
> *Perchance to hold your hand in mine*
> *I'm weakened by your pulse. Each time*
> *You smile a tremor sweeps my spine*
> *I praise God for your loveliness*

CHAPTER TWENTY-ONE
THE FINAL CHAPTER
WEDNESDAY AFTERNOON

Brick came to Korah's home later that day for dinner. After the drama settled down, and she decided that she didn't hate him for being so reckless in his defense of her, Korah decided he was somewhat of a hero. He said he'd kick some ass when he found out who was threatening their businesses, he found out who the culprit was, and then he proceeded to kick some ass, as promised.

To reward him, Korah offered to make a home-cooked meal. Brick surprised her by requesting a burger and fries.

"Really?" she replied. "A girl offers you some home-cooking, and you want a burger and fries?"

"That's not such a simple meal," Brick argued. "You can tell a lot about a cook based on the way they handle a burger."

"I can't imagine what you could learn from that."

"Well, a good burger has to have the right seasoning. It needs to be a little pink in the middle. It can't be too thick or too thin. It needs to be juicy, but not juicy enough to soak the bun and make it fall apart. And are the fries store-bought, or will you start with a fresh potato?"

Oh my, Korah thought. Never had a burger sounded like such a daunting task.

"Okay, I'll make it for you," she said. "What time can you come over?"

"I can be there whenever you like."

"I'm closing the office a little early today," she told him. "We finished up at the shopping center, so our construction crew is taking off at four. I can have your burger ready for you by five-thirty."

"I'll be there."

"Would you like beer with your dinner?"

"That would be nice."

"Alright. I'll see you then."

"Okay. I can't wait."

"Oh, and Brick..."

"Yeah?"

"Thanks again, for everything."

"No need to thank me. Are you still wearing my tee-shirt?"

"No," Korah said with a grin. She had to change before she went to the office that day, lest her team think she really had sold out. "But I can wear it for you tonight," she offered.

"I would love to see you in nothing but that tee shirt."

"Mmmm, we'll see," she said and disconnected. Her smile was big and sinful.

● ● ● ● ● ●

Brick showed up at 5:25 and waited in the kitchen while Korah finished up his meal. Rather than cook his burger on the stovetop, Korah fired up the grill to ensure the meat got a smoky, mesquite flavor. She mixed a couple of tablespoons of diced chipotle peppers and onions in her ground beef to give it a little extra kick, and she made the French fries from scratch. She completed the meal with an ice cold Sam Adams Boston Lager, which was said to enhance rather than overwhelm the taste of her gourmet burger.

They ate in the kitchen instead of the dining room, because Channel Six News was set to feature a story on Allied Construction at six o'clock.

Korah sat across from Brick and waited anxiously as he hefted his burger and took the first bite. She was worried about the bun getting soggy, because of the pickle, tomatoes and lettuce she added. But everything turned out just fine. Brick chewed quietly and let out a satisfied hum after he swallowed. Korah didn't realize she was holding her breath until he spoke.

"That's a damn good burger," he said with a smile. "You put your foot in it."

"Hurry up and eat one of your fries," she replied. "This taste test is driving me crazy."

Brick chuckled and shoved a few into his mouth. "Excellent," he announced after a few seconds.

"Great," Korah said and lifted her burger for the first time. "I'm happy to meet your expectations."

"You could've picked up something from Burger King, and I wouldn't have liked you any less," Brick said.

"I'll keep that in mind for next time," Korah said with a grin.

They chatted for a little while, enjoying both the food and each other's company, until the news came on. Korah had a flat screen mounted next to the window. Channel Six's star reporter Chad Collins opened with the construction story, as promised.

"Good evening, everyone. Thanks for joining us. Tonight we have more news on what's turning out to be a very bizarre story from the city of Mansfield. The police were called to the offices of Allied Construction and Remodeling early this morning to investigate a burglary and vandalism complaint that turned out to be much more. We've got Gabriella Sands live at the scene. Gabriella, what is going on in Mansfield?"

The view changed to a split screen of Chad in the newsroom and Gabriella standing in the same parking lot Brick and the police converged on earlier that day. The main entrance of Allied Construction was in view behind her, as was a marquee bearing the company's name and logo.

The building appeared to be deserted, and the parking lot was as well, except for a few of the larger construction vehicles Korah saw parked there this morning. Gabriella Sands was a strikingly beautiful woman with full, red lips and dark, curly hair. She wore an almond-colored blazer that complimented her skin tone.

"Good evening, Chad," she said, speaking into a Channel Six microphone. "The residents of Mansfield are in shock right now after watching this business, Allied Construction and Remodeling, get raided by as many as ten police cars this afternoon. The raid was prompted by a citizen's arrest that was made by another contractor, who's based in Dallas. That individual was acting on behalf of a *third* contractor, who hails from Overbrook Meadows."

"I'm already getting confused," Chad said good-naturedly. "Hopefully you were able to make some sense of this."

"Yes, I was," Gabriella said with a smile, and Chad was dropped from the shot, leaving only her.

"The trouble for Allied Construction came to a head today," Gabriella said, "but their problems have been brewing for years. The CEO, Mr. Solomon Gundry, is said to have a history of shady business practices, and recently he has begun to amass quite a bit of debt."

Gabriella's shot was momentarily replaced with what looked like a mug shot of the portly gentleman Korah saw that morning – the one Brick threatened to apprehend after his initial skirmish, but thankfully the police were there to act as mediators.

"Mr. Gundry founded this company in 2002," Gabriella continued. "Police are saying he recently took some drastic measures to ensure that his business stayed afloat. I spoke with Overbrook Meadows Detective Daniel Majors earlier today..."

Channel Six played a portion of the pre-recorded interview. Detective Majors wore plainclothes. The scene was filmed in his office, rather than at the site of all of the drama in Mansfield.

"We initially became involved in this case after a few vandalism incidents were reported in Overbrook Meadows," the policeman said. "Those incidents occurred at worksites for a company called Texas Builders. Someone slashed the tires on some rather expensive construction vehicles. We now believe that was done in an attempt to sabotage those projects."

"What would someone have to gain by sabotaging those projects?" Gabriella asked off camera.

"Well, we're not completely done piecing all of this together yet," the detective said. "But based on statements made by some of the men who were arrested today, Texas Builders and Allied Construction are competitors. Solomon Gundry allegedly wanted to undermine the efforts of Texas Builders, which would hopefully give him an advantage in the race for a major contract both companies are competing for."

"That contract," Gabriella said, as they returned to a view from her camera in Mansfield, "is for a new high school that will be built in Overbrook Meadows next year. As of this moment, the school district has not announced which contractor will spearhead the project, but they did confirm that Allied Construction and Texas Builders are top candidates.

"Police are saying that after the vandalism incidents at the construction sites, Mr. Gundry allegedly sent this man, Mark Lassiter, to break into the main office of Texas Builders yesterday evening."

Channel Six displayed a mug shot of the man Brick manhandled earlier that day. The creep was just as ugly as Korah remembered him. The picture made her shudder, despite the fact that he was still locked up at the moment.

"The motive for the break-in is unknown at this time," Gabriella continued. "Lassiter was caught in the act last night by Texas Builders' CEO Korah Stewart. Police say Lassiter allegedly ran into Stewart's car as he fled the scene. He has been charged with breaking and entering, hit and run and an unrelated warrant from Waco for aggravated assault. He is being held on a $50,000 bond.

"All of this culminated in a wild scene this morning," Gabriella said. "Korah Stewart, along with another contractor named Brock Avery, arrived at the Allied Construction headquarters right behind me at approximately nine am. Once here, they confronted Gundry and Lassiter, which led to a brief scuffle. Thankfully the police also arrived at this location moments later, and they were able to intervene and make the appropriate arrests before anyone was seriously injured."

The camera view returned to a split screen of Gabriella on the scene and Chad in the newsroom. He looked both amazed and still a little confused about his coworker's report.

"The third contractor," he said, "What is Brock Avery's connection to any of this?"

"According to police, Avery is not connected to this case in any way," Gabriella said, "other than the fact that he restrained Lassiter and indicated he wanted to make a citizen's arrest. I called Avery's office this afternoon, but he was not available for comment."

Brick chuckled as he watched the news report. It was Isaac's idea to keep Brick House out of the story as much as possible. He didn't even want the police to know about the incident with the scissor lift.

"We don't need to be involved with any of this drama," Isaac had advised. "I don't want to hear our name on the news tonight."

Brick knew that Isaac was watching Channel Six with his wife at that exact moment. He was probably cursing Brick for being so damned gung-ho.

Back on TV, Chad Collins said, "This is all quite remarkable. I've never heard of construction companies going to war with each other. I guess I never really considered it before."

"I'm with you, Chad," Gabriella replied. "This story really opened my eyes. These multimillion dollar contracts can make or break someone's career. We've seen time and time again that when a huge amount of money is involved, anything's possible."

"What about the other arrests?" Chad asked. "I'm told quite a few Allied employees were taken to jail today."

"That's right, Chad. I was here for most of the action. At one point it did look like everyone who worked here ended up in handcuffs. Police say most of those arrests were for misdemeanor warrants. But more charges were filed when detectives began to question the employees about the vandalism and other shady practices at this business. So far everyone is pointing their fingers at the man in charge.

"This is a developing story, Chad, and I'm sure to have more information in the days to come. As for now, Allied Construction is closed, the CEO is behind bars, and there's no word on when – *or if* – they'll ever open their doors again. Which, some say, may be for the best."

"Thanks, Gabriella," Chad said. "You do great work."

"You're welcome," she said and relinquished the screen to just Chad in the newsroom.

"Also topping our news," he said, "is the accident on I-35, which still has three lanes of traffic blocked. Thankfully there were no fatalities after a Hershey's truck rolled over and *caught fire*, spilling tons of *dripping chocolate…*"

Korah used the remote to turn off the television.

Brick was grinning at her when she returned her attention to him. His burger was completely gone, as were his fries. He brought his beer mug to his face and took a manly drink while she watched.

"You think you're all that," she teased.

He leaned back in his chair, relishing the feel of his full belly.

Korah rose to her feet to collect their dishes. "Do you want another one?" She wouldn't normally suggest it after such a big meal. But Brick wolfed his burger down rather quickly, and he wasn't a small man.

He sat up suddenly and took hold of her wrist when she reached for his plate. Korah was startled by his speed, but she knew she shouldn't be, not after watching him chase a crook named Lassiter into his own office that morning.

"I was just thinking about how I still owe you a spanking," Brick drawled. He looked up at her with a sinister twinkle in his eyes that made Korah's heart skip a beat.

"Yeah, right." Somehow she managed to sound more defiant than she actually was.

"I'm pretty sure I said I'd have to punish you when you felt better," Brick recalled.

"Punish me for what?"

"For trying to catch a burglar with your car. That man could've really hurt you, if you managed to stop him."

Oh, that.

"Well, it's too late now," Korah said. "Your window of opportunity has closed."

"Is that right?"

He had that sexy, southern swag working just right. He wore jeans with a black button-down that was open halfway down his broad chest. His rigid jaw and square chin made Korah lose her breath.

He looked so good, she began to wonder why she was opposed to something as harmless as a spanking. No one had done that to her– not since the seventh grade. That was thirty-four years ago. Surely her reaction would be a lot different now.

"I'm afraid so," Korah breathed.

I just cooked dinner for you, and you want to spank me?

This man had some nerve.

Was he crazy?

Was she crazy? Why else would she be considering it?

Brick's eyes twinkled as he stared up at her. "Alright. Generally I'm a man of my word. But I'll let you off with a warning this time, little lady. But if you keep talking noise, I'm gonna have to make a believer out of you."

Korah's chest rose and fell visibly. They maintained eye contact, locked in a battle of wills. Her clitoris began to throb so unexpectedly, she sucked air between her teeth. She knew he saw her. Her sensible side urged her to concede, but the boss in her would do no such thing.

She smirked, and cocked her head when she spoke. "You ain't gon' do a goddamned thin–"

That was as far as she got before Brick pulled her forward so suddenly she lost her footing.

"Aaah!"

He swiveled quickly in his chair. Korah thought he meant to catch her, but his legs only served to trip her up even more. She came to a rest face down, with her midsection completely on his lap. Without a pause, Brick yanked her skirt up to her waist with his left hand and yanked her panties down her thighs with the other.

Korah was mortified. She was ass-out, in the middle of the kitchen, on a Wednesday afternoon.

"Brick!"

She reached back reflexively. Brick let go of her skirt and blocked her with his left hand. He used his right hand to *SMACK!* her ass so briskly, all of the goose bumps on her butt cheeks were set on fire.

Korah's eyelids flashed open like shutters. The pure shock intensified the pain of the impact threefold.

"*Aaah!*"

Her jiggling booty massaged her clitoris wonderfully, making her whole body shudder.

SMACK!

"*Ow*! Dammit!"

She didn't know if that was a scream of pain or pleasure. Her whole body was on fire. By the third time, she didn't try to reach back and stop him.

SMACK!

And he suddenly let her go. He helped her to her feet. Korah wobbled on her pumps. Her panties were wrapped around her knees. Her ass was stinging.

Stinging so good.

She didn't know if she came, or if she was extremely wet for him. The muscles in her pussy contracted intermittently. Her legs trembled. She couldn't stand. She sat on his lap. That made her ass sting even more.

She kissed him. Her hands gripped his chest. She ripped his shirt open and ran her hands up and down his pecs. Brick moaned in appreciation. Her tongue slipped into his mouth. A million pinpricks continued to poke her ass. She reached into his lap as she raided his mouth with her lips and tongue.

Brick was so hard. His dick felt cramped in his jeans. Korah tried to get his belt off. Her fingers couldn't make sense of it. She reached with both hands. Brick grunted. His hands moved under hers. He manipulated the belt much better than she did.

Korah sucked his bottom lip into her mouth and bit down on it. She heard the belt buckle fall open. And then the button. He reached for the zipper, but she made it first. His hands flew to her chest instead. His touch made her breasts swell and stretch the fabric of her blouse.

Brick squeezed them so hard, Korah cried out. She pulled his zipper down. His dick sprang forward. Korah peeled his boxers back and grabbed hold of it. It was throbbing. She felt hot blood racing through veins that were thick and engorged.

She reached with her free hand and pulled her panties the rest of the way down her legs, so that she could turn and straddle him. Now she faced him completely. She stared at him, her eyes dark with desire. Her breaths quick and eager. She squeezed him harder. Brick's nostrils flared. His dick jumped in her hands. It grew even more.

She let it go and used both hands to grip his shoulders. She slid her hips forward until the base of his dick came in full contact with her pussy. His eyes dilated. Korah worked her hips closer, until his dick stroked her clit.

She kissed him again. Her hips continued to grind hard and slow. His dick was soon slick with her essence. He grabbed her ass with both hands and pulled her closer, making her grind even harder. His fingers dug into her skin, making the pain from her spanking flare up again.

He lifted her hips slightly, just high enough for his fat head to slip inside her. They both thought better of it at the same moment. He backed away, just as Korah was rising to her feet. She took a step back, her eyes glued to his dick. It was big and dark and pulsating, pointing directly at the ceiling.

Brick bent and dug a condom from the pocket of his jeans. Of course he had one. There was never any doubt that she was his for the taking. He ripped the wrapper open and rolled the condom down the length of his shaft.

He sat down again, and Korah immediately returned to her perch on his lap. This time there was no hesitation as she climbed him and eased down on his dick. She lowered herself until he filled her completely. Korah threw her head back and screamed when he grabbed hold of her waist and thrust his hips upwards, not stopping until their pubic hairs meshed.

"*Fuck!*" she yelled.

She leaned forward, her hands gripping his shoulders, her hair falling in her face. She began to grind on his dick, up and down, slow and sweet. Brick reached for her face and urged her forward. He began to suck on her lips and tongue. His hands skated down her sides and found a home on her hips. He caressed her as she picked up speed and rhythm, slamming her smarting ass on his thighs.

As her eruption drew near, and her glorious screams reverberated off the kitchen walls and cupboards, Korah was vaguely aware that this was a Wednesday night. And Brick really had thrown her over his knees and gave her a spanking.

A delicious smile curved her lips. She didn't know why this man made her feel so alive.

So uninhibited.

She was a rational personal, and she knew Brick was as well. But he had proven time and time again that he didn't give a damn about rules when it came to life and love. He was teaching Korah to feel the same way, and she was an attentive pupil.

Her orgasm was a mighty torrent that gained momentum as it rolled from her head to her chest. It came crashing down her clitoris, causing her pussy to grip him and suck him until he gave in to the pleasure and exploded deep inside her. Korah yelped with pleasure and pain. She felt his dick jumping, stretching her walls, every spasm.

It was six twenty-four pm.

On a Wednesday night.

A work day.

She absolutely loved her life.

EPILOGUE

On Monday the following week, Korah opened the day with a team meeting. Devin and his crew were set to break ground on a million dollar community center in De Soto that morning, so the overall mood in the office was upbeat. Today was also the day the Overbrook Meadows school district would announce which contractor won the coveted bid, so there was an underlying anxiety that made everyone a little tense.

Before the meeting concluded, Korah told her team, "I would just like to say how proud I am of all of you. The last few weeks have been very stressful. We made a lot of sacrifices for the school bid, but we took care of business.

"We completed work on the shopping center, and we stood tall in the face of adversity. It would've been easy to throw in the towel, especially when the vandalism started. But we didn't. We kept our nose to the grind, and we showed them that we're no lightweights.

"And we made the local news," Korah said with a grin. "I wish we could've been featured in a more positive story. But you know what they say; *all* publicity is good publicity. Priscilla says two of the remodeling jobs we picked up last week were from folks who saw us on the news."

Korah smiled. She wore a burgundy pantsuit with her hair pulled up in a tight bun. She was beautiful and powerful and confident. She sat at the head of the table admiring her small but commanding group.

Priscilla was as quick as a whip. No one could crunch numbers better than her. She still brought up retirement every now and then, in passing. In the meantime, she was grooming Korah's daughter to take her place.

Stephanie, for her part, was doing great in school. She was intelligent and ambitious, much more ambitious than Korah was at her age. Stephanie knew how to separate business from emotions. She was also a little cutthroat, which would make her a force to be reckoned with when she took over as VP for the family business.

Korah had yet to confront Yolanda and Devin about their inappropriate relations, but that wasn't something she considered a priority. It appeared that she had already missed her opportunity to stop it before it started, and they were both adults. There was very little Korah could do about it, at this point.

In her time as CEO, Korah had gone through several assistants, none of whom could hold a candle to Yolanda. And Devin was family, so there was no chance of getting rid of him either – not that she wanted to.

"I would like to commend Devin in particular," she said, "for his persistence, integrity and leadership skills that are growing more impressive every year."

She and her son locked eyes.

"I think sometimes I take him for granted," Korah said, "because he's my son. But every now and then I step back and look at all he's done, so many beautiful constructions. When I think about the big shoes he had to fill, and the competence and respect he instills in all of his workers – some of whom are twice his age – I can't help but tip my hat to him. Bravo, sir."

Everyone casted appreciative smiles his way, and Devin grinned sheepishly.

"Of course today is the day the school will announce the winner of the bid," Korah said. "We all know that job would propel us to heights even I've never envisioned. But the fact is, even if we don't win the bid, Texas Builders is already one of the top construction companies in this state. We will continue to expand, and we will continue to build. A decade from now, the school job will seem like small potatoes, compared to the stuff we have on our plate.

"So keep doing what you're doing. All of you. I couldn't be more proud. Now let's get to work."

The group began to applaud, which was totally unexpected. Korah's eyes twinkled as they filled with tears.

"Alright, alright, enough of that," she said as she turned and headed for her office. "Let's get a move on. Time to build something."

● ● ● ● ● ●

The call from the school district came at nine am sharp. Yolanda came to Korah's office to deliver the news.

"Ms. Avery, the school district called."

Korah looked up at her, her eyes hopeful.

Yolanda swallowed. The corner of her mouth twitched slightly. She shook her head.

Korah's chest tightened. All of her limbs went cold. She blinked once.

"Who got it?"

Yolanda sighed. "Brick House."

Korah nodded. She grinned, but it was humorless.

"You okay?"

"Of course," Korah said.

The phone on Yolanda's desk rang. She hesitated.

"We still have work to do," Korah said.

Her assistant nodded and went to answer the phone.

Korah waited an hour before she called Brick on his cellphone.

"Congratulations."

"Thank you."

He didn't sound as happy as she thought he would. Probably didn't want to gloat.

"You okay?" he asked.

"I'm fine. This isn't about me, Brick. This is a big day for you. Your time to shine. You'll be in the papers tomorrow."

He didn't speak right away. She knew he was smiling then. She could hear his cheeks spreading. She was proud of him.

"I would still like to work with you," Brick offered.

"No. Don't do that."

"I'm not trying to make you feel better. I'm serious. This is a big job, Korah. It's huge. I could hire you to build the gym or the football field, or *both*. It's a fifteen million dollar job. You're my woman. You should get some of it."

Korah couldn't say she wasn't tempted. It didn't have to be all or nothing. But could she put Devin on a Brick House site? Would he go? Her son did feel a little better about Brick, after he helped the police shut down Allied Construction. But would he work for his mama's boyfriend? Surely for millions of dollars he would.

Maybe.

"Take some time to think about it," Brick suggested.

Korah didn't respond.

"So, are we still on for this weekend, or are you mad at me now?" Brick asked.

Korah smiled. She had agreed to spend the weekend at the Avery Ranch. Brick promised her horseback riding. Fishing and canoeing. He said they could tell campfire stories, with a real campfire. He said the hay in his barn was really soft. Korah told him *a roll in the hay* was just an expression. He said it didn't have to be.

"I'm no sore loser. Of course I would still like to go."

"Awesome. You're gonna love it there. You may never want to leave."

Korah didn't doubt that. She felt like that every time she and Brick were together.

"Did you make that appointment yet?" he asked.

Last weekend Brick proposed that they get checked out by their respective physicians. Once they got a clean bill of health, he wanted to eliminate condoms from their love life.

Korah was surprised that he asked, but she appreciated the fact that he was always responsible, even when he seemed reckless. This was Brick's way of making them an official monogamous couple.

"My appointment is tomorrow. How about you?"

"I'm going today at lunch," he said.

"You sound excited."

"I'm am. I can't wait."

"To go bareback..."

"Yes'm."

"I think I would enjoy that."

"You will," he promised. "A whole lot."

She giggled. "Not as much as you, I'm sure."

"You'd be surprised."

"You're right," she said. "Mmmm... There's something I've been dying to know..."

"What's that?"

She checked to make sure no one was lingering around her office door before she said, "I wonder what your cum tastes like."

Brick dropped his phone. Korah giggled as he scrambled to pick it up.

"Sorry. What was that?"

"Oh, wow – would you look at the time."

"What?"

"I gotta go."

"That's not cool."

"Go on and get back to your work and your celebrating. I know you're eager to do both."

"I am. And thank you."

"For what?"

"For not hating me. I think if the shoe was on the other foot, and you stole this job out from under me, I wouldn't want to see your ass for at least a month."

"You wouldn't want to see my ass?"

"Well, not your *ass* – ass. Of course I'd always want to see that. You'd have to send me pictures, though."

Korah's grin was delightful. "Goodbye, sir."

"Okay. And don't forget to talk to your son about my offer."

"Why do you think I need to run it by him?"

"What other reason would you have not to accept right away?"

He was always right inside her head. So insightful, Brick was. It was hard not to love him.

"Congrats again," she said.

"Thanks. And don't worry, you'll get 'em next time."

"No doubt, baby. No doubt."

TO BE CONTINUED...

BY KEITH THOMAS WALKER

ABOUT THE AUTHOR

Keith Thomas Walker, known as the Master of Romantic Suspense and Urban Fiction, is the author of more than a dozen novels, including *Life After, Fixin' Tyrone, Dripping Chocolate* and *The Realest Ever*. Keith enjoys reading, poetry and music of all genres. Originally from Fort Worth, he is a graduate of Texas Wesleyan University. Keith was nominated for an Emma Award in 2010 for Debut Author of the Year. In 2012 Keith was the recipient of a BRAB Book Club Award for Male Author of the Year (for Harlot) as well as a SORMAG Award for Fiction Author of the Year. In 2013 Keith was the recipient of a BRAB Book Club Award for Male Author of the Year (for Dripping Chocolate). Visit him at www.keithwalkerbooks.com.